Good Little Indian Girls and Stuff

From Fat to Fab

Bina Patel

BALBOA.
PRESS
A DIVISION OF HAY HOUSE

Balboa Press books may be ordered through booksellers or by contacting:

Balboa Press
A Division of Hay House
1663 Liberty Drive
Bloomington, IN 47403
www.balboapress.com
1 (877) 407-4847

Print information available on the last page.

ISBN: 978-1-9822-1623-8 (sc)
ISBN: 978-1-9822-1622-1 (hc)
ISBN: 978-1-9822-1624-5 (e)

Library of Congress Control Number: 2018913583

Balboa Press rev. date: 05/09/2019

Disclaimer

This memoir is based on my personal experience of life. Characters names and situations have been changed to protect confidentiality.

Caution: The offerings for wellness in my story are not a substitute for professional medical advice, diagnosis, and treatments. Please seek the appropriate care and support involving any change in lifestyle, including diet, exercise, medical, and alternative therapies. The author is not claiming to be an expert on any aspect of healthcare or spirituality and cannot be held responsible for an individual's physical, emotional and mental health, or spiritual experiences based on this story.

OM

This story is dedicated to my beloved family and
to those adrift at sea in search of a safe shore.
You are not forgotten.

Contents

Background

'You must write a book,' said my counselling supervisor. I was flattered but faltered. Storytelling and ridiculing myself to get the laughs was a comfortable way of life, the tears needing expression safely concealed. But a book! Scary stuff!

Amidst the voice that said, 'Don't be silly,' another stoic voice surfaced. 'Why not?' Writing had always been a part of my expressive self. As a child, I used to scribble random stuff in a diary, such as 'Went to the seaside today' and 'He's *hot*!' Friends and family enjoyed my ramblings in letters and postcards from various holiday destinations. I dreamt of articulating something meaningful to share with a wider audience but was unsure of what that exactly was.

My Indian birth tribe with its allegiance to ancestral duty, obligation, and sacrifice underpinned a certain life position. If I was to share anything with the world, it had to be through a prestigious platform such as a 'proper job'. This meant being a doctor, dentist, lawyer, accountant, or the like. These professions equated to having intelligence and material wealth. People were interested in your story because you had an elevated status in society. Integration was possible. Oh, and marriage prospects were good, too!

This narrow world view was undoubtedly shaped by childhood conditioning. My grandfather's generation made immense sacrifices when emigrating overseas in search of the good life. Their decision to leave family behind in India, and travel across choppy seas to the land of opportunity (Africa) made them heroic. In honour of these acts of selflessness, we, the beneficiaries of blood, sweat, toil, and tears were cajoled into always 'doing the right thing'. I lost count of the times I was labelled 'good girl' when behaving perfectly. My mum still says that when she approves of me. Over five decades on, it still matters that I am a 'good little Indian girl'. Such allegiance to a forefather, mother, and the tribe ('*We*') meant alienating the self ('*I*'). But now, a birth.

A rebellious seed, sown eons ago, has awakened. I feel like a determined tender sapling wanting to grow up on my terms as opposed to genetically coded rules. I recall sitting opposite an empathic therapist, rambling on about 'my boring stuff'. Nothing prepared me for the outpourings from the 'I' concealed under the mask that is the human condition. A part of me had been suffocating beneath the tribal framework of duty, obligation, and sacrifice (as in the 'oughts', 'shoulds' and 'musts'), the strict code of 'no boyfriends allowed', arranged marriages, the taboo of premarital sex, and the strong patriarchal domination of the tribe. The latter was symbolised by a blatant bias for the arrival of baby boys over baby girls. Then there was the shame around exposed body flesh, menstruation, masturbation, smoking, and boozing. I also resented being part of a caste system in which Brahmins (priests) sat at the top of their holier-than-thou tower whilst the Harijans (the untouchables) sat in the bowels of the earth, cleaning toilets.

Once 'I' got going, there was no STOP sign to be seen. Further reflective bubbles expressed angst around the holiness of being vegetarian, the guilt of not being that, mandatory domestic excellence, the indignation of being labelled a spinster, tribal obsession with status and wealth creation, crucifying religious ideology, and a strong sense of (often forced) family ties. Having to bow down to a hierarchy in which respect for elders was considered sanctimonious, even if they had betrayed and humiliated me, felt excruciatingly unfair.

Further objections emerged. Why in a so-called civilised society, as the Indian (South Asian) one likes to see itself, was it okay to be a bystander of domestic violence, accept female foetal murder, forced marriages, honour killings, rape in marriage, child brides, female genital mutilation, and homophobia? The statistics around social justice and moral conscience, within my birth tribe, do not always make me proud to be Indian. Where has the vision 'be the change in the world you want to see' espoused by the revered Mahatma Gandhi, father of *ahimsa* (non-violence), gone? Why are we fragmented? Men and women cannot exist without the other. Why then do we violate one another, and ourselves, in the process?

Amidst the torrential rain of questions with vague answers, a glimmer of hope for understanding the tragedies of life surfaced. Attitudes, traditions, customs, and belief systems get passed down through generations. Apparently, our world view is attributable to the complexities of the *Cultural Parent* (Pearl Drego, 1983). This parent holds the 'personality of the culture' deep in our psyche. Drego developed this idea based on the cultural analysis work of Eric Berne, father of Transactional Analysis. I was introduced to this parent during my training in Reflective Therapeutic Practice. What an encounter!

This Cultural Parent lies at the core of our social conscience and drives our behaviours, attitudes, and belief systems in powerful ways. We all know the struggle of juggling with what *we are supposed to do*, and *what we have to do*, amidst the introjections from an intuitive voice that expresses what *we might like to do*—so many voices, yet so limited our choices. Why? Largely because the influence of this parent is deeply embedded in our unconscious, off the radar, out of our awareness. This creates chaos as we carry on in the world trying to be at one with it. We are increasingly frustrated as we feel scattered, misunderstood, marginalised, and dehumanised. This rupture can manifest as addictions, dysfunctional relationships, self-sabotaging behaviours, aggression, hatred, violence, or total shutdown as in deep depression. Why does this happen?

There is a quote attributed (on the internet) to Carl Jung, father of analytical psychology (alchemist and mystic to some). I struggled to find the original source but share it here as an offering towards understanding why befriending the unconscious is important for a life well lived:

'Until you make the unconscious conscious,
it will direct your life and you will call it fate.'

Indians just love sitting in the lap of fate. Worse still, fate is used to justify abhorrent practices which represent the dark shadow of an otherwise rich culture. An opportunity to create positive change is always in the air. We, the Cultural Parents of the next generation, must grab it. *I say out with duty, obligation, and sacrifice and in with compassion, connection, and co-creation.* Cultural metamorphosis is escalating due to globalisation and rapid advances in digital highways. Many practices defined centuries ago by our ancestors are past their sell-by date! Potentially, technology can transport someone out in Kashmir, Nebraska, or Uganda into our homes on a daily basis. We can become virtual neighbours. We no longer live in isolated contained communities. Social media platforms and space travel are pushing boundaries to the outer frontiers. We are one, like it or not.

This story shares the journey of establishing a relationship with my Cultural Parent and attempts to make meaning of life. It has been a conflicting ride. Being born to Indian parents (South Asian culture) in an African territory with British values has had its joys and challenges. What has profoundly surprised me is how this reflective process, drenched in intuitive writing, has taken me on a journey from *Fat to Fab.* I had no idea that a side effect of this *verbal detox* would lead to incredible healing. Pounds of fat have been shed as the story has unfolded. A new upbeat outlook has arrived.

My struggle with body weight was birthed years ago. *Fatty* was a familiar label whilst *diet* was a constant four-letter word central to my existence. Surprisingly, *Fatty* is nowhere to be seen these days. Instead, *Fabby* has surfaced. How refreshing and joyful this feels. After enduring years of pain and despair that can define the human transformational journey, *walking my talk* and *living from the heart* have become my core drivers. I cannot recommend this way of being enough, set free to be me, warts and all. I can finally breathe, expansively, amidst the suffering.

An insight. Looking *Fab* is indeed wonderful, but do not drown in the illusion that 'thin is in'. Some of the most deeply wounded people have stunning figures and look beautiful. They *appear to radiate bliss* but their *reality is far from that.* One just has to look into the world of celebrities to see this truth staring at us. In the real world, people suffering from certain medical conditions may appear slim and look great. Sadly, they do not feel that way at all. Human beings are masters of facade but thankfully, also capable of exerting choice.

What increasingly feels precious is the ability to hold a *fabulous attitude* in the face of adversity. This really has proven priceless in this journey from *Fat to Fab*. Instead of drowning in the ancestral code of duty, obligation, and sacrifice, with its underpinnings of shame, blame and guilt, my life script has been significantly revised. By courageously daring to engage with intense feelings and giving them a voice, a lifetime habit of 'comfort eating' has broken. *My relationship with food has changed because my relationship with myself has changed.*

Food used to simultaneously control, soothe, and tranquillise me when I was drowning in my sorrow, as all addictions do, be they excess food, alcohol, exercise, shopping, gambling, drugs, sex, work, or attachment to technical gadgets and social media. *The feel-good factor from gorging down chocolate cake was a guarantee, but only temporarily. Self-loathing would follow quite quickly.* It was tough. Self-loathing is toxic. It eats you up and then spits you out in disgust, leaving you feeling exposed, vulnerable, and impotent. Fat becomes a shield.

This armour can be shed. As my bruised and battered heart sobbed, intense feelings cascaded onto these pages which held them tenderly for me, without judgement or blame. Forgiveness arrived. That most powerful healing tool for dampening internal sabotage. As thoughts and feelings tumbled out, a gentle loving voice emerged. It drowned out the critical voice which used to remind me of all the times I had failed because I had 'no willpower or discipline'. This *'forgive and be honest with yourself'* process gradually led to more nurturing thoughts, feelings, and behaviours. To my incredible shock and surprise, my weight started coming down and staying off. It was a slow process with stumbles and falls but huge insight. I found a key to liberation.

Caution: This book is not a guide on healthy eating or weight loss. Instead, it encourages self-discovery through honest reflection, courageous internal dialogue, and the written word. Compassionate engagement with these processes led to life-changing personal transformation. Profound psychic shifts occurred as the *verbal detox* progressed. I became acutely aware of my four bodies (mental, emotional, physical, and spiritual) rather than just the physical one, an 'aha' moment of the most scrumptious kind.

For years my emotional body had been stuffed with the wrong 'food'. So, it numbed up. Instead of feeding it with self-love and self-compassion, I had been stuffing it with samosas, pizzas, chocolate chip cookies, and ice cream. ***Somewhere in this reflective process, my emotional body resurrected and demanded love, forgiveness, and kindness rather than self-criticism, shame, guilt, and deceptively comforting foods.*** As my heart-centred emotional 'body' received nurturing human emotions, especially self-compassion, the shield of fat started dissolving away. Fragmented parts of me starting talking to each other and journeyed towards wholeness. I could be at one with the world, even with my imperfections and vulnerabilities.

It is hard to express how amazing it feels to be my *true self* after years of walking the streets of falsehood. I share this story in the hope that illumination, transformation, and magical shifts will lead you down your street of truth, wherever that may be. You will know you are heading there as a wise intuitive voice in your head will start powering you up and the crucifying internal dialogue will start dissolving away. Seeds of self-love will be sown as you start living from inside out rather than the other way around. External validation will matter far less. Deep in your heart bursts of courage and calm will arrive. *Fearless living becomes a real possibility, and with that, nurturing relationships emerge, be that with food, people or any other entity that you are in relationship with.*

Another gentle caution. You may feel worse off before calmness, clarity, and joy arise. When I gave up my food prop, anxiety with all its *body talk* (dry mouth, butterflies in stomach, heart palpitations, disturbed sleep and feelings of dread) became a frequent challenge. I guess anxiety had always been there as I lived my stressed-out, inauthentic and often lonely life, but food addiction contained it. I rapidly woke up to the fact that there was another part of myself that I had to make peace with. *Thankfully, there are so many resources and tools available to manage and lay anxiety to rest.* You are not alone. Please do not give up. Wobbly bridges have to be crossed, if we are to be 'free to be me'.

I have shared tips for doing this in the hope they will support you. *A favourite tool is of acceptance that life is one big river of unpredictable flow.* Something or someone is always knocking at my soul's door. Acknowledging the visitor with an appropriate response (rather than knee-jerk reactions) seems central for anxiety-free and transformational human experiences. There are no quick solutions. Curiosity and awareness hold the key. Joy and calm are available, as are agitation and aggression.

To this end, *reflective questions have been posed after each chapter.* These can be worked through on your own, or perhaps by sharing them with a friend. Whether you are a spiritual seeker, therapist, teacher, parent, yo-yo dieter or from any other walk of life, I hope they generate meaningful courageous conversations. Never underestimate the power of healing from within.

References and online resources have been included in the end for further exploration. These wise fellow spiritual seekers have profoundly inspired me. The list is by no means complete but offers a diverse range of messages for healing and living an authentic life.

Finally, I encourage you to create some quiet space for reflective writing because *silence truly is golden.* In this sacred space, as 'pen caressed paper', seeds for immense growth were sown. An intuitive process was set into motion by which deeply-embedded unconscious attitudes, beliefs, and assumptions wandered into my consciousness. The latter became a powerful oasis for healing where permission was granted to be set free. I wholeheartedly wish you the same.

Out beyond wrong doing and right doing
There is a field
I'll meet you there
    (Rumi)

Bon voyage.

Introduction: Early Reflections

What's it all about?

They say life is a journey. I can get my head around that. We are born. Then we die. In between the two states, we journey — from birth to death. If we are born to die, we could ask, 'What is the point of being born at all?' The need for a plausible answer feels urgent when a baby dies within minutes of birth. What is the point of their journey, besides anguish to the parents and all involved? Add to this that most famous Shakespeare saying: 'All the world's a stage, and all the men and women merely players; they have their exits and their entrances.' This makes me think, if the world is a stage with us humans as actors and actresses, who on earth is in the audience?

Who are we here to entertain? Who writes the scripts? Who produces and directs the dramas? Do we have to stick to the scripts, or can we pen our own lines? What is the drama about? Something deep and meaningful, or just plain boring? What is the message or messages that we are here to receive or convey?

When I thought about my own life, my parents were obvious candidates for the producers' role! They did produce me after all. But who or what was directing our family drama, influencing our scripts and penning the dialogues? Was it God? Was it our ancestors? The birth tribe? The Brahmin priests of Hindu religion? Politicians? Great philosophers? The pop band Abba? Or the neighbours?

Amidst many possibilities for 'who done it', *culture* kept fiercely knocking on my door. *Religion* followed closely behind, that old faithful friend, or foe, depending on your world view. Being a child of Indian parents meant inheriting Eastern culture. Simultaneously, being born and brought up in a former British colony (Kenya in eastern Africa) meant exposure to African and Western culture through formative years. Since then, England (hence British culture) has been my home for almost 39 years. So, I consider myself multicultural with overtly British tendencies. Yet certain triggers propel me into feeling like a 'good little Indian girl'. What's that about?

The terms *little* and *girl* suggest the presence of 'child residues' within the adult. Either way, this generates emotional conflict, leaves me feeling cornered and posing the question: *how do cultural and religious ideology impact on my identity and way of life,* especially when I consider myself a British Indian with African roots, held together by religious beliefs sourced from Hinduism and Buddhism with a dashing of Christianity and Catholicism? That is before I get all body, mind, and spirited and resonate with the concept of a spiritual being having a human experience. My favourite coping strategy of late is to recite an inner wisdom which arises from the depths of my soul in my morning meditations:

The Human Being gets agitated.
The Spiritual Being sits in the knowing.
(Knowing being an oasis of grounded-ness and calm)

Eastern and Western cultures have been established for eons, as has multiculturalism. Yet the latter seems to be a newish kid on the block (again) and a hot topic on twenty-first century planet Earth. It demands an attitude of working with sensitivity towards cultural diversity, difference, and sameness within politics, education, the arts, the health industry, the workplace, the family, in society, the community, and life. It drives political correctness to the edge. For instance, I was quite happy being described as a coloured person, though I understand why this is inappropriate now. Apologies if this offends as I know it will. That is not my intention. To me, person of colour describes, well, a person of colour. After all, black, white, brown and anything in-between are all colours. Underneath the label, I am still that person, colour or no colour, with all my human frailties and strengths. *Please see me.* Whatever my colour. It changes with the seasons. Suntans and all that.

The idea of multiculturalism got me thinking about my personal view around culture. A precise definition felt elusive but it centred around holding a certain world view embraced from the time of conception, perhaps even before. My cultural life felt inextricably linked to being part of a specific tribe, heavily influenced by the rules and regulations established by my ancestors who occupied a region of India called Gujarat (that I have visited but never called home). It perplexes me how the 'good little Indian girl' inside my 'mature British Indian woman' frequently screams for attention. Living amidst a dominant Western culture, my subculture seems to demand a certain attitude towards myself and others. It holds a tremendous power over me. What's that all about?

It's about deeply held beliefs and identification with labels. The need to examine and erase those that serve me no more has become a passion. After all, the human race can only survive, and more importantly thrive, by constantly re-examining and reframing itself depending on the challenges and needs of the prevailing period.

An *ideal model of multiculturalism creates harmonious communities that live on Integration Avenue rather than on Segregation Street.* We are all chasing the same human experiences – love, laughter, safe homes, nurturing relationships, financial security, meaningful work, freedom of speech and expression of cultural, social, political, and religious ideas without persecution and endless suffering. This is an impossible mission whilst carrying generations of introjected ancestral frameworks in our psyches, which form our rule books of life, especially introjects that speak of distorted ideology, extremist views, power, superiority, entitlement, and the like. Don't get me wrong. A lot of the teachings are very wise and precious. Conversely, many are frankly just not relevant to today's society. In fact, *toxic belief systems are proving to be dangerous and making life impossible for millions caught up in man-made power struggles.*

Some missions feel possible, like this calling to embark on a journey of liberation from the 'oughts', 'musts' and 'shoulds' of outdated cultural frameworks. I propose we stop acting out of tribal duty, obligation, and sacrifice. From observations and personal experience, these drivers lead to guilt, shame, blame, fear, anger and self-loathing, where the 'we' suffocates the 'I'.

Alternatively, 'we' and 'I' can waltz in harmony. I propose a framework of *compassion* (for self and other), *connection* (based on human values such as authenticity, honesty and respect rather than gender, race, power and wealth), and *co-creation* (where we are able to express our needs and understand those of another before defining outcomes). These drivers lead to love, kindness, forgiveness, self-worth, clarity, freedom, belonging, and expansive possibilities. Utopian some may think. I beg to differ.

Mother Earth is urgently crying out for our support NOW as she births a new age, a new world order. Some are calling it the Age of Light or the Golden Age, some post-capitalism. I dream of a new age of peaceful beings. Let's face it. There is a tsunami of evidence gathering that our current model for life is not creating universal well-being. *Homo sapiens* are becoming *Homo burnouts*. Chronic stress, brick walls and plastic are the new enemies, as is the possibility of nuclear bombing. All man-made creations. Again.

As some wise person said (source unknown), 'If we always do what we have always done, we will always get what we have always got.' I would rather not, thank you.

What can we change and how? At a personal level, Mother Gaia (Earth) and Father Sky are urging me to stop residing in ignorance and the wound of the 'good little Indian girl', that deeply conditioned inner child who feels the need to stay unhealthily attached to the outdated teachings of the Indian Cultural Parent. They are urging me to step out of this role and step up to being a responsible adult, the message being, *'Drop the repetitive game and consider alternative frameworks for living.'* I would like to do that without being labelled a *betrayer*. I, from the East, passionately love many things from the West. Why wouldn't I? Look where it has taken me.

On to my stuff.

Chapter 1

Scripted by Age 7: Holy Krishna (as Opposed to Holy Moses)

What is normalised in childhood travels with us,
for better or for worse, into adulthood.

We learn a lot as children – how to walk, talk, eat, wee, and poo in the appropriate places. We learn to play, read, write, throw a tantrum, get our cuddles, and learn how to be accepted, or rejected, by the world. Child developmental studies suggest there is significant non-verbal communication between mothers-to-be, the environment and their unborn children. Absorbed thoughts and feelings matter. Research abounds around the benefits of pregnant women listening to soothing music, and how babies can be persuaded to emerge waltzing into the world in calmness and serenity. Having no experience of childbirth, or recall of whether I danced or stormed into the world, this is hard to verify. Calmness and serenity do not seem to be the language of the new mums I know. More like wild white-water rafting and white-knuckle rides alongside gory blood and detached placentas. Yuk.

Eric Berne, the father of Transactional Analysis psychotherapy, suggests we already have a detailed life plan etched into our seven-year-old brain, which determines how we engage with the world into adulthood. Holy Krishna (the Indian version of exclamations such as holy Moses! or Jesus Christ!). That's scary! Apparently, ancestral, parental, tribal, religious, and environmental messages sponged up consciously or unconsciously by our tiny brains go on to shape our thoughts, feelings, behaviours, and attitudes into adulthood. I became curious about what I may have absorbed by age seven. I felt helped along by a melody.

There's that famous Doris Day tune, 'Que Sera Sera,' the one that goes,

> When I was just a little girl, I asked my mother what
> will I be?
> Will I be pretty? Will I be rich?
> Here's what she said to me.
> Que Bina Bina.

'You will be a good Indian girl with impeccable moral values and principles. You must have a "proper" job (none of that arty, creative talk) which brings honour to our family. Your arranged marriage will result in domestic bliss with a charming, handsome, and clever GLIB (good little Indian boy) born into a well-to-do (as in loaded with wonga) family. This arranged union will produce two beautiful, perfect, fair-skinned children (one of each sex of course) who will grow up with doting grandparents and a nurturing extended family.'

'Little Bina, you will also be a pillar of society and a wonderful ambassador of your mother country (India), as in the queen of *chapattis* (Indian flatbread) and vindaloo curries. The *good life* will equate to a jet-set existence with holidays around the world. Home will be a house with its beautiful trimmed hectares of luscious gardens set around a fountain feature of waterfalls, holding your dreams and ambitions intact. Whenever you are frightened, pray to God. He will always protect you. Visit the temple regularly, say your daily prayers, honour customs and traditions, and no harm will come to you.'

What a load of nonsense. More poignantly, what a lot of truth there is within the nonsense. In fairness to my mum who came from a very humble background, the tune sounds more like what my ancestral Cultural Mother sings, that deeply embedded 'parent' in the psyche whose song has travelled generations. The lyrics may have been written centuries ago, most likely by the patriarchal Cultural Father, but they are still what millions of Indian girls and women are singing to this day.

I recall a recent conversation with Sweetu, a friend's twenty-five-year-old British-born daughter who was addicted to the lyrics of this song. Her grandmother had been streaming this melody into her psyche from the time Sweets (my endearing term for her) gushed out of her mother's waterways. She strives to be a dutiful (grand) daughter by adhering to the tribe's rules but happiness is an illusion. Her curries are great but the 'no premarital sex' code of Hindu good conduct was keeping potential husbands at bay. The formula of 'the way to a man's heart is through his stomach' was not working. Additionally, the current economic and political climate was making life difficult for her generation. It really wasn't fair. She lived in a tiny flat (which she owned courtesy of daddy's tax efficient approach to business) but, as her peers, she craved for a big house, a flashy car, and fancy holidays. Now. What was the point of slogging through their private education otherwise? The tears spoke volumes to me. Sigh.

Indian soap operas viewed by millions, on a daily basis, add fuel to the fire of discontent. Every storyline has a perfect family of three generations living in a palatial house with regal architecture set amidst gardens that mimic the glorious rolling hills of England. Rambling bushes of jasmine, roses, and exotic lilies abound. There is always a fountain to be found. The perfect daughter-in-law, draped in a beautiful sari or some ridiculous East-meets-West (fusion) outfit with matching, dangly, sparkly Swarovski jewellery, is usually found slaving away in the kitchen cooking up the family meal or being the perfect wife, mother, daughter-in-law, sister- in-law, God worshipper, and pillar of the community – the hostess-with-the-mostest sort of thing.

Behind the soapy scenes, mother-in-laws pamper their husbands and sons (their beloved Princes) by wiping their brows and serving them cups of tea with Bombay mix and diabetic-inducing sweet snacks after their hard day at the 10am to 4pm office. This reception is usually preceded by the meet-and-greet ritual at the palace door where a chilled glass of water is served to hydrate their male egos and remind them of their superior genetic make-up. Whenever there is an existential calamity (such as when the aesthetically perfect, but biologically choked daughter-in-law cannot fall pregnant), the temple in the home, usually larger than a semi-detached, three bedroom Edwardian house, becomes the focus of incessant prayer and summoning to the gods. As the crescendo of Holy Krishna chants reach dizzy heights, suddenly thunder and lightning abound, the chandeliers start dancing, and a son is conceived. And people think immaculate conception is exclusive to Mother Mary! *Why can a woman just not be loved and accepted? Son or no son?*

Under the joviality lies a deep personal annoyance at such a stereotypical portrayal of Indian family life in the twenty-first century. This is the framework I was brought up on forty years ago. It holds too many painful memories of watching my mother damaged by such a superficial life script assigned to Indian women. By age seven and certainly by age fifteen, I had learnt a lot. It was not all very pretty.

I arrived into the world as my father decided to move away from the extended family. This was a taboo act within a culture that had unshakeable allegiance to ancestral cohesion. Dad was the second youngest of eight children. It may have been difficult for his needs to mean much, or for his voice to be heard amidst a gathering of siblings. My late uncles, as the elders did traditionally, defined the rules by which the extended family would live. My father did not want to play happy families and live in an inter-generationally occupied house (as per the soap operas). His was a classic case of the *potential for toxic fallout when East meets West in a strongly patriarchal Eastern family.* We resided in an African country which had just become independent of colonial rule. The political scene may have changed, but British culture was everywhere to be seen. There were different ways to be – African, Indian, British. Choose your Pick n mix.

Whilst my dad pursued freedom, my mother resigned herself into married life, leaving behind her deepest dreams and desires to another realm. Sadly, this is a common theme within her generation, where women had limited autonomy (a theme that shamefully continues to this day). Young Indian girls from humble rural families were frequently married off into richer households to experience the grandeur of city (and a better) life. These families were often rich in material terms but rather poor in terms of manners and humility, it seems. A late aunt of mine got rather upset with me when her feelings of superiority about being born into a 'royal Indian family' were gently dismissed. It fell on me to remind her that we lived in a country with an established royal family called the Windsors. We were the Patels, an ordinary middle-class and middle-caste family. Now there's some labels for you! *What is it about the human need for hierarchy and perfection? To be extraordinary and not embrace the ordinary? I struggle every day.*

Back to childhood. My father abandoned the framework of tribal duty, obligation, and sacrifice, and decided to individuate and move out of the joint-family home in his quest for freedom. As we lost connection with parts of our blood family, our nuclear family unit formed new relationships with other members of the expatriate Indian community in Nairobi. What a gift. What a joy to have genuine relationships that kept our hearts beating. Life felt on the move again.

My brother and I were enrolled into some of the finest schools in town. This meant we went to institutions in which the curriculum was based on British standards, Oxford and Cambridge, you know. We were awarded prizes when we did well. I was learning that my worth was based on a reward system. Dangerous stuff, as I got addicted to receiving prizes by always trying hard to be the best at everything – best daughter, best granddaughter, best sister, best friend, best pupil, and God's favoured child. This was the beginning of a distorted way of being, of denying who I really was and violating my true nature. It has taken years to soften the addiction. I am in recovery. It feels good.

Thankfully, what could have been a traumatised childhood became a rather adventurous one with our 'adopted' extended family. Memories of holidays by the seaside, picnics in coffee plantations and amazing wildlife safaris abound. My parents felt a bit different from my friends' parents, especially my father who wanted to embrace aspects of British culture rather than drown in imposed Indian rules from dominating siblings who held the family power. We survived.

What did this mean from a cultural point of view which undoubtedly shaped me? My father obviously had an affinity for the prevailing British culture that was integral to life in Kenya, which was a British colony till 1963. This culture was threaded through the educational, judicial, and railway systems, the agricultural and tourist industries, and even politics. The education system exposed us to middle-class British ideas and values which spoke of certain privileges and a certain way of life, such as eating scrambled eggs on toast with forks and knives!

I recall fond memories of my parents teaching me how to appropriately use these shiny, bulky eating tools, and how to precisely position them to say, 'I'm done,' or 'Still eating,' a very important etiquette especially when we went for Sunday lunch at the grand old colonial Norfolk Hotel or attended formal occasions such as dinner dances in the New Stanley or Hilton Hotels. Got to get it right. We were ambassadors representing our mother country, India. We could be proper. We could be polished. How superficial.

Embracing British culture meant horse riding, piano lessons, going to the cinema to see *Abba: The Movie*, disco dancing, and frequenting Angus Steakhouse. The latter was not in keeping with the 'good Hindu code of conduct', as beef is a seriously forbidden food based on religious teachings. They were one of my favourite outings! The restaurant served the most amazing veal steak and garlic sauce to die for. Oh dear! There goes the halo of the 'good little Indian girl'! As for the English accent, considered rather posh and revered by many, I have lost count of the number of times people have commented on my apparently perfect British accent. Not as posh as the Queen I say.

A particularly wonderful British society image is deeply etched in my mind. We were attending a dinner dance in a five star hotel downtown. There was my dashing suited-and-booted father gently grooving away with my mother, who was draped elegantly in a beautiful silk sari with a red rose in her perfectly coiffured hair. They were holding hands. They were living their dream. My grandparents would have been shocked and disapproving. Such overt exhibition of intimacy and physical contact in public was not appropriate. At least they had some clothes on, unlike some of the more recent images being relayed out of Bollywood (cousin to Hollywood) in India where semi-naked writhing bodies have unfortunately become the norm. Now there's a judgement for you.

Whilst a lot of our friends confined themselves to life within the Indian community, my father had a mixture of friends and business associates that included Indians, Europeans, and Africans, too. This caused him internal conflict and led to unhealthy habits such as fibbing. I have some sympathy for him.

I recall how, in spite of being in his forties, he was still anxious about being able to enjoy alcoholic drinks in the home as my mother, and the prevailing Indian culture, disapproved of such indulgences through bad Western influences. He would therefore conceal the truth about the beers or gin and tonics (G&Ts) he had knocked back with his mates before heading home. Imagine being labelled a bad boy for just wanting to enjoy a refreshing gin and tonic, whilst watching a blazing orange African sunset lighting up the sky, speaking of wonder and joy. This is the stuff of dream holidays. I do not know what all the fuss was about. He never overindulged. There's a time for a *lassi* (yogurt drink) and a time for the G&Ts!

Apart from the piano lessons and disco dancing, which could be seen as the more superficial expressions of Western culture, I sensed my father's soul had a deep desire to be set free. Western culture permitted self-expression, whereas Eastern culture promoted tribal advancement, especially with blood family. The latter can be suffocating. Don't get me wrong. Narcissistic autonomy is undesirable. The importance of community and belonging is essential, but it is not necessarily everything. The *Self ('I') is not a traitor when it wants to step aside from the tribe, individuate, and express its uniqueness.* Man walked on the moon because someone dared to dream boldly, outside the box, beyond the tribe's dreams.

My father wanted to express his individuality rather than embrace the identity of his clan – to drink alcohol, eat meat, travel abroad, have diverse friends and experience their world view without being accused of abandoning his tribe, and being a bad boy. I feel he had a deep sense of adventure and a genuine passion for travel, often mistaken as an inflated ego state needing to show off his wealth rather than being understood for what it was. This adventurous streak culminated in my brother and I, aged eight and six respectively, going on a grand tour of India with my parents and our English friends, Barry and Irene, jammed into my father's pride and joy – a big white Mercedes Benz imprinting its identity on the dusty roads of Rajasthan and Deradoon.

When visiting ancestral villages, our genetically extended family would come pouring out of their homes to greet and welcome us. It was important to them that we had not forgotten our forefathers, not pulled out our roots entirely and become totally *pardesi* (foreign), not become coconuts, as in white (westernised) on the inside and brown (Eastern) on the outside. I have been called a coconut. I assure you it was not meant to be a compliment. Am I a coconut? Perhaps I am. And even if so, is that such a bad thing when, not far from my beloved England, whilst writing this, war is raging, bombs are killing little children, and homelands are being ravaged whilst people flee in terror. *Identity matters, but not when it tries to survive whilst crucifying others in the process.*

Amidst the joys of my largely sunny childhood, unlike those shelled children, there was a disturbance. A sense of guilt and shame sat with me. We were privileged to live in a wonderful home. My father had it built from the ground up based on the architectural talents and 'stylish living' vision of a Danish man, a significant European in our lives. I never met him, and yet he shaped my childhood experiences through those bricks, mortars, wooden floors, huge balconies, and majestic walls. We had a sprawling home with that inevitable fountain, floors of the most exquisite polished wood, intricately patterned mosaic terrazzo with fine furniture and light fittings from foreign lands. I can vividly recall the luxurious feel of the beautiful golden carpet (sourced from India) beneath my bare feet in the living room. The acre garden was a mini botanical paradise adorned with exotic flowers and foliage amidst the endless carpets of grass. It was mum's pride and joy. Then there were the servant quarters. Ouch. I have said it now. That felt shameful. Servant. Awful. Awful. Awful! Let me explain.

Part of my childhood multicultural experience was to accept that the majority of the people of the land, the Africans (Kenyans), were far from liberated by gaining independence from the British Empire. It was standard practice for the Indian community to have local African domestic support which included housekeepers, gardeners, cooks, nannies, car washers, and a general dogsbody. People routinely spoke, often ungratefully, about their *servants*, and of course, we had our share. Johnny was his name.

Our wonderful Johnny spoilt us rotten. He was barely out of his teens when employed by my parents as a general housekeeper and multi-tasker. I have heartfelt memories of him. Johnny, my brother, and I behaved like the three naughty musketeers in the absence of my parents. Us siblings would have wrestling matches on that beautiful regal carpet with Johnny, the referee, merrily jingling my mum's prayers bells to begin and end rounds. Naughtiness was not confined to indoors. My mum once noticed how her car looked bashed in. The truth eventually emerged. Johnny had been teaching my brother how to drive my father's Mercedes-Benz, and the pair of them had ended up knocking my mum's car in the dodgy process. How they thought they would get away with it, only Johnny knows. So now not only was he our housekeeper, but he was a driving instructor. And who taught him? He could not afford driving lessons. Trial and error with my dad's car, on the sly, methinks! My parents trusted this angel of a man (quite rightly) and left the car keys lying around. Who can blame Johnny for taking my dad's vehicle for a spin around the gated compound? He could only dream of owning his own car and riding it along the streets of his land of birth. Some dreams just do not materialise. Little boys are drawn to cars almost by gender default. Sadly, to this day, there are millions of boys in the world who just play with toy cars but never grow up to own one. This makes me feel so sad. Actually, this really makes me furious.

At Diwali (Hindu festival), dad would buy tons of glorious fireworks. We would have the most colourful firework display within our garden, including rainbow-coloured fountains, spinning wheels, rockets, and bangers. Johnny, oblivious to any health and safety issues, would fearlessly ignite the dangerous things for our pleasure. I recall cowering behind a garden bush before bursting into gleeful delight at the spectacular sights in the magnificently lit-up, sparkly sky. *It looked like a thousand stars had emerged from nowhere to greet us, speaking of endless heavens and possibilities.* I love stars. What a warrior Johnny was. We were lucky to have him in our lives, and then the luck ran out. Circumstances changed. He left, leaving us distraught. He was such a significant carer in my childhood, and his sudden loss was like a bereavement. Death arrived, but the body was nowhere to be found. I remember going to his living quarters, looking for him, only to find that Patrick (new multi-tasker) had moved in. Sob. He was not Johnny. Where was he? Where is he? My brother and I often think of him with great affection to this day. We have been unable to contact him. I hope he is in a joyful place. The tears have arrived. Excuse me for a bit.

On reflection, this relationship had a profound effect on me. When little, I saw past the colour of skin. Johnny was not 'black' to me. He was a decent human being with warmth, kindness, and compassion who happened to be darker skinned than me. I refuse to use the word *servant* anymore. It feels abhorrent unless one is a *servant of peace*.

As a child, confusion abounded around the colour of skin and what it represented to me. There were so many mixed messages being hurled my way. Our servant (of peace) who scrubbed those mosaic floors was African. Yet my father had an African friend who lived with the same privileges that we did. Uncle Sam, his wife, and five children were welcomed into our home with open arms. They shared our sparkly knives and forks and ate from my mother's finest dinner service. They were a joy to be with, and we visited them in their home, too. No snobbery there in spite of their African heritage. Ah, but you see they were middle class. That meant having wealth, education, and a nice home in a nice area. That fitted. If you were poor and black, you were 'still shackled in the chains of slavery and servanthood', but if you were rich and black, you were 'liberated and free' and cool to hang around with and most likely from the Kikuyu tribe, the King of all tribes.

In the African culture, it mattered whether you were from the Kikuyu, Luo, Kamba, Maasai, or other tribes. There was a recognised hierarchy which resonated with the Indian caste system and the British class system. *Power-based systems are obviously a toxic human need.* Depending on your tribe or caste, you were destined either for the parliament buildings, the servant (of peace) quarters, or anywhere in between. Sadly, on the other hand, black skin represented violence. We, the Indians, lived in a culture of fear, always bolting our doors and windows, be it in the home or the car. Security guards were routinely stationed outside our homes. The majority of crimes were committed by local people or bandits who invaded from neighbouring African countries. *The truth is that amidst the political unrest brewing in the region, we, the foreigners, were often fuelling the violence.*

Indians in pursuit of the 'good life' had thriving businesses and plunged their wealth into gigantic sprawling mansions and fancy cars. Holidays meant going to posh hotels and animal game reserves to be served 24/7 by African waiters and porters. We wore designer clothes (as in Levi's) and decked our bodies with 22-carat gold whilst our servants (of peace) polished the carriages which rode us to the ball. Work out the balance of power there. Frighteningly, there was an armed robbery in my home when fifteen years old. I managed to hide from the robbers in my mum's pantry but sat with my heart in my mouth as gunmen threatened my parents with death if they did not deliver them rich goodies. Thankfully, we survived, but sadly prejudice was born.

My father took it to another level and would pull rank in restaurants for the best tables and get demanding if things were not going his way; a recurrent theme amongst his generation of Indian men who had bought into some sort of elitist ideology on foreign shores. It was all very embarrassing, and once, when a bit older and bolder, I recall storming out of a restaurant in protest at my dad's poor behaviour.

There I was, perched on the lawn outside, crying in fury. He eventually came running out to find me inconsolable. Whilst sobbing, I managed to articulate (well, actually yell at him), 'How can you treat someone like that? How can you treat any man in his own land and place of birth right and privileges like that? How can you? No decent father of mine would do that!' All this through a snotty nose and shrivelled up eyeballs that could hardly be seen for the crying.

My father just looked at me speechless and then mumbled something like, 'I'm not sure why I do it,' and promised to try and improve his manners in the future. In time, I understood why he did it. He had absorbed messages of superiority as part of his childhood conditioning, unconscious processes so out of his awareness. This does not condone his behaviour, but it has shed light on my behaviours, which can appear rather superior at times. Ouch! Gradually some of this misguided conditioning from his past dissolved. He was softer and kinder to waiters. In fact, he went the other way. They became his mates to share a beer and kebab with!

I feel grateful that my intuitive child sense held what was right and wrong. My true nature did not buy into all the 'well, we give them jobs' and 'that's life'. You know, the haves and the have-nots. In those tender years of growing up, I had limited understanding about this complex phenomenon, but it seems that within my soul, there was a sense of something *primordial and innate* that spoke of respect for humanity – black, brown or white. This is what I am referring to when I speak of *true nature*. It refers to that uncontaminated part of us, that knows intuitively deep in our beings what is right and wrong, but that which has been annihilated by man-made ideology to suit humanity's needs. A most cherished letter I still have somewhere in my 'beautiful memories box' was the one that my headmistress, a Catholic nun, wrote to my parents when I left Kenya, at age fifteen, to come to England: 'Bina's most beautiful gift is that she cares a lot for those less gifted than her.'

Has my ego emerged, that part of me that seeks validation and loves feeling superior? It certainly has. Kindly indulge me for a second or two. Thank you. My attitude around ego, which is often seen as a negative aspect of personality, is that we need it to survive. It helps us create boundaries and fight our corner. The ego is rather territorial in human beings, whereas our true nature recognises that the territory is formless. So, I say:

Let ego enjoy the success yet not distract us
from the Highest Good for All.

This gift of caring for others is universal. We, human beings, have the potential to genuinely cherish another from the depths of our souls and heart. Sadly, in the disillusionment that can be life, and depending on our personal experiences, this aspect of our nature is often abandoned or damaged. Gifts can be anything from a gentle touch to a smile, to hugs of reassurance, to sharing of knowledge, skills, chats, tears, pain, dreams, stuffing our faces with yummy cupcakes, and so much more. Whilst bound to my childhood and youth, I did not know how to energetically and consciously make the world a better place. Now the fire pit feels ignited and a passion for creating a world of 'the haves and the haves' is ablaze. Move over default settings. *Move over Cultural Parent. No need to suffocate us with out-of-date stuff.*

These are glimpses of my childhood. What has shaped you? Why do you see and experience life the way you do? In terms of life script, by age seven and certainly by my early teens, it was obvious to me that human beings could be incredibly harsh, vile, brutal, violent, and unkind. Paradoxically, they could be loving, funny, enterprising, compassionate, and kind. I also learnt that colour of skin matters. I am not talking about potatoes. Growing up, white skin and the attitudes that went with it alluded to entitlement and a superior power. Black skin was loving, kind, suppressed, agitated, and sadly, also to be feared. Then there were us in-betweeners, the brown-skinned Indians. Brown skin meant affection, joy, laughter, privileges, community, belonging, safety, security, family rifts, boring religious rituals, patriarchal oppression, hypocrisy, duty, obligation, sacrifice, and a deep love and fear of God. Brown also represented no smoking, no spirited drinking, no boyfriends, no snogging and no premarital sex. Worse still, every boy in my life was my brother except that perfect 'good little Indian boy' who would arrive in time to wed and bed me. The horror of it! Ultimately, the good life was defined by having an elevated status in society, usually based around private education, materialistic wealth, and a proper job; a liberating and yet simultaneously suffocating ideology.

Oh yes. What about mixed race? Who are you?

The script runs even deeper. At a personal level, it seems like little Bina decided that it was her job to make everyone smile by always being upbeat and happy, particularly when Mother was sad. Extended family conflicts created a lot of angst in Indian households. Ours was no exception. It was a central theme of conversation when my mum and her contemporaries reflected on life. Sadly, the same theme (conflict) is threaded into current society. My mum's eyes held a certain pain and a huge well of tears as I grew up. At times, her body held frustration and anger. I saw it in her facial muscles, those little twitches, so subtle and yet so voluminous. Illness arrived and, with it, I felt an increased need to rescue my significant carer. I do believe that, at some unconscious level, I had started rejecting the life script being presented to me. My intuitive radar seemed to connect to another truth. That of my true nature, the pure uncontaminated self. I could not buy into the illusion of playing happy blood families and look forward to married life. People seemed to just make up their happiness as they went along, pretend all was well, their masks intact, the storylines rehearsed and original thoughts, feelings and dreams abandoned for fear of the consequences of not belonging, for the terror that is isolation and loneliness.

In my teen years, girlfriends got soppy and soggy over boys. They started dating behind their parents' backs. I liked a boy, and he liked me, but commitment meant accepting a golden heart on a chain from him. No behind-the-shed snogging stuff for me, not what 'good little Indian girls' did. Got to hold on to the virginity for the husband. *Never mind that his had been abandoned eons ago.* In sticking to the ancestral code of good practice, I was consumed with trying to be perfect, always trying that little bit harder to be validated. These driven behaviours for acceptance are the stuff of counselling and psychotherapy. I became everyone's little Florence Nightingale, caring and sharing, rescuing. BUT, amidst the softness, there was a mighty concealed rebellion brewing which was to lead to amazing liberation, but not before years of struggle, pain, guilt, and shame. Better late than never, I say.

My mother had a few favourite rhymes in her world. She would often say, 'Suppression leads to depression, and no voice means no choice.' Oh. Then there was 'man proposes; God disposes.' She was a wise, fatalistic lady, my beloved mother. She often said her life was a journey of *'badhu gari javanu'*. Translated from Gujarati (mother tongue) into English, it means 'everything must be swallowed'. Welcome to the origins of my comfort eating, years of dieting and pet names such as Fatso and Fatty. Charming? Not.

Reflections

Who has significantly contributed to your *life script*? What messages have they conveyed to you that have been profound?

What specific childhood experiences influence your adult world view?

What does the colour of your skin represent to you? What prejudices or privileges do you feel you experience because of it?

Chapter 2

Parents: Papa, Mummy, Dada, Ba, and the Cultural Parent

Our ancestors matter far more than we ever know

Imagine the shock of discovering that you have hundreds of parents. It is hard enough trying to cope with the emotional challenges of being in relationship with our biological parents (Papa and Mummy - as in dad and mum) in whom we seek perfection but usually cannot find it. Apparently, that is because they are human beings. The latter come in mixed bags of the good, the bad, the mediocre, and the rather ugly, all inseparably rolled into one. Pick your mix.

Our minds house powerful scripts introjected from parents, teachers, actors, actresses, pop stars, philosophers, political and religious leaders, and since 1989, the World Wide Web. These messages profoundly shape our world view, for better or for worse. Then there is the mighty vision of the *Cultural Parent*, the father and mother of all parents. Pearl Drego, a transactional psychotherapist, published an article in 1983 with this very title. This 'parent' conceives the 'personality of a culture' which holds inter-generational and collective thinking, feeling, and behavioural systems that mould the individual towards tribal allegiance. The *group's song* is a potent force.

Evidence of group identity can be traced back to generations of ancestors, right through to more recent relatives and our grandparents. It is plausible. Who has not seen mannerisms and characteristics that run vertically and horizontally in families? A dear cousin is often mistaken to be my brother. When asked if he is, 'no' is the polite answer. 'But your cousin looks like, and has mannerisms, just like your father.' I agree, but he is not my father's son. His mother is my father's sister. The power of the gene pool is strong. We share characteristics with relatives long dead and gone. I am often likened to my well-departed paternal aunts in terms of a happy disposition and creativity, and my physical attributes are mirrored in extended family members. Bizarre features like the bushiness of eyebrows, lip morphology, certain mannerisms, ample hips, or the angulation and contour of a nose speak of inevitable connection.

Ancestrally transmitted frameworks for 'correct living' abound. In all cultures, as in the Indian one, family customs, traditions, and rituals are kept alive for generations in honouring the ancestors, hence the power of joint-family systems, arranged marriages, the dowry system, child brides, religious pilgrimages, specific death rituals, and family gatherings, especially around holy festivals. How may I have been conditioned by my ancestors? Let me introduce you to my grandparents. I never met my paternal grandfather but feel him ever-present in my psyche, especially of late. My father has shared some poignant childhood memories with me.

My paternal grandfather (Dada) died in the year I was born. This was a big blow to my father. My grandfather had a fierce presence and what sounds like a mighty spirit. It was around 1910 when he sat sail from India to Africa in search of a better life. The British presence in India was in full swing, with opportunities for Indian men to go to Kenya (a former British colony) and help build the railways. The potential rail workers were enticed by financial rewards. My grandfather felt responsible for securing the family's future, which had promising potential abroad. This meant leaving my grandma (Ba) behind in India. Their marriage became a cycle of intermittent relationship resulting in the birth of around ten children – India, the land of fertile soil and all that. A couple of children were lost on the way. With no bereavement counselling for my Ba to address her grief and loss, she probably just got on with it amidst the sorrow of longing for her breathless children and imagined all that they could have been. The facts are sketchy.

Dada managed to get to Kenya via the railway worker route but somehow landed a job in a bank, a most pivotal moment. The ancestral seeds for freedom through education (and holding proper jobs) were sown. At this point I feel the need to shout out a huge 'thank you, Dada, from the bottom of my heart.' His foresight, sense of responsibility and vision for a better life have gifted me that most priceless of human needs – freedom. I used to take it for granted but seem to cling to, and prize it ever more, especially in the current climate where freedom and democracy are being attacked in ways that are unimaginable. Hope abounds. The human spirit is heroic. *It seems like my grandfather's spirit has introjected a sense of life with purpose in me.* Thank you, Dada. Thank you.

Recollections of my maternal grandfather are fleeting, having met him once on visiting the village of Dabhoi where my mum was born. Her childhood home was a humble dwelling with little dark rooms and not much light. This offers a possible explanation as to why my mother loves washing up in dim light and likes her curtains closed just so. *We really are so present in our childhoods whilst in the depths of adulthood.* My maternal Dada died at the age of fifty four. I feel he is resident somewhere within me through the stories my mother has narrated about him. He was a gentle man who toiled the land and managed to tick things over. My mum is great at ticking things over, as I am. My mum's eldest brother was the family hero. He studied into the night on dusty roads lit by the village street lamps, and went on to become a medical practitioner with a rewarding career. Education was a man's privilege and right. Shockingly, it continues to be that way in many communities even today. Welcome to so called twenty-first century modern day living.

I am sure if my mum had been given half a chance to pursue higher education, she would have excelled professionally being the smart cookie that she is. In the end, being a girl and feeling like a burden, as finances were scarce, she decided to marry my father, leaving her family with one less mouth to feed. That could have been my fate if I had been born in India where millions of women are still treated as second-class citizens, if citizens at all. The statistics around domestic violence and gender inequality in India are horrendous. Actually, let me correct that.

They are pretty horrendous in Britain, too. One only has to look at the number of organisations within the country that are dedicated to this cause. The incidence of physical, emotional and sexual violence is rife behind closed doors in British Indian (South Asian) communities. The potent power of family *izzat* (honour) and *abru* (reputation) means an individual can be silenced with ease. My ancestors may have left behind their motherland, but sadly, they did not leave behind primitive thinking and a patriarchal need to dominate, suppress, and enforce a script of 'no voice, no choice'. Thankfully, not all ancestral conditioning is soul destroying.

The Universe has been far more tender towards me than I can ever explain. So here I am, Ms Eternally Grateful.

With the passage of time, human values such as respect, dignity, and compassion have become an important part of my script. Welcome to my beloved maternal grandma. Our paths crossed only briefly, yet her gentle magnetic eyes remain memorable. They gave me a profound insight into her inner world. Her body housed a beautiful soul. *She could not read or write a word but was highly educated about matters that really count on earth school – dignity, wisdom, and compassion.* Mum has shared stories of my altruistic grandma who would get my mother and her siblings to sneak out food, through the back door, to any frail elderly people in the village. She had *a sense of community.* I feel my mum learnt about courage and resilience from my grandma, characteristics passed down to my brother and me through the tapestry of experience and conditioning. Not all ancestrally transmitted qualities are negative. Best embrace and celebrate them.

My maternal grandma came from a poor family. She was orphaned when six years old and brought up by an aunt, no servant (of peace) to wash her clothes and hydrate her ego like mine was. Her childhood story is full of arduous walks to the village lake for water collection and laundry duties. My mother and her sisters did the same. Lakes are still used as washing machines in Indian villages where hardy women perch on the edge of pools of water and literally beat the dirt out of cloth. Such scenes, depicting a traditional way of life, have been brushed by painters for centuries. I wonder what conversations are had. What is expressed? Is there joy? Is sorrow shared? What about hopes and dreams? How much does the body ache from those beatings, and more so, from culturally inflicted wounds that do not permit the pursuit of dreams?

Taking my cynical hat off, and based on my mother's accounts of her youth, there is a balanced view. Many women were blissfully living this life. Really? Back then there was no rapid communication from the external world as to what alternative lifestyles were available, as is our current situation, due to digital magnificence. *What did not exist could not be missed or hungered for.* Who am I to judge, with my westernised lenses and ways of being? Perhaps there was a huge sense of camaraderie and connection in these daily tasks, as there often is when human souls come together and share of themselves from a common ground, from the heart, with a unified vision, whether it is doing the daily laundry or creating world peace.

What about Ba, my paternal grandma? I did spend quite a lot of time with her over the years. Those eyes, I see them right now, fierce as they pierce, windows to her soul. My paternal grandma was a little woman with huge presence. She had an aura of authority which oscillated between many judgements. The latter feature daily on my menu of life too. They can be discriminating. Ouch and Sigh! I often wonder what she would have made of the current situation especially around our cultural norms? We have a huge extended family embracing inter-marriages which have brought American, Australian, Afro-Caribbean, European, Middle Eastern and Oriental blood into a previously dominant Gujarati gene pool. All change, as they say. What would my grandparents make of all this? Words such as shame, shock and betrayal do come to mind. Or perhaps understanding and acceptance would prevail? One can only imagine.

From a personal point of view, I am not surprised by these shifts because human beings are always in transition. That is the basis of evolution. *We are all products of millions of permutations of liaisons through history.* I often think about my forefathers and wonder, 'What did my grandfather's grandfather's grandfather look like? And what about my grandmother's great-great-great-great-great-great-grandmother. Who was she?' And sometimes I keep thinking back even further and imagine what my family of origin (Adam and Eve kind of concept) looked like? Was life blissful or predominantly about survival and suffering? Were they darker skinned, lighter skinned, hazel-eyed or brown-eyed? Were they short or tall? And who on earth put ample hips and chunky thighs into the gene pool? The angst of my life! I would love to have photographs of these parents. There's something about black and white faded images that create nostalgia and transport me to another intriguing lifetime where life was perhaps far more tranquil than what we have made it into.

One thing is for sure. The human race is on the move, reorganising itself, trying to reach a new equilibrium. The transitions within the Indian culture could be viewed as nothing more than just a by-product of this oscillating force, just as in other cultures. After all, as per anthropological records, the human race has its origins in Africa. Now we are scattered all over the World Wide Web, so to speak. Diversity is a product of nomadic life. We march on. *But it feels important to pause and honour our past.*

My Ba (paternal grandmother) faced tough challenges in her time. Sadly, a couple of aunts left their marriages, which was unheard of in those days, the shame of it all. Yet my grandma bore it with a certain resilience, perhaps gratitude, too. One of these (late) aunts went on to care for my grandmother to her death. This was rather unusual for an Indian family. Daughters did not normally look after their parents. They went off to live with the in-laws to look after them, and the husband, who was part of the marriage package. There is a poignant song that was played at every Indian wedding in my childhood. It would be timed perfectly with the final goodbye as the bride bid farewell to her parents amidst the wailing and howling befitting the occasion. Let me own up to my own fair share of howling on such occasions. One just got taken over even if one hardly knew the bride, or her fate. Blame it on a song. It went something like this in Gujarati, my mother tongue:

*Bena re, saseriye jata jo jo pakhan tari na bhinjai, dikri tho
parki thapan kehvay*

I understood most of the language to make the Gujarati-to-English
translation but had to search the meaning of *thapan* through a certain
engine. Thank goodness for instant technology. The translation of
thapan, from Gujarati to English, produced the following words:

Thapan = capital, deposit account, capital, funds, stock, deposit.

Basically, allowing for 'slight loss in translation', the song being belted
out to the bride was:

'Daughter dear, as you head off to your in-laws, do not drench your
eyelashes with tears. Since after all, daughters are only transient foreign
investments for their parents.'

Aarrrggghhh! A foreign investment? Really? Is that all that I am? Sorry,
but some allergic reactions do persist.

Now this is definitely NOT the type of song one wants to pass down to
future generations. *Delete.* I wish to be a far more progressive Cultural
Parent than that. We cannot define ourselves through man-made
institutions such as marriage. Having not made it to the altar myself, I
have lived with the angst of being single in a world that is obsessed with
coupledom. On reflection, observing how many marriages are falling
apart within my community, I know in my heart that I have come good.
In fact, I have thrived rather than just survived, unlike some dear sisters
and daughters who have endured domestic violence.

One can only imagine how my grandmother felt when two of her
'transient foreign investments' returned to her doorstep, leaving their
marriages behind. Something tells me it was not a warm fluffy feeling
at all. I am curious about whether it was more acceptable to her that at
least they'd tried married life, unlike me who just shunned it altogether
and embarked on an alternative way of life, you know, that one labelled
'spinster'. I cannot be bothered to react. Which was more shameful?

Which to her was more culturally acceptable – having tried and failed or just breaking the code of good conduct, as in her eyes little Indian girls were just born to marry? I will never know. What a shame.

How else can she be recalled? My Ba was widowed quite young. A constant memory of my paternal grandmother is of her being draped in a crisp, white cotton sari with her head permanently covered with cloth. Her beautiful hazel eyes represented the only outwardly colourful expression of the mixed Eurasian and Aryan blood of our ancestors. Being widowed meant her forehead was devoid of the red powdery spot (*chandlo*) she would have regularly adorned when my grandfather was alive. It is the signature of a married women. Who would have thought a little red spot could so strongly shape a woman's identity? But it did. Not anymore.

The cultural tide is changing. At times, it feels like a roller coaster without any brakes. Revolution is steaming ahead. Evolution is plodding along behind. The introjects of the Indian Cultural Parent with its long-standing social, familial and gender norms is being ferociously challenged. New systems are emerging, interestingly not only in foreign lands but in Mother India herself. Traditional family life is diluting as families are getting smaller and adopting Western culture. Even my mum and her friends wear pants and tops (as they so dearly like to call them as opposed to trousers and tops), with *saris* (traditional gear) increasingly confined to special occasions. Denim jeans are probably the number one favoured garment amongst urban and many rural Indians, like the rest of the world. Now there's globalisation for you.

Regarding professions, it seems like the long-held ancestral theme of 'proper jobs' is disintegrating slowly but surely. A job these days can lie beyond the traditional seven (doctor, dentist, accountant, pharmacist, optician, engineer and lawyer) that were offered to my generation by the tribe. One world ideology and advances in speed of travel and communication means that the dream is ever-expanding. Cyber talk abounds. The opportunity to travel and work in places afar presents the opportunity to mix with people from multiple backgrounds and create 'new blood' through inter-marriage or no marriage at all. There goes the taboo on premarital sex! In fact, pre-nuptial sex amongst the younger Indian generation is rife, and denial amongst traditional and so-called westernised parents even stronger. Time to wake up.

Then there is religion, revered by my ancestors for centuries. Hinduism is over 3,000 years old. It does not have a grip on modern Indian children in the same way as my generation. God is often not worshipped, acknowledged, or feared any more. Technological gadgets and all the possibilities they present are far more worshipped than Lord Krishna. Search engines know it all. As for nourishment, meals are not just about rice and *daal* (lentil soup). Welcome to Fusion Land – Indo-Chinese, Indo-Italian, Indo-Mexican, smoothies, juices, sushi, superfoods. You name it. We devour it. What about languages? The common language is becoming English rather than ancestral native dialect. Many children in my family do not speak Gujarati. This is not a criticism. They are a product of the power of the prevailing dominant Western culture in their less prevailing subcultural Eastern lives. The loss of an entire language in time; it is a possibility. But not English. For now.

It really came home to me the other day. Sharing a common language with my grandparents' and parents' generations enriched my knowledge of ancestral history, which ultimately shapes me. By speaking a common language such as Gujarati, we have been able to share precious narratives of the past which has helped me understand the personality of my birth tribe and what a part of me is all about. The current generation, with language barriers, may be missing out on a wealth of understanding about their lives as they cannot communicate with people that hold important narratives affecting their psyche. *Our ancestors hold precious understanding and wisdom which can shed light on our repetitive limiting storylines and dramas that we keep playing out without any understanding of why.* This knowledge can help liberate our spirits and underpins many contemporary therapeutic approaches.

The power of language, especially English, is irrefutable. A young Spanish shop assistant recently said to me, 'Where did you grow up? You speak perfect English. I wish I could speak like you.' On commenting to her that her Spanish accent was charming and her English was very good, she quipped, 'It doesn't help me in my job. I think I can sell more things if I had your accent.' This sounded incredible. Now the so-called English accent has become an economic currency, the Indian accent being confined to call centres. Ever come across one of them?

Reflecting on my ancestors glaringly revealed something of great importance to me. I am an amalgamation of so much more than is obvious to me at first glance. Belief systems and attitudes which have been attributed to my parents and birth tribe are actually social constructs and cultural norms that were probably birthed by my Cultural Parent centuries ago. Western psychology, understandably, places much emphasis on the role of biological parents in shaping the world view of a person. There is often great focus on trying to make meaning of the dynamics of these relationships when things go terribly wrong. What I am beginning to wake up to is that my biological parents are only a part of my world view contributors. In my mind, the Cultural Parent feels huge. *The 'oughts', 'shoulds', and 'musts' of life have cascaded down generations and speak of a profound tribal power, far superior to the will of an individual.* That is why atrocities like female foetal murder, honour killings, rape in marriage and female genital mutilation exist. They should not. Nothing justifies such violence. The following felt revealing:

"……Unconsciously they (children) remain loyal to unspoken family traditions that work invisibly. Family Constellations are a way of discovering underlying family bonds and forces that have been carried unconsciously over several generations." –Bertold Ulsamer

(source: hellingerpa.com)

This makes me wonder about what aspects of my Cultural Parent do I love and frankly cannot stomach anymore? More importantly, *what responsibility do I have as a Cultural Parent to future generations in ensuring that the 'belief' seeds I sow help them thrive rather than suffocate their dreams and ambitions?* How can 'I' live harmoniously with 'we'? Before answering that, it seems cultural practices that are nourishing, and cultural myths that are toxic, must be identified. I wonder what all this means for you?

Reflections

How were your parents shaped by their parents' views of the world?

Are there any obvious patterns of behaviour and attitudes prevailing between you, your parents and your grandparents or extended members of your blood family?

What does your Cultural Parent look like? Does 'it' promote multiculturalism or tribalism?

Chapter 3

My Precious Daughter: Domestic Goddess and Rescuer Extraordinaire

Women are not born just to serve. We are also born to receive.

My dear girlfriend Pushpa and I were sitting in a cafe in the heart of vibrant London, putting the world to rights, as you do. Amidst the lattes and mochas being frothed up, we acknowledged that South Asian culture was being dramatically redefined, literally, as we spoke. How could we define what being Indian, amidst our British existence, meant to us? In my mind, there was no clear definition any more. All was in flux.

'What does being Indian mean to you?' I piped.

She flashed her pearly whites at me and said, 'For one, I can't cook!' What? Did I hear that right? Why was I surprised? Or more to the point, I was not surprised. The ability to cook is a statutory requirement to qualify for perfect wife and daughter-in-law material. Every little Indian girl is expected to have the capacity to roll out the *rotis* (flatbread) alongside the exotic curries and *biryanis* (rice-based dishes) in minutes. You would understand what this means if you ever watch an advert on an Indian TV channel. It goes like this:

The telephone rings. The wife, in her finest embroidered sari, with matching dangly earrings, colourful bangles, sparkly sandals, and manicured eyebrows, picks up the phone to hear hubby say, 'Lata, darling, so sorry for the delayed request, but I have invited my mates over for dinner, and we are parked in the driveway. Is that ok?'

'Of course, Ramesh dearest,' breezes Lata as she starts dancing around the kitchen to a famous tune and manifesting a feast fit for kings. The advert usually ends with a bag of *chapatti* (Indian bread) flour splashed across the screen with the happy diners, all twelve of them, gyrating their hips and mimicking some dance sequence out of a Bollywood film, digesting that feast, no doubt.

How contrasting this feels to the Western culture which appears far more formal when it comes to bonding dates. In the early days of my British residency and connection with English friends, I was a bit miffed that popping in for tea unannounced was not the norm. Indian homes (and, hence, kitchens) are open to visitors 24/7. No need to phone. Just drop in. I like that. Well, sort of, until someone knocks on your door at some unearthly hour. 'Just thought I'd pop in for a quick cup of *masala chai* (spicy tea) and some gossip,' they pipe. Indians do struggle with boundaries, be they between neighbouring countries or themselves. English friends, on the other hand, usually get their diaries out to formalise the process of *the* visit which gives them time to gather the meat and two veg. That sounds patronising, and it is, and I apologise.

To justify my poor attitude, a true story is offered. Meet Harry and Edith, our angelic English friends who invited us around for the annual supper. The latter is a term learnt in England. For Indians, it is foodie time at any time! We tend to eat a lot and resist being confined to eating times such as high tea, brunch, and supper! Anyway, back to the Smiths. Well, there we were in anticipation of the great British spread. Following on from the glass of wine, meat and two vegetables, and chocolate and pear pudding with no seconds in sight, my mum, brother, and I were found to be stuffing our faces with cereal within an hour of returning home. We were still hungry. No worries. We Indians are smart, and have good memories. The following year, we loaded our stomachs with Bombay mix before we went around for the annual English supper. All was well, no top-ups needed to satisfy the extensive Indian bellies.

Back to that conversation with Push (don't they just sound great these shortened terms of endearment), what did it mean to be an Indian woman these days? *We all seemed to be rescuing everybody but ourselves.* She, of numerous sisters, went on to explain how her parents did not glorify education. Her mum clearly prized cooking skills instead. Push and her sisters would inevitably be married off to some GLIBs (good little Indian boys) to conjure up a daily dose of artery-clogging meals full of flavours from the Ganges, night or day. In my extended family, the daughters were expected to be domestic goddesses (DG) from a young age. Gold standards in cookery, sewing, dusting, flower arranging and social entertainment were expected. Indians just love gold, as do burglars, all 22-carats of it.

One of my endearing cousins was the ultimate DG, from age zero. She would still qualify for the award of global domestic goddess to this day. A very distant dream in my case. My paternal grandmother (Ba) was rather unimpressed with my progress in this department. In her eyes I was more like DC, as in domestic chaos. She sternly told me to stop having too much fun and focus my mind on these crucial golden homemaker tasks. Who would marry me if I could not cook? Well, I can cook but nobody married me. My house is in pretty good order, adorned with neat cushions, ornate, dust-free (well, sort of) furniture, creative artwork and flower arrangements, all signs of domestic competence. My guests are always warmly welcomed and well fed. I am assuming she would be proud of me today. That is until she hears about my love for the bubbly stuff, gay marriages, premarital sex, and rock and roll. Would she approve of this young, free, and single fifty-six year old who resides on her own? Especially as good little Indian girls only leave their parental home on marriage? There goes my halo. It is culturally rather fragile these days. A rebellion has been brewing.

For instance, at age forty-three and closer to peri-menopause, I decided to buy my own home, a stone's throw from my parents. My mum's friend (busy body *auntiji*) objected. 'What's the need for you to leave your parents' home at this age?' she said. What she was actually saying was, 'Why are you abandoning your parents?' I heard it loud and clear. The same undercurrents were rippling in parts of our community when my brother decided to emigrate to Australia for a better life. How could he abandon his family? My parents did not object. After all, how could they? They had left Mother India to go to Africa for a better life, leaving their parents behind in the homeland to be cared for by extended family. For my parents, it was a case of checkmate. *But guilt and shame are sneaky and creep into our psyches through the back door.* I managed to suppress them somewhere in my fat body. I was moving out. Period or no period.

In addressing what being an Indian woman means, in modern-day Britain, the word *conflict* arrives. My generation has been force-fed, as a duck or goose is for foie gras, the seeds of 'premature parenting' from babyhood. A clear message is planted into our childhood life script which instructs us to dutifully look after our parents forever. I can understand this when they are older and perhaps frailer, but to expect it from when they are in the mid-fifties to early sixties (official Indian retirement age from life) is rather ridiculous. Religious ideology in this department does not help. There are a lot of Hindu devotional songs which espouse the virtues of seeing God in your biological parents, and worshipping them as you would the Almighty. Please, change the tune. It feels suffocating, especially if they really struggled with good parenting skills and you were the brunt of such inadequacies. And slaps.

An Indian girl's life script can be inevitable. There is a ceremony, still honoured by many Gujarati families, called *chhati*. *Chh* refers to the number six. Apparently, the God squad writes our soul's journey when we are six days old. Central to the theme seems to be valuing duty and sacrifice. It is what soldiers do for their country. I am hardly a soldier. Sulk! This journey can be translated into aspiring to domestic goddess status and living in extended family homes with several bodies under one roof, or certainly along the same street. It means respecting elders who have done nothing to earn your respect, being tribal rather than individualistic. Your own needs and desires come second to the family's needs. It means no room for personal space. What's that bizarre concept? The harsher side to this ideology is that it makes good little Indian girls grow up into Rescuers Extraordinaire. In extreme cases, burnout is inevitable manifesting in chronic illness, debilitating disease, anxiety and depression. It is on the rise.

My Indian girlfriends and I have shared endless conversations around the angsts of expectations from parents and relatives alike who want us to be a certain way. It does not matter whether you are married or left on the shelf and labelled 'next time around'. Whether you live in Europe, Asia, Africa, America, or Australia, there is a thread of expectation to serve, serve, serve, an unconditional sort of service that leaves the mind, heart, body and spirit depleted. In the end, rescuing others does lead to deafening applause. A dangerous side effect is an addiction to external validation. *Praise becomes a drug.* I am only acceptable if I am dutiful and selfless (sacrificial) – serving the family, society, community and God. I am only okay if others say so, no room for self-care or self-love and self- acceptance. What's that?

The increasing conversation amongst my generation, especially women, is around the physical and emotional exhaustion of caring for extended families. This can amount to over fifty human beings. I do not jest. In many families, when planning to have a small, cosy family birthday party or wedding celebration, the guest list starts with the number fifty one, as fifty people, 'the family', are already permanently etched on the Patel party list. It is only a question of when you start abandoning relatives. The ones who do not get an invite feel betrayed and often express it. To top it all, many women feel obliged to cater for the guests by producing the party feast in the 'home-cookery school'. This means arising at unearthly hours to cook the sweet treats (*ladwas, jalebis, eggless cakes, baklavas, gulab jamuns, barfis, shrikhand*) and the savoury treats (*dhebras, puris, shaaks, mogo, paneer tikka, biryanis, aloo samosa chat*) with little time left for curling hair and painting the masks on. You only have to observe the mother of the bride on the wedding day, or mother of the toddler at the first birthday party (and their female 'support acts') to understand what I mean. Whilst everyone else looks a treat and smells like a deluxe-fragrance room diffuser, the 'up at the crack of dawn' posse of women have a weariness about them concealed under the best foundation and hastily applied deodorant. The smiles are held in place (as if by an infusion of Botox) because even though the mind, heart, body and spirits are drenched in fatigue, the show must go on.

Why have Indian women become awash with this level of stress? Talk of feeling overburdened and depleted is a recurrent theme. An insight. We reside with a generation of parents whose rule book for life states that 'a family unit never fragments, rain or shine.' Undoubtedly things have changed for a lot of so-called modern families. Separation of units is happening, but there is resistance. Underneath the veil of acceptance, ageing parents expect their children to keep up their social life, meet their increasingly complex needs, and generally see them to the crematorium. This is a tough ask, especially when coupled with the trials and tribulations of raising children who see themselves as westernised and who struggle with their Indian cultural identity. Whilst men may be supportive in their role as provider of practical solutions, the majority of the physical and emotional burden of this drama falls on the shoulder of women who adhere to the *Manual Of Domestic Goddess, Excellence & Acceptance*, authored by the Cultural Parent. This drives an automated need to rise to every occasion, repeatedly, at the expense of their physical, emotional, mental and spiritual well-being. Is it worth it?

The sinister side of this cultural normalisation of *being born just to serve* is seen in the horror of abuse. This can be physical, emotional, mental, or sexual or anything in between. The official figures for these atrocities amongst the South Asian community, especially against young girls and women, in India and the United Kingdom are shameful (just go onto the World Wide Web and you will see what I mean). Sadly domestic violence is not confined to my community. Research suggests that women and men from all cultures with histories of domestic violence in their childhoods may grow up to become bystanders, perpetrators, or victims of this crime themselves. Violence is normalised in children, and so the cycle goes on.

Stopping the repetition.

I recently read the outcomes of an academic research study, *Abuse going unreported in Britain's South Asian Community* (https://www.theguardian.com/society/2015/sep/19). It made for some sober reading and highlighted how misplaced collective cultural ideology such as the patriarchal system can be so destructive.

The difference between domestic violence in the South Asian community compared to that in Western culture is underpinned by the extended-family-system framework of Eastern culture. Indian victims, largely women, will be violated not just by members of their own family, as in a father, mother, or brother as seen in honour killings, but often by members of the extended family. Not only does a husband act despicably towards them, but so do the in-laws (father, mother, sister, brother,) cousin next door, and so on. United-we-stand is a force to be reckoned with in these situations. How vile and disgraceful. The Cultural Parent should know better. This framework for life is unacceptable. *Women are not born just to serve. We are also born to receive love, respect, dignity, and freedom.*

Central to domestic violence lies an abject lack of self-esteem and self-worth. One buys into the psychology of servitude and subservience. Victims of abuse, irrespective of gender, often cannot talk about their horror or walk away from the violence for reasons of *sharam* (shame), *abru* (reputation), or the *izzat* (honour) of their family. They are held to ransom by a strong internal dialogue along the lines of 'What will people say? This will shame my family.' Essentially, *individuals are spat out to keep the tribe victorious.*

I am grateful that in spite of developing the habits and symptoms of a Rescuer Extraordinaire, my sense of self-worth and self-esteem were not completely obliterated. I have been able to fight my corner against aggressive men. Sadly, I am aware of many women in my community who have suffered domestic abuse. My heart aches for them. They become slaves to a deeply rooted cultural attitude of 'Now I have laid my bed, I must lie in it even if I am harmed.' My mum has shared with me how she was told in gentle but firm terms by her father that she 'must make her marriage work no matter what.'

She has succeeded and made it work through the rain and shine. *Self-sacrifice being her formula for success. That framework stops with her as I have no intention of following in her footsteps.* Self-love and self-compassion are becoming more my style.

The whole scenario of domestic abuse really pushes my button of ethics. If I know someone going through this but do nothing about it, what does that say about me? Am I being a bystander? Or worse still, a perpetrator by not intervening? Abuse of any form should not be a family affair. We cannot abandon ourselves ('I') for the reputation of our families ('we'). We cannot become the 'walking dead'. Nothing justifies that level of sacrifice, surely. I respect that it is a complex issue. When fear hangs over a victim like a dagger, it must feel impossible to see a glimmer of light in the eternal darkness that is life, and take that first step to break the chains of imprisonment. Technology may be the way ahead.

This was brought home to me when listening to a recent radio show on the BBC (British Broadcasting Corporation) World Service where they reported on the results of a competition held in Mumbai (India) for developing a 'violence/abuse detector gadget'. This was instigated to help address the terrible atrocities of domestic abuse, sex trafficking, gang rape, and the like against women in India. I was uplifted as it was obviously becoming an important issue for social change, yet I felt deeply sad. The winner was a gadget developed by a man. How more humanistic would it be if men could re-programme their own gadgets, as in their minds and below-the-waist weapons of mass destruction, to bring an end to these terrible crimes rather than rely on an inanimate gadget void of empathy or compassion to resolve the issue.

Gender inequality challenges are tough. In spite of my steely exterior and being raised in a relatively progressive family, serving dutifully for years has been part of my script, too. Having been unconsciously fuelled by the Cultural Parent's stereotype script of what Indian girls are expected to do for acceptance by the tribe, I know what a depleted mind, heart, body, and spirit feels like. Do not get me wrong. It has not all been confining or downhill. I have travelled extensively, bought my own home, had a rewarding career, been on top of my game in my field, and so on. But the unconscious has been working its unravelling wheel unbeknownst to me. This reality emerged during personal therapy as part of my counselling training. Part of this obsession with serving, besides the introject from the Cultural Parent around what a good little Indian girl abides by, seems to be wrapped up with *negative emotions associated with not doing the marriage thing*. My parents have never made me feel a failure because of my lack of marriage, but I probably have been harbouring feelings of guilt and shame (those toxic emotions again) at not getting married and failing to produce those beautiful grandchildren for them. I say *probably* because talk therapy has revealed that nothing is for sure when it comes to psychologically motivated aches and pain. It is usually a multifactorial malfunction. There are so many theories, confusion galore. Heartache and dysfunctional behaviour seem far more complex to resolve than toothache. I was once a dentist. I should know.

There are supposedly several reasons for my behaviours. Some are attributable to unconscious scripts learnt as part of my childhood in which I was introjected with this-is-how-to-be-accepted-by-the-tribe messages by my parents, culture, religion, the media, environment, education system, and so on. This is commonly referred to as conditioning, or brainwashing, if you are a total cynic. Then there is that primordial phenomenon which prohibits a child from completely breaking free psychologically from a parent. It may be to do with the fact that human babies are dependent on their significant carers far longer than other species. There is more time to be 'needy' and 'dependent'. *We want to be loved and nurtured no matter what.* We engage in emotional and psychological warfare in an attempt to make our relationship with our significant carers (usually parents) ideal, whatever that means. The ugly side of this is seen in abused children who will accept a daily bashing from a parent rather than be ignored. At least the physical pain confirms 'I exist'. Sob.

I find great solace in John Bowlby's attachment theory, described in his classic book *A Secure Base*. This attributes our adult behaviours to the type of bond we formed with our significant carer (usually mothers) when young. So we can be predominantly secure and confident (ab fab), anxious and ambivalent (take it or leave it: like me sometimes), or anxious and avoidant (often labelled as antisocial). Worse still, we can be disorganised, which equates to chaos. Finally, we can experience differing styles from each parent and have bits of each style. Confused? How normal.

So back to my processes – they just love that word in the world of counselling and psychotherapy. Process to me is about making transitions and finding meaning. It offers a path to a progressive life, rather than to a stale one. Change can lead to feeling anchored and simultaneously floating free. It is not as rosy as it sounds.

Assumptions when one is unmarried abound. People thought that my 'spinster's life' was rather laid back. I used to get all hot and bothered about being labelled a 'spinster' but notice that the label evokes no discomfort anymore. Trust me. This writing process is so healing. A label is after all only a label. We do not have to have an allegiance to it. I am reminded of Shakespeare's famous quote from *Romeo and Juliet*:

A rose by any other name would smell as sweet.

Sorry, I digress. Back to my rosy narrative. Many assumed that being without husband and child left me with plenty of free time to be running here, there, and everywhere, attending endless social gatherings, every weekend, just off the choked M25 motorway, meeting every cultural expectation. My generation was coerced into showing up at all extended family occasions be they weddings, religious ceremonies, birthday or dinner parties. It was rude to say no. One must not offend. I often asked my mother, 'Why must we go?'

Response? 'That is how we will find you a husband.' This attitude was not confined to my mum. It was deeply ingrained in her generation. Essentially, it was all about networking to find that suitable boy and keep tribal cohesion going. Obligation was another theme. 'Well, we must attend this ceremony because the host's grandfather was your grandfather's best friend. He helped our family in the 1800s when they were in need. It would be rude to say no.'

Really? I did not even meet my own grandfather, so it seems a bit unreasonable to expect me to keep such liaisons going. But because it was important for me to be a 'good girl' and being Ms Popular was an addiction, I inevitably showed up.

Intellectually, all was well, but the truth was that my emotional imbalance was being diverted into body fat. I literally ate and talked my way into happiness with endless defensive video tapes (DVDs if you are young) playing out in my head. I was deeply unhappy about this way of life. Instead of being able to rant and rave about it, and express what I really wanted from the heart, I had this little voice (actually, it was rather big), saying, 'You should be grateful. You could have ended up with some chauvinistic husband with an extended clan who expected you to produce several children, stay at home and sparkle the dishes after dinner time. Be the perfect dutiful traditional wife.' Yawn. 'Worse still, you could have become a victim of domestic violence as many Indian girls are.' The mind completely took over when really it was the heart that wanted to run the show. It does make me think. *The mind, our best friend or foe?*

The internal movies went on. There was that additional dialogue in my head which said, 'And how much nicer it is to look after my parents than some other good little Indian boy's parents as per Indian family customs.' If I charged an hourly rate for listening to the theme of 'the unreasonable demands of in-laws' (often referred to as out-laws), I would be living on an exotic island with Adonis by my side, massaging aromatic oils into strategic body parts and having an abundance of naughty but nice fun and frolic. Wake up, Bina. Sigh!

At an unconscious level, at which we all reside far more than we ever realise, I was driven by a deep desire to make things right. For who?

Certainly not for myself. For whom then? Reflections galore, and there it was. As previously acknowledged, though my parents never directly expressed disappointment at my lack of a wedding band, my mum would often say, 'Well, it's not in her destiny to marry, or perhaps God has retained her in our lives so she can look after us.' Just like my aunt who was left to care for my grandmother in India whilst her brothers lived the good life in Africa, free of any parental responsibilities. Please do not judge my mother harshly. This is how she managed her wounds. Religious balms can be so numbing and simultaneously feel healing.

There was some feeling of failure on my part gurgling somewhere deep within. Unmarried and childless, that's a potent duo. I tried to make up for it in any possible way. My home was only a few yards away from my parents' house. Dropping in every day and catering for their physical and emotional needs became a ritual. Daily visits to friends and relatives at weekends to reduce isolation and loneliness became the norm. Compulsion seemed to be the driving force, but I wonder if I was also seeking forgiveness because my beloved parents' scripts had been somewhat torn apart by my lack of marriage and the absence of grandchildren, usually a given for my parents' generation. Perhaps duty and sacrifice were driving me to care for them so intensely, as written in my soul's journey when six days old. I really would rather be driven by love.

Most of my parents' friends had an abundance of grandchildren. Understandably, that is all they talked about. My mother felt she had no stories to narrate as nothing had progressed in her life since she had changed her own baby's nappies, so to speak, stuck in time and space. Though she never said it and used the 'destiny balm' generously, I sensed she suffered deeply from feelings of abject betrayal as my brother and I are childless. So, *moi*, Ms Rescuer Extraordinaire, tried to give my parents the happiness that grandchildren may have given them – how naive, how impossible. I saw how both of them came alive when we were around babies or little ones. It broke my heart. I tried to be their supportive son as their only son, my brother, was oceans away. He and my lovely sister-in-law called and visited whenever possible, but transient physical presence and a distant voice do not hold much power in the day-to-day scheme of our lives.

It was like being on a hamster wheel. The more I did, the more praise was bestowed on me by the extended tribe, who labelled me the most perfect daughter one could wish for. This led to an addiction for external validation as true self-love was lacking. It was part of my reward system. My extended family saw me as a rock who could be completely relied on in a crisis. I would drop everything to soothe others and make it better. I became a Rescuer Extraordinaire, just to be accepted, just to be forgiven for letting my ancestral, biological, and Cultural Parent (s) down. But my view is changing as self-care and self-love are demanding my attention. With that, *duty, obligation and sacrifice are being abandoned as they are no longer my driving forces for acceptance.*

Why? Because when we starve ourselves of self-love, self-worth, and self-care, we betray and abandon ourselves, adrift in a stormy sea, vulnerable to the elements, drowning our bodies, mind, heart, and spirits, never to realise our authentic nature, that uncontaminated part of our self that already knows the truth. The latter is not some man-made truth with all its distorted labels and ideologies but a universal truth that every human being aspires to, which speaks of emotional and psychological freedom and a sense of joyful meaningful purpose for our existences, not fragmentation and a constant inner struggle which leaves us feeling depleted and purposeless.

While at it, I would like to have a little moan about the current rage of *developing resilience*. Don't get me wrong. It is a valuable life skill. But so is owning our vulnerability. Both are equally essential to ride the tsunamis of life. To be honest, the need to develop some sort of stoic-superwoman capacity that can always ride the storm feels tedious. In fact, far from developing resilience, which to be honest has been my norm for years, learning to accept my own vulnerability and say 'no' is a growing edge. I am not always in the mood for resilience. Can you please just see me as strong anyway, strong in my moments of weakness, softness, self-doubt, and confusion?

I share an entry from my diary not so long ago:

It is okay to say I am tired. I am weary. I need to rest. I can't give you any more support today. I can't run that extra mile today. Please ask me tomorrow, but today, I cannot do it, and it is okay. More than okay. Like a weary traveller in a hot desert barren of an oasis, I am parched. I am weary. I need to rest. Please, may I rest? Please may I rest and still be okay as a human being?

Make that a 'yes'. Thank you.

Thought for the Day:

Dear Life, please support me as I hold an attitude of loving–kindness that honours the interconnectedness of all beings without abandoning myself.

Reflections

What gender-based responsibilities have been assigned to you in your culture?

Are you a Rescuer Extraordinaire? If so, what's that all about?

How can your external life be balanced against your personal needs for well-being? How can you develop self-care and yet still care for others?

Chapter 4

My Precious Son: The Right Honourable Good Little Indian Boy

Compassion for Men

There is an attitude held by many women: 'all men are bastards', as in nasty and horrible. Is that true? No, not in my experience, though it is understandable why this attitude may prevail. Prisons house men who are mass murderers, rapists, drug traffickers, paedophiles, and all other unmentionables. The current barbarism by terrorists on humanity are predominantly male acts (but not exclusive to them). Biological programming seems to seed more softer and nurturing qualities in women, but it cannot be denied that harsh female energy harms men, women, and children in unimaginable ways.

Another derogatory label used by women is 'typical men'. This emanates regularly from fellow good little Indian girls when having a domestic moan. *Typical* referring to men's lack of sensitivity or being 'mummy's boy', with an inability to multitask.

Igniting compassion for men can be challenging, especially when we are constantly bombarded with their shadow side. Evidence abounds that damaged, broken, and sadistic men are not behind bars but threaded into society. They secretly beat women up, sexually violate them, and treat them as second-class citizens, if citizens at all. Brutal rulers, predominantly men, murder their own blood brothers, sisters, and children with bombs and chemical weapons to meet some horrific need. Suicide bombers, predominantly men, randomly kill people in airports, marketplaces, train stations, public events, and on pavements. This rips into the fabric of society and sows a deep seed of hatred in the hearts of women towards men. Rational thinking reminds us that men are also violated by such atrocities, but the unconscious is notorious for creating fear-based distortions in our thinking.

What life script drives such hatred and violence? These men often have a personal history of terrible neglect and abuse in childhood. That does not condone their behaviour, but does that exclude them from compassion, a basic human right and need?

What makes a human being so disconnected from being human? Assuming being human is about having qualities that support the loving and progressive continuation of the human race, rather than its extermination. In patriarchal societies like mine, men believe they are superior to women. At some level, they may be. They are physically stronger for sure and therefore more amenable to certain tasks than women. But what else? Oh yes. They produce the sperm for future generations. In the Indian culture, they are highly revered for that. Women's eggs seem to be just taken for granted. *Sperm cannot birth into human life without egg, a trivial fact, so it seems.*

Boys will be boys. 'So, what's going to happen to your dad's line?' said my dear childhood male friend who was born in patriarchal India and now lived in America. Having fathered magnificent children, he was content in the knowledge that he would live on through them after death. His curiosity was obviously related to our family status quo. My brother and I are childless.

My response? 'Dad's line will end with him, and there's nothing tragic about that.' This sounds harsh. How can I hold such a view? It is because an alternative view on reproduction exists. The fact is that though my father possesses human qualities worth leaving behind on planet Earth, a part of me accepts that not all of us are born to expand the ancestral line.

Some of us are born for other accomplishments as stated by Paramhansa Yogananda in his famous book *Autobiography of a Yogi* (288): 'He who rejects the usual worldly duties can justify himself only by assuming some kind of responsibility for a much larger family.'

Interesting how I am happy to embrace 'much-larger-soul-family' duties but struggle with tribal ones. *This expansive view feels supportive as it gives me permission to fail at reproduction and live the bigger dream.* Luckily, there was no insatiable desire on my part for spreading the Patel seed. I know of women who have resorted to sperm banks to realise motherhood. Thankfully, with no man in sight, or marriage for that matter, spinsters like me are let off the hook. We simply cannot even consider having a baby without marriage. Where would the family hide their shame? In any case, my seedlings would not matter. In my birth tribe, a son is revered because he secures the ancestral lifeline and is automatically bequeathed the title of the Right Honourable Good Little Indian Boy. 'Golden balls' comes to mind. Relief. The tribe can flourish. Testosterone-driven attitudes, traditions, customs, rituals and cultural habits can go on. Gujarati girls, like *moi*, on the other hand, are left to carry their father's names as middle names, and on marriage, daddies' names get swapped for husband's names. How these men cling to us. Please stop clinging. Shower love. But do not cling.

In my heart of compassion, I acknowledge it can be tough on Indian boys. They are under pressure to do the honourable thing for the family, to be Providers Extraordinaire. My father struggled in breaking away from his family. What is incomprehensible is how my dad, in spite of wanting to do his own thing, still expected my brother to follow a certain familiar familial script. Hello, Cultural Parent. That unconscious force ever-present. We were a family of many doctors. This was considered to be a prized profession. Health meant wealth! My father wanted it for my brother. Doctors need to stay grounded at the sight of blood. My poor brother is usually horizontal on seeing this body fluid, not much use in a medical emergency. Sadly, acquiring appropriate status and affluence to honour the ancestors means a lot in my culture. In fact, Indian boys have been dished out messages for generations which would go something like this; expressed as a letter from a father to his son.

My dear Jignesh,

Your mother and I are so happy you have secured admission in medical school in the best university on this planet. You are the first child from our village in India to do so. God is great. Now we know that all our sacrifices have not been in vain and you will go onto bring glory to the family. I look forward to retiring soon once you can take over running of the family. As an elder son, you know this is your duty. We must also give your little sister Priya a good dowry when she marries. She will definitely get a rich, educated husband because we will be a family of doctors with honour. Your little brothers are so excited at the thought that they can travel abroad and also be like you. A family of doctors, how wonderful. Your grandfather would be so proud. In the end, all sacrifices will lead to a happy, healthy, and wealthy life. I dream of the day I can get that nice foreign car like Chambubhai next door. You boys, my clever sons, can build a hospital and serve the community. We can call the hospital Saraswati District Hospital after your grandmother. You know how much she looked after you when you were *chhotu* (little). She always said that, one day, you would make her proud. You owe her that. Otherwise we are fine. God is great.

With unconditional and conditional love,
Yours,
Father

Please give a thought to women who produce only daughters. What a failure that can feel as the family name will die with them. What is to become of those parents who have no son to rescue them into old age?

Whose mercy must they rely on? What of us who are childless? Is old age to be something that we should become petrified about? Who will support me in that vulnerable stage when end of life is around the corner?

Suggestions on a postcard please.

Though the letter is slightly tongue-in-cheek, the theme of duty, sacrifice, honour, expectations, and God's role in the family drama are very real to this day. There are over one billion Indians on the planet, predominantly living in India. The reality is that the majority of our fellow brothers and sisters are still held ransom to patriarchal systems. I recently read an article on 'How India fails its women' (*The Economist*, 7 July to 13 July, 2018, 10). The irony is that wealthy families often prefer women to stop working outside their home. This is used as a marker of status. How pathetic. More shockingly, Indian women are less likely to do paid work than any country in the G20, outside Saudi Arabia. That does not mean that life is luxurious. What about the unpaid work they do 24/7 throughout their lives? In conclusion, ancestral rules are hard wired. They keep repeating in our psyches leaving Indian girls being programmed into Rescuers Extraordinaire and young Indian boys into Providers Extraordinaire.

For men, this provision is based on the capacity to earn sufficient amounts of money to maintain a certain lifestyle. An Indian man is often defined by his postcode, the size of his mansion, make of his car, his job title, and his capacity to look after his parents and extended family. It is a tough act to follow. Many men rise to this challenge. For others, though, this is a distant dream. They simply cannot achieve it. They have not had the supportive families, privileged education, and opportunity to manifest a grand lifestyle. Alternatively, those who are creative (artistic) are drawn to professions where the rewards are not financial but personal. For them, the overriding feeling can easily be 'I feel a failure'. Even when they are not. Most definitely not.

Thankfully, in spite of the depressing statistics, a momentum of change is brewing. Attitudes are changing, some out of willingness, and a lot out of necessity. Add to that human evolution, migration, and energised feminism. A cultural framework that worked years ago in traditional rural life in India cannot be sustained in the leafy suburbs or not-so-leafy council estates of Britain or other Western lands. *The Indian male species and, for that matter, men in general are being threatened in a way like never before.* They cannot, at some primordial level, handle the surge in the domesticity of their tapestries, living with women who have a voice and use it. What about masculinity? And all that goes with it? The problem is that evolution has never kept up with revolutions. There is always a time lag involved. This creates space for uncertainty and apprehension which is often played out as aggression. Men are increasingly encountering women, be it at home or in the workplace, who want to exert their choices and create more balance between the male and female roles of old. Men are having to load up and manage baby buggies at a faster rate than the speed of their broadband connections. Wives, partners, and girlfriends are saying, 'I am not your mother. And just because your mother did it, don't expect that from me or put that on our daughter. And by the way, you are on child duty tonight, and baby needs a nappy change now. Thanks.' Nothing wrong with that. But balance matters.

The pressure is on. Slickly dressed women, in onesies, are tapping away at their laptops, with perfect shellacked nails, creating monetary wealth, be it in their kitchens, on social media platforms or in plush companies in the public and private sectors. This is all very threatening and confusing stuff, feminism at the fore. *Whilst there is a long way to go until gender equality reigns, momentum is gathering* where women are, quite rightly, demanding change by exerting more choice. NO MORE is the theme. I sense that a lot will change for men out of no choice. Do not misunderstand me. Condoning any patriarchal behaviour that disrespects and tries to extinguish rightful female expression is not an option. Equal pay, same opportunities, freedom for self-expression, respect, and dignity in every sphere of life are every woman's right. I abhor acts of male violence against girls and women. It makes my blood boil which runs into conflict with my compassionate heart which says 'but...'

Feminist ideology that reduces men to sperm is unjustifiable. On the other hand, as the author Chimamanda Ngozi Adichie eloquently highlighted in her TEDx talk titled *'We Should All Be Feminists'*, it is necessary to uphold the word *feminist* as women have been excluded and oppressed as a group for centuries. It is not merely about fighting for human rights. It is about female human rights. A gender-based war is raging out there. The success of the #MeToo campaign is evidence of that. The lid on gender-biased pay by large corporations has also been lifted. We need to be cautious. Nature versus nurture matters. Little boys are impressionable. As Adichie points out, 'We must raise our daughters differently. We must also raise our sons differently.' Her point of view being that *men and women must all be feminists.* 'We must all fight for equality.' Too true.

To some extent, I am a product of this view. On reflection, my parents (so proud of them) played a pivotal role in my liberation from the choking grip of the birth tribe. My father granted me the jewel of permission to do whatever my brother wanted to do. He always treated me equal to my brother. I recall him asking me if I had met any 'nice young man' (as in potential husband) at University? Whilst most fathers were pushing arranged marriages, my father was gifting me choice. In spite of this, *the Cultural Parent, a fierce ancestral code (of how to be accepted) that seeps into our blood and every cell in our body, had already caged me.* I possibly could not tell my father about my lust for a man who did not fit into the tribal code of what good little Indian girls do to honour and exult their families. This potential husband was the wrong religion, a person of another colour and an artist. I could not let my beloved parents down. I could not bring shame to the family. I chose silence. Checkmate.

My mother, whilst putting a lot of effort in trying to birth the Domestic Goddess as opposed to the Domestic Chaos in me, expected my brother to help clear the table, make his bed and keep things tidy. She did not sprinkle him with 'prince syndrome' fairy dust. He is quite the domestic goddess and yet, bursts of testosterone-fuelled patriarchal behaviour linger on.

In my eyes, *potent seeds of feminism are sown* when every father says to his daughter, 'you are loved and cherished and can do whatever your brother (boys, men) can do too' and where sons are taught by both parents to honour and respect female energy in every aspect of their lives. *A non-negotiable rule for life.* When we cherish another, we will not harm them.

Easier said than done. It can feel challenging to show any compassion for men if you have been violated by them. On the other hand, I believe it is important to understand what is going on for men whilst we women stand up for our rights. As Martin Luther King Jr, the inspirational leader of the American civil rights movement wisely said, 'That old law about "an eye for an eye" leaves everyone blind. The time is always right to do the right thing.'

Come on men. Do the right thing. Honour female energy in all its ages and forms. After all, it birthed you into existence. No womb, no you.

Why must women hold a balanced view? Well, there are signs that all is not well in the patriarchal camp. For instance, there are more men than women committing suicide than ever before, which signals that men are struggling too, terribly. I read a fantastic blog (www.centreformsc.org/ultimate-courage) recently by Daniel Eilenberg titled *Ultimate Courage* where he highlights that whilst women are more likely to seek help, men will suffer in silence. He attributes some of this to the fact *'Boys learn to so fear being called a girl early in life that they will go to great lengths to avoid this. Think blustery, aggressive defences.'* Yet there is a bias in psychological support services for women and children rather than for men. Gender bias and stereotyping around mental, physical, emotional, and spiritual health does us all a disservice. Recently, when highlighting one of my well-being workshops to girlfriends, I wrote, 'please pass on to anyone who may be interested. Men might find the content too fluffy but they are welcome, too.' On reflection, I was reinforcing stereotyped ideas around how 'men don't talk' and 'men are not interested in talking about their feelings' or worse still, 'men's feelings don't matter'. But they do. They matter a lot.

It feels more crucial than ever before that we all understand each other from the depths of our souls, rather than the contents of our minds across all genders and spectrum of ages.

Growing up, I observed how Indian boy's life scripts were all about working towards 'proper jobs' and elevating to at least middle class status in society. Just like Jignesh (in the letter) was expected to do in the future. Poor soul. What of men who fall short of these expectations? What of men who work hard but cannot afford the swanky SW3 postcode? Or chose not to?

My brother is a shining example of choice and one who conquered those toxic human emotions, namely guilt and shame. When my father struggled with empathy for his son's dizzy relationship with blood and disinterest in a medical career, he propelled my sibling into a rebellion. My brother was different from the macho types of his generation. Even as a little boy, he was far more sensitive and prone to angst and feeling deeply for those less well off than us. He had a softness about him and would cry when upset but was told not to. He was definitely a victim of the big-boys-don't-cry campaign. To shed tears was to be weak and not in keeping with the male species. Psychological research shows that suppression of painful feelings has negative effects. The pain has to go somewhere. Is this why men are so angry and feel the need to lash out, dominate and control? In extreme cases, the tears seem to be shed through bloody wounds rather than the eyes.

Vulnerability can be a strength. My sibling is deeply inspired by Mahatma Gandhi, father of *ahimsa* (non-violence), not fleetingly, but at a heartfelt level. This attitude is deeply embedded in his soul as expressed in his professional life. His job choices have mirrored this virtue consistently. He cares about humanity, not about materialistic wealth and position in society. As a child, he thought deeply about the lives of children left behind in orphanages, as we drove away, after having made our donations of clothes and food. My mum would periodically expose us to poverty, to appease the gods, I suspect, but also to give her children a reality check about life – to make us appreciate our secure homes, friends, and family life. My mum knew about monetary struggle having grown up in a minimalistic home. My brother is comfortable being this way whereas I on the other hand, have some rather princess-like qualities and am more than happy in the material world. Time to rise above it, a little bit at least.

To do that, it may help to abandon the idea of keeping up with the Joneses. *Strength of character lies in rejecting being a slave to the conditioning and definition of what success for good little Indian boys and girls means.* The ability to exert choice against the expected norm can be liberating. This attitude is desperately needed more than ever before. Material wealth is seen as a marker for success. It is often chased after to remain at the altar of praise in the parents' and the tribe's minds. If you meet any Indian parent and ask after their children, they will usually define their well-being by their positions of affluence (eminent cardiologist, president of the Anglo-Asian region of the world, CEO of the Moon, political candidate for the Special R Us party, etc.) or the area they live in: 'Hampstead, darling' or 'Mayfair' when really it is Kilburn. They seldom mention their sweet natures or kind hearts.

I recall being embarrassed when my dad would go on about my professional achievements. His chest size would increase by three inches, inflating with pride. That's appreciated at one level, better to have a loving father who expands his chest with pride than a sickly one who expands other body parts in abuse. The reality is that anyone can achieve what I have given a chance. The problem is that not many get an iota of opportunity to express themselves. It really is a world of the haves and have-nots. As Oliver James puts it so aptly in his book titled *Affluenza,* we are suffering from the *affluenza virus* fuelled by selfish capitalism. Wants are surpassing needs. Affluence is being prized more than the emancipation of men, women, and children.

The virus is even to be found in so-called sterile hospital units. A European friend, who is a medical consultant, has observed how male Indian doctors, junior or senior, are obsessed with creation of material wealth. I can only hope they are equally passionate about creation of health. After all, that is what their medical education was all about. It seems like they have been told, consciously or unconsciously, the 'good life' and success is measured by *what they have* rather than *who they are.* There is constant pressure to elevate their status to the haves, leaving the have-nots on another realm. The stereotypical questions Indian people ask a young man on completing his education are, 'Have you got a proper job?' 'When are you buying your home?' 'When am I coming to your wedding?' As for questions put to young Indian girls? 'When are you getting married?' And once she has done that, the question becomes, 'When are you going to make your parents into proud grandparents?' These markers equate to success. Rather claustrophobic, isn't it?

Besides restricted cultural attitudes, where men are seen as the 'breadwinners', the current global economic climate is unhelpful. The whole work scenario has changed due to political uncertainties (which impact the socio-economic climate) progressing faster than the speed of lightning. Competition for jobs is rife. Changing demographical landscapes by the migration of people is creating national and international turbulence. The migrants, the human beings, are not necessarily the problem. Lack of political vision, corruption and a rampant spread of the *affluenza virus* in capitalistic societies fuel unimaginable human suffering. In previously stable and wealthy nations, infrastructures are heaving, salaries are stagnant, and the cost of living, especially basics, such as housing, are escalating. Couples are putting off marriage and abstaining from having children due to economic restraints. People are struggling to buy their own homes in spite of working really hard towards the promised dream. There is joy in owning a home and sitting in a temple of your very own making, however small and humble, not to mention the security that comes from the asset that may make old age a bit safer and softer.

My capitalist feminist friend chides me for my restricted viewpoint. Indian men do not have to feel under pressure to own homes. Why not just rent as the rest of Europe do? The problem is not with renting but with *lack of choice*, not just for Indian men but for all people irrespective of gender, race, or colour. It hurts being part of a society where, in a financial hub of the world, there are approximately a thousand d banks, where homelessness is on the rise. People cannot afford a meal shop, let alone the weekly shop. My struggle extends to being part of a society where old people are being forced out of their homes to pay for their care as they fragment physically and emotionally. They sweated day and night in their youth for comfort in old age which is proving to be rather uncomfortable. It feels exhausting to live in a world where young people are spiralling into debt, where success is defined by celebrity status and being size 0. We are all being bombarded with material, via social media platforms, that create unattainable aspirations. Frustration, lack of opportunity, and stagnant earnings are creating depression. The goon show that has become politics is not helping. Stress-related illnesses abound. Do forgive me if I sound full of pessimism. I am not. Just laying bare the facts. No intention for 'fake news' here! The prediction by the WHO for 2020 is a world in which mental health issues are going to predominate above other health issues. I just got an email about a conference looking at the rising tide of suicide ideation in universities. An equally frightening statistic is that 50 per cent of those born after 1960 will get cancer. That just makes me suffocate with anxiety as I am a 1963 child.

What is going on? I thought the human race was progressing towards a better way of life with advancing science, technology, and extra-terrestrial conquests. Man landing on the moon is evidence of the exquisite capacity of human intelligence. Yet we are in an intense struggle. Why, oh why? My beloved mum's saying comes to mind:

'No voice, no choice,' which also means, 'No choice, no voice.' Back to Oliver James's take on it. The *affluenza virus* (selfish capitalism) leads to suppression, oppression, and depression. Add to that alienation, isolation, and marginalisation. Add to that war and terror. I do not want to be part of such a world without at least trying to create some positive change for children even though I have birthed none. Children are our future. How can we abandon them? I highly recommend his book as he offers some down-to-earth advice on 'how to pursue our needs rather than our wants'.

What truly makes for a *good life*?

It best not be about men being pushed to become Providers Extraordinaire. Indian parents are still obsessed with their children joining professions within medicine, dentistry, accountancy, pharmacy, optics, engineering, or architecture. The work place is much more diverse than that. Professions embracing technology, alternative energy sources, cyber security and artificial intelligence (AI) are the new kids on the block. I understand that it is important to be in well-paid jobs. Food needs to appear on the table. The bills have to be paid. We need a decent roof over our heads. But perhaps we could look at what amounts to being 'well paid'?

Messages coming out of the motherland around wealth are incredulous (*The Guardian*, Tuesday 10 July 2018, 10-1). The Bollygarchs of India are on the rise. In the mid-nineties, two Indians featured on the Forbes billionaire list. By 2016 this rose to eighty four. Additionally, 'the top ten per cent of earners now take fifty five per cent of all national income, the highest rate for any large country in the world.' The presence of endless slums amidst these riches make for some sobering reality. We must collectively wake up. Let us stop bleeding to an illusion. Surely, human existence is more than just about perfect lives based around materialistic wealth. I do struggle on a daily basis. I like my material stuff, but I also know deep in my heart it is not what makes me truly happy.

This is a calling to start living differently. Not all men are bastards. I have a plethora of wonderful men in my life. There is a growing feeling amongst many women that it is sometimes extreme feminist thought and behaviour that is more frightening than the challenges of speaking up against unacceptable male attitudes. Women use their sexual prowess for power and glory. Scantily clad women are plastered all over mainstream magazines' centre pages and dominate advertising. This gives wrong messages to young girls who essentially are being told that sexual allure and a beautiful body equate to acceptance and success. *Where are the important conversations about women on women happening?*

In fact, the concept of empowering women has been misinterpreted by young impressionable girls who now go around in gangs violating their own gender. Conversations with teenage girls often reveal vicious bullying of peers through social media. Top model agencies and fashion houses have women in senior positions promoting distorted body sizes and shapes, which continues to fuel eating disorders in young girls. The message that needs promoting is 'health is wealth.' NOT 'thin is in'. Self-harm is a constant feature of girls referred for psychological therapies. Worryingly, anorexia and bullying is on the rise in young boys, too. Let's not be blinded by distorted feminist ideology. I fear it will alienate young boys and men from promoting feminism with equality, respect and dignity across the board. *Men and women need to work together in all walks of life to create a fairer society.*

There is ample room for change. Politics is a male-led affair. Woman hardly feature in top companies. Professions such as aeronautics, physics, mathematics and engineering are male dominated. Until the gender balance changes, testosterone-fuelled ideology will prevail. I do not underestimate the challenge. Romantic utopian ideas cannot be adopted. Can we at least try to live with courage, passion, and joy from the heart rather than from the shadow side of the Indian Cultural Parent which spreads patriarchy and the *affluenza virus* like wild fire? Can we thrive rather than just survive the day, the week, and the month? How can we do this?

An Offering

How about being able to express oneself and be respected, seen as a success and thought a worthy member of the human race, irrespective of gender, whether a cook, cleaner, retailer, house husband, website designer, fashionista, social activist, *chaiwala*, street cleaner, or gardener.

Indian society must realise that it is okay, more than okay, to be a builder, pilot, barista, administrator, hairdresser, nail consultant, florist, man with a van, carpet fitter, human resources manager, counsellor, social worker, psychotherapist, rehabilitation officer, practice manager, DJ, singer, ballerina, or deep-sea diver. Need to take a pause? Pause.

Or be a market stall holder, electrician, nanny, highway engineer, train driver, charity volunteer, foster parent, prison officer, yoga teacher, body worker, teacher, headmaster, drain cleaner, scaffolder, footballer, dancer, choir singer, conductor, priest, nun, monk, and anything else in between.

I am not naive. Money is essential for a decent quality of life. I believe there is a way to achieve that if there is a *will for a fairer world*. Society at large needs to shift its moral compass. Any job should earn a decent wage in keeping with the cost of living. The financial hub capital that is London cannot function without an entire army of hard working people who keep the infrastructure going. Wages need to be determined not according to the fat-cat ethics but based on the idea of fair play.

The reality is we need us all – from deep-sea level to street level and to what goes on in the air.

Potent belief systems defining stereotypical gender roles drive prejudice and discrimination, especially when they have been carried around for what feels like forever. Masculinity should focus on 'are you someone who respects women?' rather than on 'what powers you up?' *More importantly, men should be encouraging men to step up to treating women equally and with the utmost of dignity. They are the ones who should be saying 'NO MORE'.* Surely?

Compassion for men is needed whilst they reframe themselves in a changing world where masculinity has lost its identity. Parenting has a crucial role to play in this movement of 'all change'. Domestication need not be confined to the female race. Boys should be encouraged to share all domestic tasks from a young age. *The song saying they are somehow superior to their sisters or other girls is best not sung at all.* The idea that women are born to cook and men to work really belongs to the dark ages. What always amuses me is how the so-called best tandoori and gourmet chefs in the world are men, and yet in daily life the majority profess to culinary amnesia. In the gender game, education should be an equal right for boys and girls, as should being able to wear blue and pink and play with dolls and cars. *And the message for young girls? How about 'let your healthy mind-heart-body be your most prized asset rather than the size of your waist, bust and butt'.*

Creative connection and co-creation rather than ferocious gender competition may be the way ahead.

Perhaps life is far simpler than what men and women have made it into. The Universe's truth feels so far removed from what we believe to be true. I want to live my truth which means rejecting a lot of attitudes, beliefs and ideas taught to me by my Cultural Parent. Yikes! Anyone out there who can help me? Perhaps God can.

Reflections

How do you view masculinity and the role of men in contemporary society today?

What does feminism look like to you?

What aspects of gender bias create division, rather than positive relationships, between the sexes?

What does the 'good life' mean to you?

Chapter 5

Religion: The God Squad and Dodgy Priests

Religion: Friend or Foe?

Religion and God are central to the life of Indian girls and profoundly impact our world view. My mum introduced me to God in utero, but memory recalls an introduction when I was around six years old. We had a little temple in our house. It was a pink plastic version of a classical temple found in India with tall domes and pseudo marble interiors housing the images of certain gods and goddesses. Daily offerings of a diva (oil lamp), incense sticks, and prayers were a ritual. My ramblings whilst standing in front of this Life Force usually consisted of the following:

> Dear God,
>
> Thank you for everything. Bless my mother, father, and brother. And all my friends. And Johnny and Tipu, our Alsatian dog. And please help me pass my exams. And mummy buy me that bag ...(Sigh. I started young!)

And so on.

At around age thirteen, I decided to abandon prayer in this numbing way. Put it down to the pubertal spurt. I sensed that Divine Intelligence was terribly bored with my repetitive themes, as there was no genuine heart in my ritual. I was also getting disgruntled with God, and man, as *puberty and menstruation brought obvious discrimination into my life.* It was considered inappropriate in my culture for a menstruating female to take part in anything vaguely holy as the body was considered 'impure' at this time. Superstition had it that participation in religious ritual would create bad luck. It was best to stay away from the 'pure' crowd. By not showing up whilst the rest of the family did, it was announced to the world that the 'painters were in'. I might as well have been plastered with a wet-paint warning sign. This all felt very humiliating. Surely, no loving God would ban me from Her presence, especially when they had made me the way I was. Why would they be offended by their own creation? These were all men-made rules to keep us women in our place, and they sucked! So there.

My wise mother decided it was okay for me not to pray to the plastic, but she sneaked God into my life in another way. She started buying illustrated magazines on Hindu mythology, along with my favourite magazine, *Pink*. The latter provided me with the vital statistics of Donny Osmond on a monthly basis, that blue-eyed, large toothed singer from the USA who belted out endless love songs, the famous one being 'Puppy Love'. I was beside myself, with Donny, not Hindu mythology. I remained faithful by showing interest in the mythological tales of Lord Rama, Lord Krishna, Hanuman, Mirabai, and the regal Prince Siddhartha Gautama, who went on to become the enlightened Buddha. My young soul had unconsciously tapped in to an energy called Religion. A particular favourite was the Buddha's teachings. He made such sense, unlike those adults and religious priests who made no sense at all.

God is usually affiliated with a religion as in Christianity, Islam and Hinduism, and is seen as a beloved parent, creator of the universe, an expert on humanity and a moral guide for appropriate conduct and living. This Force is often characterised by qualities of omniscience (infinite knowledge), omnipotence (unlimited power), omnipresence (present everywhere), and omnibenevolence (perfect goodness). What intrigues me is that Buddha never acknowledged God, and yet Buddhism is an established religion. *Human beings' interpretation of ideas and concepts always need to be held to inquiry in the mind.* Did God say that, or is man saying that? Do we really know? How do we know? What is the evidence? Where is the evidence?

Sometimes, the evidence is in the experience like when attending Friday mass in my secondary school. This was optional for us non-Catholics. My friend Bhakti and I would regularly position ourselves in front of the holy altar, belting out hymns and listening to sermons about the good, the mediocre, and the rather bland. To be honest, I hardly remember a word (sorry, Sister Augustine), though I vividly recall the experience of being in contact with something (an energy, a feeling) quite intangible yet profoundly uplifting and healing. This house of God was a beautiful chapel radiantly illuminated by large pillar candles and gently shimmering stained-glass windows. I cannot walk past a church forty years on without the urge to go in, light a candle and embrace a moment of quiet contemplation. I did it just the other day. Religion is a personal experience. Not one to be forced on others. And certainly not something to be used to annihilate humanity.

Amidst my confusion, clarity emerged in that quiet, gothic calm and paradoxically energetic space. Honouring God was not an introjected childhood habit or mere fantasy. Even at a young age, comforting and nurturing whisperings of protection from 'beyond' were most real for me. I am not alone in describing this feeling having read about it, and hearing it repeatedly from diverse sources, from people of all faiths and those surviving dire circumstances. Viktor Frankl, a Holocaust survivor and author of *Man's Search for Meaning*, described his experience a few days after liberation in this way. 'I had but one sentence in mind-always the same: I called to the Lord from my narrow prison and He answered me in the freedom of space. How long I knelt there and repeated this sentence memory can no longer recall. But I know that on that day, in that hour, my new life started. Step for step I progressed, until I again became a human being' (p.96).

The most wonderful thing about Hinduism, a polytheist religion, is that there is a God to call upon for every eventuality, a bit like how it is in Catholicism with the saints. Buying a new house? Call on Ganesha, the elephant god, remover of all obstacles. He can optimise the negotiation skills of the legal team. In your favour, of course. Once settled in your new home, call on Agni, the god of fire, to extinguish residual unwanted mouldy spirits from the chambers. Lack of money? Try the goddess Laxmi, the Hindu goddess of wealth, fortune, and prosperity. Struggling with fertility? Pray fervently to the goddess Parvati. Most importantly, know that in death, god Yama will come to receive you and light your path to the source, back to Brahma, one part of the Hindu triumvirate who are believed to have created the universe alongside the gods Shiva and Vishnu. Lord Shiva, also known as the Cosmic Dancer, is held responsible for destruction and reconstruction of life on earth. It might be helpful to engage in dialogue with him at this volatile time on planet Earth. A lot of destruction seems to be going on with not much reconstruction in sight. You may challenge this view if you are a successful property developer.

Lord Vishnu is seen as the preserver of life. He is believed to have reincarnated into Lord Krishna and subsequently Lord Rama. Hinduism embraces the concept of an eternal soul and rebirth. Both these gods are highly revered by Hindus and obviously impressed George Harrison of the famous Beatles band. He became a devotee of Lord Krishna and played a significant role in keeping the ISKCON (International Society for Krishna Consciousness) movement alive to this day. *I do love a daily chat with Lord Krishna, a most empathic counsellor.*

The Hindu scriptures are encapsulated in the Vedas, meaning 'knowledge'. Holy passages include the Upanishads, Bhagavad Gita, Ramayana, and Mahabharata. Hinduism is considered an oral tradition. Messages for humanity (from the Creator, I presume) have been passed down through the ages, via the sages, around four to five thousand years ago. It is a way of life rather than a religious ideology. The scriptures contain mythological stories of good always conquering evil, as well as codes for right conduct, right action, and good practice that are threaded through all the great religions. Central to Hinduism resides non-duality of existence (we are all one), waking up from *maya* (illusion) and living from *atman*, the soul. The latter is considered to be eternal and carried in the physical body through many cycles of human births, hence the idea of reincarnation.

I recall reading Nikki de Carteret's book *Soul Power* around fifteen years ago. Her journey was drenched with stories of her experiences of God, many of which I related to. We simply could not have made it up. If you are a non-believer or of another faith, you may be losing interest or thinking, 'What a load of nonsense.' That is okay. All views are respected except extreme religious ideology that murders in the name of God. Please stop it.

Even in belief, there is a constant struggle. What is God? I have mostly inferred this entity to be male even though there are many female deities in Hinduism, another symptom of gross patriarchal influences whilst growing up. One could ask if there is a God community sitting around in Starburst cafes in the heavens, observing us mere mortals and planning endless cycles of rebirth based on our moral codes of practice? Do these cosmic forces really influence the earthly experience of all living creatures, great and small? Are we at the mercy of them? That is what I believed when younger. That is the power of the Cultural Parent. *We buy into what we are told as children as our choices are limited. As adults, we have will and choice.* I seem to have developed a far more expansive understanding of the whole God-squad phenomenon, based on my earthly experiences.

It seems that whether an individual embraces God, or not, is rooted in the individual's innermost physical, mental, emotional, and spiritual experiences, embodied rather than intellectualised. This connection can be an external or internal event, a collective experience or a deeply personal and individual one, a rather complex, multi-layered affair.

I increasingly see God as an energy called *breath*. Often known as *prana* in Sanskrit. The reality of breath, often referred to as the Life Force, is powerful. A baby comes into the world and is pressured immediately into taking its first breath as a sign of life. At death, we are pronounced breathless. *Prana* infuses and communicates with every cell in our body. When depleted of it, a cell starts to lose its identity, choke, and die. Breath-related events are evident in daily life. Who isn't familiar with the idea of 'breath being knocked out of them', or becoming aware of holding the breath when anxious, feeling choked up, or hyperventilating in panic? In this moment, the mind feels elusive, but in my experience, if I stay anchored and connected with breath, I will survive. Everything passes. Just as the wise Buddha said it would.

Breath is central to mindfulness practice, which is a powerful tool I use to manage anxiety on this journey of existential attacks. Jon Kabat-Zinn, considered a pioneer in bringing this practice from the East to the West, paves the way to understanding and implementing this practice in his book *Wherever You Go, There You Are*. The mind and body hold all our angst. We cannot escape suffering by going on holiday or relocating because a lot of our painful fear based 'stuff' lies in our unconscious (out of awareness) mind-body, and it will surface at the most unexpected moments in the form of anxiety (threat mode), with all its torment. No need for shame or blame. It is a common problem and it is okay to say 'I am anxious'. If at this time we can engage in moment-by-moment experience of our breath and suspend judgements made by the body and mind, anxiety subsides. As we breathe calmly, fear which drives anxiety starts fading away. This is because the body's own natural calming system starts to kick in. Try it. Chip away with quiet determination. Headspace (www.headspace. com) is an excellent online resource. Alternatively, join a mindfulness course or class. Seek help from professional resources. Do not let anxiety conquer you. Do not underestimate your ability to help yourself.

Note: If your anxiety is part of a more serious mental health condition, mindfulness practice may not be appropriate.

Back to God. How else do I see this controversial figure? There seems to be a common world view. This omnipotent presence is symbolised through figurines, symbols, mandalas, mosaics, paintings, sculptures, talisman, amulets, and so on across all religions. This cosmic energy resides in churches, mosques, synagogues, and temples, or can be accessed through pilgrimage to holy sites. God may be felt by immersing ourselves in nature. Indigenous cultures revere Mother Earth and everything that she cradles – plants, birds, animals, flowers, trees, mountains, rivers, oceans, air, earth, wind, and fire. Intimate contact with this Life Force can transport us to a higher consciousness where, in spite of the challenges of life, at some level, all remains well. God can be right there with you on lighting a candle in your pyjamas. This symbolic act can connect you to Him or Her via your personal intercom system. Other channels of communication include rosary beads, prayer, chants, contemplation, and meditation. Sound, especially through music, is often seen as a vehicle through which God travels from heaven to earth. The same vehicle can transport us from earth into heaven. Who has not listened to music that takes them into a heightened nurturing and rapturous energetic realm?

Personally, a connection with this Life Force has meant the journey from stagnation to transformation, from being adrift at sea to being anchored on a safe shore.

My adult self also sees God as the truth which came into being well before the dinosaurs and *Homo sapiens* inhabited Mother Earth. This reality soars above man-made rules and regulations, especially the suffocating ones. It is devoid of all agitation and aggression. I may have experienced an essence of 'it' in the stillness during meditation. 'It' also feels tangible when the moon, suspended like a giant pearl in a dark indigo sky, appears out of nowhere to take my breath away, or in that blink-of-an-eye moment when the sun dips into the horizon leaving a blazing trail of crimson-red sky. I definitely see this truth in the eyes of a new born baby and have seen it in the eyes of a dying person. I cannot define it at all, but 'it' exists for me.

What increasingly draws my attention is the fact that I seem to have disconnected from the goddesses (Gayatri Ma, Lakshmi Ma, Amba Ma, Durga Ma) of the Hindu religion. Why have I bought into the idea that God is predominantly male energy? In Hinduism, goddess Chhaya is the Shadow Goddess. How interesting that the shadow, often seen as the dark and sabotaging side of our psyche, has to be female. I wonder which man thought of that.

But, 'all change', again. Religion seems to be falling out of favour with the human race, whilst metaphysical principles and the possibility of manifesting positive attitudes, beliefs, and experiences has created a huge self-help industry. The umbrella term *spirituality* seems the way forward. So instead of God, there is talk about the Universe, Life Force, Divine Intelligence, the Source, the Absolute, the One, *prana* (breath), Physis and Chi (energies), and the Force of Star Wars. Love it. Diverse views are welcome.

I tend to talk a lot about the Universe these days rather than focus on the word God. The Universe will provide. God will provide. Are they one and the same thing, the Universe representing a huge laboratory of amazing phenomenon based on spectacular energetic reactions which feel so soothing and healing? Wind caressing my face against the gentle warmth of the sun as it lights up my face feels magical. The patter of rain against a window pane whilst wrapped up in my warm cosy duvet seems to say, 'All is well.' I find myself in the most nurtured and safe space when sat gazing at the moon and the stars. In the stillness of the night, these balls of energy speak volumes to me. They whisper messages of love, comfort, peace and connection. We are all residents of the Universe. I am a part of it all. I cannot not be. If I am the Universe, I am God, and God is me. And God is eternal, so I must be. Do I die when I die?

Answers on a postcard please.

If this is not making any sense to you, I am not surprised. It has taken me years to formulate these ideas, and they keep changing with time. What has really transpired for me in these reflections is that the truth of the matter is *God can be whatever we chose Him of Her or 'It' to be, including non-existent, as an atheist would believe.* To my dear cousin, an eccentric scientist, who once remarked as if he found it offensive, 'There's God everywhere in your house' (he was referring to my numerous altars decked with religious and spiritual paraphernalia), I say, 'All views and beliefs respected except those that kill and murder in the name of God. Kindly stop it.'

People are being brainwashed into unhelpful ideologies by dodgy priests. I want to moan about people of the cloth. There goes the halo of the good little Indian girl. Meet Father Berry.

> *Father Berry was a man of God*
> *Obscenely judgemental and rather odd*
> *Who believed that only Christians went to Heaven*
> *Leaving us Hindus to rot in hell*
> *Which really made me want to yell*
> *Prat!*

Why do I hold this attitude? Experience, of course! When on a multi-faith summer camp in my youth, Father Berry advised us impressionable teenagers that abortion was a sin even when a child was born through rape. Basically, it was not enough that rape violates a woman's body, dignity, sacred space, and soul, but now she must go to hell and endure the fires that burn down below. Shouldn't she decide, without any pressure from others, what the fate of the burden she carries should be? Free of guilt and shame. Surely?

I must share a little naughtiness here. Some of us were so full of indignation with Father Berry that we secretly took the air out of his car tyres leaving him stranded on this farm until help arrived. Back in those days, that could mean a few days. I recall feeling vindicated and victorious as we merrily departed on our journey home, cheekily and most insincerely waving to him from our school bus as he stood akimbo in the distance. I was glad for his suffering. He should have known better. Fancy condoning rape. The grown up in me is a bit aghast at my childhood behaviour but if I am being honest, the memory of this holy man with four flat car tyres makes me giggle even to this day. The idea of rape does not.

I met another similar priest in my later years who implied that the only final destination available to me was hell as only Christians go to heaven. Another prat. The sad reality is that such tunnel vision does a disservice to the millions of wonderful Christians out there spreading a message of love, respect, and tolerance central to religion. Meet Judith and Tom, our wonderful Christian friends.

In the 1980s, when my mum arrived in England, long before the Indian TV channels and dancing tandoori chicken adverts for company, isolation and loneliness could be soul destroying, as they are now. Culture-friendly television shows are a godsend for so many South Asian people, especially the elderly, who are easily cut off from the fast-paced society of today. Tom and Judith gave my mum much needed support by inviting her to their Christian fellowship meetings and into their home. I can hear the Hindu holy cynics say, 'They were probably trying to brainwash her.' What nonsense. They were practicing their faith, walking their talk, by holding an attitude of acceptance, openness, and respect for a fellow human being, an attitude so needed today in our global world of bombs, resentment, and extremism. What I loved about my mum was that she was open to new experiences so far removed from her previous existence. She did not line up her Hindu religious or cultural ideologies in defence as many of her contemporaries did. She embraced their hospitality and Christian messages enthusiastically, so much so that the 6.30pm programme, *Songs of Praise*, became a regular feature in our home. We love it, and any version of it, to this day. *God feels inclusive. It is man who feels the need to be exclusive and rage and be at war.*

Dear Judith and Tom, thank you for not sending us Hindus to hell and down Segregation Avenue but showing us heavenly qualities and Integration Street instead. Love, respect and tolerance. Priceless.

The thing is Hindu Brahmin priests are no better. Years ago, on a family trip to the motherland, we visited a beautiful temple in South India. It is a splendour of art and scientific endeavour, as the chambers are aligned in such a way that at sunrise, the shimmering sun rays light up the statue of dancing Lord Shiva stood majestically in the deepest chamber. It really is a spectacular event, and in that moment, one knows that God is real; a very sacred meet-and-greet-your-creator event until, that is, the priests trivialise it. There I stood amidst the crowds waiting for this wonderful sacred phenomenon, the cosmic dance, to shake me to the core. My eyes were shut fervently in prayer whilst waiting for the sound of the temple bells to announce the earthly landing of Lord Shiva only to find, on restored vision, a small group of worshippers lit up in the chamber together with the Lord's statue. This was unusual as normally, in Hindu temples, only the priests are allowed to enter the deeper sacred chamber. I rubbed my eyes in case still in slumber. No, it was real. Later on, when inquiring directly with these people how they had managed to get so close up to the Lord, they confirmed gifting (as in bribing) the priest with twenty dollars. The fury of it. How dare they violate a holy place with corrupt acts? But, of course, dare they did which sadly is a common practice in my religious Mother Land. Money and the power that goes with it can break all the rules, holy or otherwise (think Banks, hmm), with no consequences. Sadly, a common phenomenon globally these days.

It gets worse. On visiting a temple in later years, a Hindu priest informed me that I would be gifted with a wonderful husband and beautiful children if I followed his advice and donated money towards maintenance of the shrine (as in his upkeep). That was after spending a mini fortune on flowers and incense sticks as part of my offerings to divinity. He was implying that I would be cursed with misfortune if his instructions were ignored. As if He or She cares. Gods and Goddesses are far smarter than shallow rituals. Little did this unholy so-and-so realise that I was having a hot flush right in front of his very eyes (as part of my daily menopausal routine) and my ovaries had been redundant for a while. I was not about to birth his lies or any children for that matter. Victory! Good always prevails over bad. Can you hear the trumpets?

This belief system is what I desperately hold onto in the current climate of terrorisation spurred on by (spiritually) lost men and women. The ones who wreak havoc are a minority. Their weapons of mass destruction are rather ferocious and randomly directed and make us, understandably, believe that the world is just one big, awful place. Journeying to this dark place is something I resist daily. It is tough, but worth persisting. I would rather journey into the light and make choices about the path taken. The reality is that many of us do look to sacred scriptures and texts for inspiration and guidance on how to imbibe religion as a positive force in our lives, not to terrorise us into fear and switch us off God. In my experience, there has been nothing more powerful and anchoring in my life than the presence of a higher force, an omnipotent and omnipresent energy that is a constant fellow companion. In sickness and in health, in war, as in peace, forever and ever. Amen.

The reason I moan about these priests is that they do mankind a terrible injustice. This sort of corrupt behaviour puts people off religion. There is concern at the falling rates of attendance of people, especially the younger generation, to churches and temples. Yet there are millions of people who identify with a particular religion and embrace its wisdom. The latter has supported my ancestors for generations. Many thorny paths have been negotiated by sitting in the knowing of this Force in my life. Omnipresence can manifest in diverse ways: by following my intuition, my heart centre, and gut feelings particularly when the going has been rough. I can sense omnibenevolence through tears and soggy noses. It is most omnipotent in the sound of silence, deep contemplation, and heartfelt prayer.

Sometimes, when feeling utterly helpless and hopeless, human beings are just not enough to soothe the pain or help balm up the wounds when there is a deep ache in the heart, a hollow feeling in the gut, a sharp pain in the neck, a burning mass of muscle tissue and a stinging sensation behind the eyes. No doctor or alternative therapist can comprehend my angst. In this instance, I have survived by sitting at the feet of the Force and listening to what comes through in the silence. Time and time again, a gentle whisper starts easing the pain: 'Surrender. Give it all over to me. Just be.'

I have not lost the plot. Eckhart Tolle, a most revered contemporary teacher of modern day living, has a chapter titled 'The Meaning of

Surrender' in his epic book *The Power of Now* which supports this view. I quote, 'Surrender is the simple but profound wisdom of yielding to rather than opposing the flow of life. The only place where you can experience the flow of life is the Now, so to surrender is to accept the present moment unconditionally and without reservation' (71).

PS. This does not mean that if you are suffering deeply and need medical support you should ignore it. Keeping any 'alternative' idea in context is important.

I have learnt that dropping resistance to suffering is often the key to calm. Occasionally, I get the hump with the Universe who, after hearing my grovelling and petitioning, replies with a booming message, 'It's very easy to love me and revere me when all is smooth and going to your plan. The challenge is to stick with me when all seems out of control.' This is all about testing the quality of my faith and knowing that, at some primordial level, this is my journey. Contradictory beliefs are challenging. It is okay. I am not going to beat myself about not comprehending something that is so complex.

As always, a balanced view is necessary. I concede that religion in contemporary societies is becoming unfashionable. There have been awful scandals on abuse associated with people of the cloth. Childhoods have been ripped apart because of it. The very institutions that were meant to protect vulnerable beings have violated them. Disgraceful. Additionally, multiculturalism has escalated intermarriage between people of different faiths causing dilution of belief systems. That, and perhaps just because of the forces of evolution and technological love affairs, religious fervour (of the loving kind) does not feature on the menu of life these days. I notice my own hesitation in admitting that I am religious and prefer to dress up my liaison with some higher force under the umbrella of spirituality. In this way, I am not some boring holier-than-thou person who has become a preacher of some brainwashing ideology. How uncool. My perception is that being spiritual, rather than religious, leads to more acceptance. I find this rather jarring. Why must I be embarrassed to share my belief in the healing power of prayer? That most wonderful sacred dialogue with the Force. Why must I be secretive about the fact that contemplation on God, on this powerful energy, is central to my daily existence? That without my beloved Buddha, I would be half the women I am? No need for such denial. I am religious. So there!

For anyone sharing this angst, I would highly recommend accessing the wisdom of Caroline Myss (www.myss.com), a medical intuitive and authentic spiritual director of the most endearing kind. She says it the way it is with no whistles and bells attached. Some may struggle with her directness. I find her rather inspiring. She reminds us that before the Age of Enlightenment when *reason* gripped mankind, *life was lived by a mystical truth.* In the latter, there was no need to work things out. There was a deep acceptance of a higher force orchestrating the symphony that was life. Reason has obliterated this connection.

Finally, the anti-religious feelings amongst the next generation of Indian children causes me sadness. I hope to gently encourage them to open their hearts and minds to certain Eastern belief systems. These stem from a religion so rich with knowledge and wisdom on how to live one's life in harmony and balance. *Eastern wisdom, particularly from Hindu and Buddhist sources, has taught me that embracing suffering is equally important in life, as is bliss.* We cannot have one without the other. Nothing seems to be able to exist in isolation. That is the law of nature, tall and short, thick and thin, shiny and dull, earth and sky, sun and rain, love and hate, fear and courage, peace and war, good and bad, beautiful and ugly, Breath (God) and humans.

Perhaps it is this viewpoint that prevents me from drowning in complete sorrow at the state of the world, particularly in the current climate of terrorism, war, fear, and poverty. Records show that these phenomena have been deeply etched in the history of mankind. Prior to the World Wide Web, there was significant time lag before news spread to inform people of these horrors. But now, these challenges are right on our doorsteps, on a daily basis, in a technologically hijacked world. My view of God has changed since being a child. He and She are no longer fleshy divine forms sitting in heaven ruling my destiny, or yours for that matter, but a form of dynamic ever-changing, ever-present energy and higher force which speaks of the possibility for choice, transformation, and hope.

Hinduism has served me well. It has connected me to my *atman* (soul), whilst Buddhism has taught me to understand the workings of my mind. These collectively make a powerful cocktail for relief from existential angst. Hinduism (as other religions) espouses virtues such as honouring family life, engaging with community, and using contemplation, prayer, and meditation for self-understanding and personal growth. The continuation of the soul's journey (carried in many bodies through reincarnation) are central to this religion. 'Right action', 'waking up from the illusion', 'letting go' and 'impermanence' are key messages I associate with the Buddha. 'Right' can mean different things to different people, but one does not need to be a rocket scientist to work out whether one's behaviour is harmful or helpful, or perhaps one does, as wounded humans walk the earth in their billions. A wound for a wound is causing chaos.

Hindu-based Eastern philosophies such as yoga and Ayurveda have gradually filtered into Western culture. Daily yoga and holistic nutrition can create incredible healing. Add to this the power of sound in the form of ancient chants. I just love chanting, especially when anxious. The repeated sounds create energies of a healing frequency. I can feel the centre of my chest, my heart chakra, bursting into calm. 'You are safe' says the mantra. 'I am safe' says the mind to the heart and body. 'You are secure' says the mantra. 'I am secure' says the mind to the heart and body. 'You are grounded' says the mantra. 'I am grounded' says the mind to the heart and body. Eventually, all feels well.

Have you ever sat in a room with fellow human beings chanting Om (Aum) from deep within the bellies, this being the sound (apparently) that resounded when the Universe burst into being? Try it. It will blow your mind. Well, not literally. It is a safe practice. As sex can be.

Reflections

How strong a role has religion played in your life script and view of the world?

What sustains you in your time of vulnerability when no one seems to understand your angst?

How do you view religion in the current climate? Does it provide an anchor or simply add to your confusion or even despair?

Are there any symbols and rituals that are particularly significant for your well-being?

Chapter 6

Sex and Sexuality: Blush, Hush and Flush

We are born naked. What's the fuss?

It amuses me that Indians are so coy talking about sex and its associates, such as menstruation, masturbation, vaginas, and penises, commonly referred to in slang terms as periods, wanking, fannies and willies. Ironically, one of the greatest manuals on sexual intercourse, or should I say the art of lovemaking, the *Kama Sutra*, was penned by an imaginative Hindu man from India, my mother country. I once bought a copy for a friend to help spice up her love life, as you do.

Let us start with menstruation, often referred to as *periods*. I wonder why? It may be to do with the fact that one had to suffer periodically from this body response. The shame and embarrassment associated with this force of nature within the Indian culture is real. As highlighted before, a menstruating female is not allowed to take part in religious ceremonies, as she is considered 'soiled'. If you do not turn up to a holy event as expected, everyone assumes that you are busy manufacturing red paint, even if you are not. Lovely. I have funny memories of my mum teaching me how to hide sanitary towels under jumpers when making the short trip from my bedroom to the bathroom, hush-hush. Hush, my dear mum would say. It was not lady-like to flaunt the fluid absorbers around in public. The latter referred to the gentlemen in the house, which included my father, my brother, and dear Johnny. Additionally, one never had a tummy ache from periods. It was always a headache. Funny that, considering my ovaries and womb are located in the bottom half of my body and not in my head! As I got older, things became more interesting. Tampons came into my life. Those willy-shaped, woolly vaginal inserts that some genius thought of provided much-needed relief from the gory mess of soiled towels. Some friends started using these fluid absorbers driven by the need to be hygienic, or so I thought. It never occurred to me that there may be other reasons for why they might prefer these sanitary tools until a couple of them told me about their first sexual encounters. 'It just feels like using a tampon.' Cheap thrills. Without the complexities of relationship. I'm in. Grin.

Motivated by the need to spice up my life and hygiene, a request was made to my dear mum to buy me some tampons. Quite a straightforward process, one might think, until I overheard her having a conversation with a gynaecologist about the woolly inserts and issues around virginity. I can only assume the fanny doctor (as my naughty-but-nice girlie friends and *moi* like to call these amazing clinicians) reassured my mum that my hymen would remain intact for that first night of marriage. I was expected to be a virgin bride as per the tribe's requirements. Indignation has arrived. Humph! On a practical level, there were genuine concerns around toxicity when the engineering principles of tampons malfunctioned. I know of women having to visit the doctor for retrieval of these absorbent inserts (from passages down under) as the cord for removal of the foreign body broke. Help!

My mum did her best to be communicative around these matters. An explanation of what to expect when periods started, how normal it was to experience mood swings, belly aches, and the like helped immensely. What could have helped further would have been discussion around the fact that *menstruation was a sign of motherhood and a feminine principle to be proud of,* as opposed to something that the tribe ostracised you for. Saying that, I am eternally grateful that she did not say to me, 'I will have to ask your father about the tampons,' as she did for my other outside-the-box requests! That would have been a really blush-hush-flush moment! I remember being rather shy around these matters with my father, and turning bright red in the face if I ever encountered him whilst running to the bathroom with that towel concealed under my jumper. How things have changed. My dear dad now jovially listens to my ramblings about the association between constipation and haemorrhoids, the inevitable gas after eating chickpeas, as well as hot flushes and sleep deprivation as signs and symptoms of the menopause. I do reassure him about the benefits, though. My heating bills are noticeably reduced, and all the money spent on the woolly inserts in the past can go, guilt-free, on gathering those must-have-but-not-really-needed shoes and bags. The Princess has arrived. Grin. Again.

On a serious note, it infuriates me that a menstruating woman is culturally labelled as 'soiled' or 'dirty'. I am sure there is an explanation that could be offered by some holy man as to why this should be the case. Let us ignore him and talk biology. Physiologically, this process is part of the female reproductive cycle. It can be very frightening. I vividly recall waking up in a foreign land, without my mother at my side, and noting that my Bridgets (a term I later came to use for my very large panties based on that fantastic Hollywood screen character Bridget Jones) had changed colour overnight! Additionally, there was a deep ache in my belly, gnawing away at my insides. I really did feel unwell. This was made worse by the sense of shame in spotting the bed linen in someone else's home. 'Where's my mummy when needed most?' The horror of it.

Saying that, I was eternally grateful to my aunt who kindly explained that my periods had started and showed me how to make a sanitary towel from absorbent cotton cloths and a piece of string as Indian women did. This conjured up images of hunter-gatherer ancestors who covered their private parts with little G-strings fanning out at the appropriate parts to conceal their you-know-whats! I had to wash these cloths and reuse them. Whilst an ecologically friendly task, it felt grim as not a disposable glove was in sight and health and safety rules were broken. Funny how when these body fluids were concealed in my body, I had no aversion to them and unconsciously embraced them. However, when emitted externally, outside my control, they became a foe, something to disown, something to dislike intensely, like unhelpful unconscious behaviours. How disillusioned is the mind and the games it plays.

Symbolically, menstruation is sacred. It represents fertility, the body announcing that it is setting the scene for reproduction, preparing for motherhood, that most precious gift and necessity for survival of the human race. Periods meant the possibility of birthing a soul from the cosmos onto planet Earth. It is something that should be considered sacred and deserving of respect, not something that increases a person's sense of shame, guilt, and isolation on a monthly basis for years. Interestingly, when rejected by men, my periods have temporarily stopped. This rejection seems to pierce at the very heart of my identity as a woman. That hurts, terribly. Thank goodness for the relief of menopause.

Regarding sex, I remember learning about reproduction at school and looking at diagrams of vaginas and penises. It all looked rather bland and boring in black-and-white. Bananas hanging off their stalks felt far more exciting. I thought my parents had only done 'it' twice, once to produce my brother and then to produce me. It gets worse. I had no idea that people did 'it' for pleasure or in pursuit of an orgasm until encountering that scene from *When Harry met Sally*. It really was a what-transpires-when-Willy-meets-Fanny, aha moment. Sex education can be fun, but someone must be willing to talk about it, especially the Cultural Parent.

I learnt about sex and its associates, such as masturbation, by reading novels describing vivid foreplay and sex scenes. These books kept being passed around the classroom when I was about twelve years old. No need for a bookmark. Once you received the novel and hid it behind a large geography atlas (so that the teacher could not see what was actually a sex manual), the pages would fling open like clockwork to the point where intercourse was well on its way. Words such as *shuddered*, *gasped*, *surrendered*, *moist*, and the like would stream across the page. One could only imagine these things until a certain age when the body started reacting to these streams. I did get a lot of itches down under but thought it might just be the warm summer heat – or thrush. Sigh. Denial. Dangerous.

The problem with all this sex-related stuff was that none of it was talked about openly or sensibly. My mum could understandably not go there.

She wasn't even allowed to talk to boys outside the family in her youth. There was a prevailing unhealthy attitude in our culture, and most cultures to be fair, around sex. Oh no, not that subject please, blush, hush, flush. I recall my father gently chiding me in my teenage years for reading romantic and escapist books from Mills & Boon. Apparently, such literature was unsuitable for a good little Indian girl like me! Yes, he used the word *literature*.

Add to the mix restrictive messages from the Cultural Parent which reminded me that men in my life, who may tickle my romantic circuit, were to be experienced as my brothers, except the one who would marry me. It was obviously a way of desensitising sexual feelings and needs, putting it underground, so to speak. How toxic, just like stuck tampons. It was all about keeping us females under control, wielding power over us so that we did not bring dishonour and shame to our families. The indignation of it was that it was okay for men to have non-Indian girlfriends and lose their virginity before marriage. These hypocrites then wanted virgin brides to marry and care for their mothers and families. It made the whole issue around sexuality so biased in favour of men, as if their sexual needs were more important and urgent than women. Do not get me going on about rape in marriage.

True story coming up.

When my mother arrived to live in London, it was in the middle of the HIV (human immunodeficiency virus) and AIDS (acquired immunodeficiency disease syndrome) epidemic. As a dentist, I was immersed in the whole debate of whether fellow professionals should have the right to refuse to provide dental care for people with the disease as it could be transmitted through body fluids. I was firmly in the camp of 'every person is potentially an infected patient' so best just get on with professional compassionate care for those affected, implementing the usual protocols for safe practice. Essentially, manage the fear.

The truth is that human fear is a monster that disguises that other human monster called prejudice.

The HIV epidemic forced humankind to face up to its attitudes towards sexuality. In the early days, gay men were predominantly affected by the disease. Suddenly, the word *homosexual* was in your face wherever you went. The reason I mentioned my mother was because, around this time, she asked me what all this 'homo-sex' talk was about. Gulp. My mother had struggled having an honest and open discussion with me about anything to do around below-the-waist matters. Here she was asking me to explain the fact that certain men chose to be in mental, emotional, physical (sexual), and spiritual relationship with other men in preference to women. *ET*, of Hollywood fame, might as well have arrived into our home. I made an honest attempt at explaining homosexuality to her, to which she replied, 'I can't get my head round it. It sounds all a bit unnatural to me,' which sadly summed up a lot of people's attitudes.

I could understand this coming from my mother who grew up in a village in India asexualised by her Cultural Parent. What really shocked me was when friends and younger members of family asked me if my hands had been washed properly before mealtimes (as I was treating people with HIV) and, worse still, say things like 'no son of mine is going to be a poof'. My haughty response? 'I have a spare room. He can come and stay with me.'

On reflection, it may have been more helpful to engage in constructive dialogue and be curious about what was driving their attitudes. I was equally defensive about my position as they were about theirs. We each had needs to be met. Our individual needs could have been healthily discussed through mutual respect and dialogue. *Judgements and prejudice just impeded progress.* I can see that now but could not back then whilst consumed by another force. It was a bit holier-than-thou, but it served its purpose at the time. It was around the HIV epidemic that the Buddhist teachings of loving-kindness (*maitri*) and compassion (*karuna*) gripped me. It negated my fear, and by coming together with like-minded colleagues, a dental clinic to provide care for people with HIV was established. The need to be loving, kind, and compassionate to a group of people who were suffering a ghastly disease and hurtling towards death in the most painful way possible was what mattered to me at the time. Sexual preferences did not matter to me then and they do not matter to me now.

In my experience, which is the only truth I can speak about, heterosexual women are often drawn to gay men for friendship because they seem more emotionally available to any situation. My wonderful gay friend Chaz gets it that a girl needs her shoes and handbags and that shopping is therapeutic. Gay men and lesbian women are some of the most creative people on earth. Just look around the world of entertainment, fashion, and arts, and you can see their genius everywhere. One of the most poignant experiences in my professional career has been to observe the dignity and courage with which one of my patients journeyed from being a man to becoming a woman. No human being would change their gender just on a whim. In a world where being heterosexual is considered to be the norm, the amount of angst a person goes through to be who they are, whether homosexual, lesbian, bisexual, transgender, intersex, or any other permutation is tremendous and should not be underestimated. They have to overcome prejudice and ridicule as well as suffer physically, psychologically, emotionally, and spiritually to just be accepted in mainstream society. I deeply admire them. When anyone says to me heterosexual is the only way to be, I say, 'Really?' There are horrendous crimes committed by heterosexual people, including child sexual abuse, rape, and the like. In my mind, *gender and sexual inclinations do not define you as a human being.* I have learnt that what makes us truly human are the qualities of tolerance, kindness, compassion, and emotional intelligence that embraces diversity, rather than a draconian attitude which wants to box us all into some restricted man-made ideology.

On a personal level, I have always been attracted to outside-the-box stuff from a young age. How on earth did I, a good little Indian girl, firmly introjected with cultural ideology forbidding sexual diversity and alternative expression come to adore the flamboyant Boy George central to 1980s pop culture? I used to swoon to his music like there was no tomorrow. I notice he has just produced a new album. Must get it! The dressing up and flamboyance reeked of a sense of freedom very different from the shackles of my rather prim and proper culture. I liked people with piercings and weird hairstyles. S&M (sadism and masochism) made me curious. I did not find it repulsive as so many people do, well, at least the bits that I am aware of. The *truth is that people need to express themselves in different ways*, just like I needed to. But did not.

Clarity has arrived. The reason for my deep empathy with all that was not mainstream was because, in my gut, there was a sense of *not belonging* to my birth tribe. An inner voice, an inner compass, was trying to guide me along a more authentic journey. I did not want to live my life by all the man-made rules of my patriarchal dominant birth tribe. I DID NOT BELONG. Everyone else seemed to be towing the line. I did succumb but at the expense of abusing my body. The more fat I layered on, the more numb I became to this sense of feeling lost. No more. My body truly is my temple now, and I honour it. Lumps, bumps, stretch marks and all. Within its sacred space, holding a more expansive world view than ever before is becoming the norm.

Another true story coming up.

Late one night, whilst driving down a motorway with an endearing cousin, we were chatting away about this, that and the other, as you do. Suddenly, he went rather serious and said, 'Can I ask you something?'

'Of course,' I replied, waiting for him to ask me for support with his choice of a girlfriend who did not quite tick the Cultural Parent requirement boxes, or ask about a Buddhist retreat he had wanted to accompany me on. One of the treasures I cherish in my life are young people. Having birthed none myself, I seem to revere them even more. It gives me a warm, fluffy feeling when they seek my view around existential angst, especially to do with breaking the tribe's rules. Rebel with a cause and all that. The ego obviously enjoys the ride, but more importantly, it gives me a chance to walk my talk. Having successfully negotiated my life around many tribal restrictions which has allowed me to thrive at many things rather than just survive, I am happy to share a tip or two about how to start chipping away at limiting labels and rules without totally upsetting mums, dads and culturally stuck beings. Life is for thriving, not something to be dragged through. So back to the question.

'You know how you never married. Is that because you are the other way?' He was asking me if I was a lesbian. Well, the shock of it. I was not prepared for that in spite of my affinity for Dr Marten boots, England rugby shirts, and boyish haircuts.

I found myself saying, 'No. I am not.'

'Oh' he said. 'It's just that I wanted you to know I would support you if you were.' Such heart melting moments are the stuff of life, aren't they? This conversation has become even more precious to me since I lost that cousin to sudden cardiac death over ten years ago. His memory is even more poignant because he had gifted me a DVD of one of my favourite Bollywood films *Kal Ho Na Ho* which, without much loss in translation, means 'Tomorrow is or is not'. The irony of it has never left me because soon after our precious midnight ride together, his tomorrow, as we know it on earth, was over. He died, leaving a whole trail of heartbroken souls behind. His commitment to my happiness was a sign of unconditional love, precious, something to be cherished. Thank you dear brother, wherever you are. Recalling this conversation takes me to the whole question of my own view around sexuality.

I was brought up to be heterosexual and identified comfortably with this way of being. My response to a friend who revealed her I-am-a-lesbian secret to me years ago was 'that's no problem unless you fancy me'! Defensive behaviour or what? This explorative journey has forced me to address my sexuality and feelings around all the possibilities. Like hundreds of women who find gay men attractive at all levels mental, physical, emotional, and spiritual, I have graciously accepted the fact that they just do not fancy us. What a waste. Sigh. This not-available situation can be tragic. A work colleague shared a story of how a lady she knew almost committed suicide on discovering that her best male friend, whom she passionately fancied, was gay and out of reach. Ouch.

That makes my eyes sting. I know the sorrowful feeling of adoring someone to bits but them not being available for relationship.

The topic of sexuality evokes strong emotions. Many women just do not feel comfortable around gay women. My dear girlfriend Dolly (yes, I know) finds the idea of being in relationship with a woman quite repulsive, contrary to me. I have admired women not just for their charisma, talents, and sweet natures but for their sexual allure, too. Awareness around an attraction beyond the platonic has arisen, but I have never consciously felt the urge to act on it. *Sexual-acceptance-code programming by the Cultural Parent will have made damn sure that I would never act on it.* Imagine the shame and the guilt. The usual monsters.

The truth is that there are are wonderful citizens in every community who go about conducting their lives with dignity and respect, and who identify themselves as lesbians, gay, bisexual, transgender, queer, or intersex (LGBTQI). Gay couples engage in loving relationships, whilst many heterosexual couples have violent ones. I know which couple I would rather be.

Saying that, being culturally introjected as heterosexual means I have had far more urges to romp around with men. My romantic crushes, sexual fantasies, dreams, and longings have been largely around bodies with dangly bits below the waist. It makes sense that from an evolutionary point of view if a key primordial need of human beings is to reproduce and go forth, then heterosexuality is essential. It can be considered the norm. That does not mean it is abnormal for other forms of sexual expression and preference to exist. Diversity is Mother Nature's second nature. The same principle seems to apply to the human, animal, and plant kingdoms. It feels important to connect with that fact. *Diversity is all-embracing if we are allowed to see it through uncontaminated eyes absent of man-made constructs*, especially those of the Indian Cultural Parent which struggles with anything to do with physical intimacy and sex. One really does wonder how the *Kama Sutra* was birthed in my motherland. If we could embrace difference with unconditioned abandon, the world would be a better place, for you and for me. It's my daily struggle.

So how can we engage with talk around sex and sexuality without developing a prickly rash? Well, just talk about it! It is one of the hottest topics on the planet at the moment. Gender talk abounds, especially as the categories of sexual expression are increasing in a society that is beginning to lose the stiff-upper-lip attitude of days gone by. Conventional belief systems held for eons around gender are being challenged. Any-sex toilets are popping up here, there and everywhere. There is a certain boldness and daring attitude that is emerging in young people all over the planet. They are not all lost and without vision, as the older generation sometimes like to view them. I own up to my fair share of discrimination here. 'When I was young' is a statement best reframed, especially when it is used defensively rather than creatively. I hope that young people's passions create a more loving, just, and peaceful world, for the human, animal, and plant kingdoms and any other realm that lies outside our awareness.

We need to engage earnestly with young people around identity and sexual preferences. It may be helpful to say, 'Well, let's explore what that means for you,' and 'Let's talk about safe practice around sexually transmitted diseases.' With heterosexual experimentation, sexually transmitted illnesses as well as unwanted pregnancies would be top of the let's-chat-about-it list. Sexual urges are normal when pubertal spurts begin. Apparently, it is rather normal for little boys to walk around with 'stiffies' (erections) – my friends with sons tell me so – a normal biological response which needs expression, as does masturbation for boys at a certain age. *Girls needs are no different.* Who has not had a mad itch down in the nether regions, which feels better once itched, or been excited by sexually tantalising input through the sensory channels? I can own up to it, but again, because no adult was willing to talk to me or explain what all these multiple itches and pert nipples were about, I just ignored them. The sensations were managed in the best way possible amidst that critical voice (Cultural Parent) which said, 'Don't be dirty.' Perfectly healthy and normal human feelings made pathological, associated with guilt, secrets, shame, and made unnecessarily toxic. They need not be.

Sex to me is a very sacred act, the mingling of two souls, the combination of two life forces, a merging of body fluids like having a blood transfusion. With the right soul partner (match), it can be life enhancing, with an unconnected one (mismatch), life depleting. Worse still, when infected, it can be deadly.

This sacredness around human fusion is expressed in tantric sex, an old Eastern tradition often misinterpreted as something naughty or dirty. My understanding is that with the right sexual partner, higher levels of consciousness can be accessed through sacred sexual union for the betterment of both the souls. How wonderful. I have no personal experience of it, but it feels right up my street. Sadly, in real life, such intimacy would prove challenging to me. Commitment to a romantic partnership has eluded me all my life. When my friends were daringly canoodling boyfriends behind their parents' backs, I was busy being the perfect good little Indian girl who did not break the rules. Later in life, I tried to have the odd fling. *Tried* being the operative word. When introduced to potential husbands through the arranged marriage system, genuine connection with them was impossible. Their biological urges had a tendency to want to get into my pants for that 'When Willy-meets-Fanny' experience, whereas soul-to-soul connection came first for me. The ghastly thing about these arranged marriages was that one was expected to get into bed with a man you hardly knew and let him have sex with you – the horror of it. I just could not bring myself to do it, which takes me right there next. I have healed.

Reflections

Whose responsibility is sex education?

What are your views around gender and sexuality?

How comfortable are you talking about sex and sexuality particularly in regard to your own needs?

Chapter 7

Arranged Marriages: Karma, Destiny, Hobbies, Dowries, and, Oh, Love!

Sacred Unions Hijacked

Marriage conjures up a plethora of images in my mind. Some are not that positive. They range from the more acceptable adult liaisons labelled 'an arranged marriage' to the unacceptable barbaric acts of forced marriages involving little children and young teenagers. In traditional Indian culture, marriage is primarily a family affair. The couple's needs ranked secondary. It may mean no choice (just do as we say), to disguised choice (well, we won't force you, but …), to limited choice (choose between the three potential suitors we have shown you), to genuine freedom of expression (only marry the person if you really feel it is right for you).

The tide is turning somewhat. Westernised Indian children are individuating from their birth tribe and ignoring the arranged marriage options by dating people from diverse cultures. They are comfortable cohabiting minus the nuptials. Hurrah to you. Sadly, this causes huge conflict for my generation who are still firmly gripped in the clutches of the marriage rule book as defined by the aged Cultural Parent. I know of parents who will acknowledge that their child has moved out into their own pod (home) but struggle with saying their child has actually moved in with a partner. Shhhh. That means sex is taking place – shame, shame, shame. Many parents of my generation still prefer their children to marry within the tribal boundaries as per the old established system. Ancestral blood diluted by mixing gene pools and skin colours is not an option. Family honour remains a powerful force. If we looked beneath the skins, we would see that mixed blood is red, diluted or not.

My father witnessed *ghodia lagans* (baby-cot weddings) in the village he grew up in. The heads of the family, which means men, arranged such liaisons between their respective families. Financial, social, and religious attitudes played a crucial part in the decision-making. The bridal dowry comes into its own when considering the economics of marriage. It refers to the monetary and material possessions the bride's family is expected to donate to a groom's family to seal the marriage, a ritual honoured to this day. For rich families, it presents an opportunity to show off their wealth. For a poor man, it can amount to selling his daughter on to a better way of life. It does not always transpire that way as is seen in the case of domestic abuse. Worse still a poor father will go into further poverty (debt) just to raise the money for these contracts. *How sad that a daughter cannot be thought of as being priceless, like a rare jewel, a human being with all her divine potential and feminine qualities that are wealth in their own right, rather than goods priced up to market value.*

Generally, Indians have good business sense but they are often devoid of fair-trade attitudes. In *ghodia lagans* (baby-cot weddings), a child's fate is sealed long before his or her dreams materialise. Shockingly, such marriages are still performed in India today. Equally repulsive is how young girls in Britain, in spite of laws that prohibit such acts, are taken to foreign lands, promised glorious sunshine holidays, only to be trapped into ghastly marriages with aged men. Thankfully, my family has done away with such awful customs and traditions – gratitude, gratitude, gratitude. That does not stop my heart aching for child brides married off to young boys barely in their teens, and for young girls sold off to families so that parents have one less mouth to feed. Essentially, they are sold off to physical, mental, emotional, and sexual abuse. Sob. Worse still, girls on reaching puberty are expected to become mothers. Little girls giving birth to little girls. I cannot get my head around it. This represents a very dark shadow of the Cultural Parent. How can a parent be so cruel?

Marriage seems to define success in life. It did not matter to many that I was thriving in other areas of my life in spite of the lack of a solitaire ring on my wedding finger. There was an assumption that an unmarried life was a life half lived. Judgemental attitudes around coupledom and marriage are not confined to Eastern society. Worldwide, being a couple is equated to happiness. One only has to log on to social media sites for evidence of this man-made rule. Life is about having that perfect partner with the perfect family and so on. The escalating divorce rates in many cultures, especially the Indian one, obviously speak of another truth. What felt even more offensive was being called a *spinster*, which has such a harsh ring to it. It speaks to me of being incomplete and a failure. This label further added to the humiliation disguised within my flabby body. The emotional void and feelings of being incomplete when going to social gatherings were real. Couples would go off to smooch and dance intimately to some romantic love song whilst I found myself sitting on my own, staring on with a heavy heart, feeling deeply unloved, or sitting with some other poor unfortunate spinster, making small talk whilst suppressing our raw emotional wounds. We could have danced together. So what if we were both women? Sigh! Man-made rules. So suffocating aren't they?

Religious ideology in this instance was very harmful, too. I grew up with *karma and bhagya* (fate and destiny). Sounds like some bohemian pop band. Sadly not. These can be crucifying ideologies if misunderstood. *Karma* can be understood in the Christian context of *reaping what you sow*. It is a key concept in Buddhist and Hindu doctrines. There is a saying that I cannot recall accurately but basically says:

> If you want to know how you acted in your past life, then
> look at your current situation. If you want to understand
> your future, then look at your current situation.

Essentially, actions create effects (and with it consequences), across past and future lives. If you do not believe in reincarnation, matters are simplified. Enjoy the freedom. You have one life. Live it well. I have a few rounds to go.

This cause-and-effect concept implies that I deserved my humiliating spinster position. Behaviours in previous lifetimes (as per Hindu doctrines around reincarnation) had left me unworthy of marriage and motherhood in the present one. Reflecting on my current circumstances, *karma* and *bhagya,* on the contrary, seem to have been kind to me. Life feels good. I do not want to be arrogant about it. That feels deeply disrespectful to fellow human beings whose lives are filled with horror and tragedy. How does any human being deserve the agony of a forced marriage, crushing disability, rape, murder through honour killings, violent abuse, traumatic death, and painful diseases? How can that be put down to fate or destiny? What did they sow in a past life to deserve this thorny one? Who would knowingly self-harm and sow such seeds? I still struggle with both ideas.

Perhaps *bhagya* can be liberating. We can create a better destiny by exerting free will and choice, whereas *karma,* in my mind, offers a resigned attitude, likened to taking the victim position where one sings 'poor me, no lucky stars around when I was born.' Destiny, on the other hand, offers belief in a bigger universal plan for our presence on Mother Earth which can be modified through appropriate action. *We have choice. Even in dire circumstances, we can use our minds to exert the most favourable choices for our survival*, as Viktor Frankl did. In his classic account of surviving the Holocaust in *Man's Search for Meaning*, his ability to hold onto his mind even when he was stripped bare of everything including his freedom, clothes, physical health, and dignity was the key to ultimate liberation.

This is what metaphysical manifestation threads into. Thoughts become things, as in you reap what you sow, oh no! That *karma* thing again. Help.

My mum recounts her experience of having an arranged marriage with my father with some hilarity, but underneath the humour lies an echo of helplessness. She made a decision to marry my father so that her family had one less mouth to feed. Her dreams of a professional life never materialised. In credit to my father, he refused to accept a dowry from my mother's family. Bravo, Dad. Bravo. Rather proud of you. My mum recalls the comments made by various in-laws when they first set eyes on her. As opposed to welcoming stuff like 'she is sweet natured' or 'has a lovely smile', it was more like 'oh dear, she's taller and darker than her husband', as if my mother being taller and darker was detrimental to their cardiac health.

The truth is that women of my mother's generation had very little say in who they married. A girl's fate was sealed by the elders. A dear (late) aunt recounted her story. She was taken to a neighbouring village to meet her potential husband. There sat two young men, side by side. My aunt's eyes locked on to one of them (Mr Heart-Throb) who was rather handsome and appealing to the romantic senses. She held his image in her heart as she had chosen him for her wedding ceremony. Imagine the deep disappointment on discovering that her groom was the puny little boy sitting next to 'the chosen one'. The latter, Mr Heart-Throb, would be given to another girl. The sadness, betrayal and violation she felt was palpable in her voice as she narrated her story.

Thankfully, she was rescued. My paternal grandfather (Dada) has my respect in spite of our paths never crossing. Sadly, he died around the time of my birth. Why wouldn't I honour him? His courage and actions are worthy of such accolade. In the 1950s, the word *divorce* did not exist in our community. When my grandfather realised that my aunt was really miserable in her marriage, he brought her back home to where she belonged by terminating her marital ties, burdens, and hardships. He did not care about the shame and loss of honour it would bring on the family. He challenged the Cultural Parent (hurrah) and shrugged off the threat to the family's reputation which would be tarnished because of this action. I wonder if he rescued his daughter out of love or duty. I choose to believe it was love. After all, only love is real.

Regarding marriage, my generation benefitted from the migration of our parents to westernised lands holding freedom and democracy at the heart of their political and social manifestos. One does wonder these days. Arranged marriages could be more flexible. Instead of being forced into marriage because of the one-less-mouth-to-feed syndrome, my peers and I had some choice about whether we agreed to marry some fella or not. The word 'choice' is controversial because there were always ropes, as opposed to strings, attached. For many of us, the potential husband had to come from a certain caste and family background and have a certain standard of posh education. It helped further if he looked like something out of a Mills & Boon scenario by being dashing, handsome, rugged and fair-skinned. I guess there was some degree of choice, if you could use that word. Potential brides and grooms were asked to make a marital decision after a couple of meetings. Imagine agreeing to marry a man after having just met him a couple of times. Arrrggghhh. Sorry. That was a bit of a reaction. The idea felt anaphylactic back then and feels the same today.

There were general protocols for arranged marriages in my time (and still in many traditional families to this day). The initial meeting between families and potential suitors was set up at one of the family homes. The bride-to-be would dress up in her finest Indian outfit (*sari* or *salwar kameez*) and adorn her demure female mask as she prepared to be some sort of exhibit for the future in-laws. If you were pretty, fair, of a certain height in centimetres, slim, and trim, you were in. Education was a good bonus, as this meant you would boost the family status and income. If you were fat, dark-skinned, and of a poor family, it was all very hard going. Not many people wanted you. On the other hand, if you were fat, dark-skinned, but from a rich family, the light could shine again. Your family could marry you off by sending along a truckload of goodies to the in-laws who would shamelessly accept the microwaves, the Rolex watches, the Mercedes-Benz, and tons of 22-carat gold as part of the dowry. I do not exaggerate, having witnessed these exchanges in my time. Woman could be sold off. Just as child brides are today.

Thankfully, it is not all bad news. I never got sold off. *Gracias*, Mum and Dad! My experience of arranged marriages was rather different. Having been exposed to British culture, my parents were more progressive about finding a suitable husband for me. They must have got a whiff of the rebellion brewing deep inside their child. I was not some exhibit at a wedding show and would certainly not be doing the demure bride thing. This amounted to serving cups of tea with *samosas* and onion *bhajis* to prospective husbands and in-laws in either of our front rooms (as some of my friends agreed to do). I, Ms Do Not Belong, threatened to develop a limp and have a twitchy eye if forced into the traditional way of viewing a husband with family and the entire kitchen sink on show. No one would want someone with a disability. On reflection, this was very insensitive on my part as it just reinforced stereotyped ideas towards people who are disabled and discriminated against. *Apologies abound. I was foolishly young and fighting for survival.*

The alternative that was negotiated with my parents was being permitted to meet these prospective husbands over a coffee or dinner, and then deciding whether there was any mileage in the relationship. Was I attracted to them? After all, one had to produce babies with these men and a certain intimate act was required for that process. Did we have a similar outlook on life? Did we share hobbies? Indians just love talking about hobbies. Many a time, I would sit with these blokes, or blocks (grin) as my mum called them in her strong Indian accent, and talk about my hobbies. Conditioning spoke of a love for cooking, sewing, reading, and travelling. Being vegetarian and alcohol free were often revered. Yawn. Rebellion meant being honest about a love for eating everything that moved (joke) and a penchant for the bubbly stuff or gin and tonic (no joke). I also shared my passion for learning. A potential husband on hearing about my interest in furthering my career by embarking on a master's programme judgementally piped, 'So, you are a career girl? I'm looking for someone homely.' It gets worse. 'Like my mother.' How pathetic.

Behind the scenes, there was an informal marriage bureau in operation amongst the community, with a strong code of 'right conduct' and a territorial alliance. Though a lot of us had emigrated to England from East Africa, the Indian roots and ancestral pull regarding marriage was stronger than ever. My family's roots were associated with the Gujarat state in India. From my understanding, the Patels were a community of farmers and organised themselves into a hierarchical group. Economics and the power money yields drove the layering of the Patels. The larger wealthier towns were known as the *mota chh gaams* (big six villages), the middle range of twenty-seven villages were referred to as *satyavis gaam*, and then came the *nana gaams* (smaller villages). Somewhere in this man-made snobbery, there were people from the *panch gaams* (five villages). There were seriously a lot of Patels about. Like the Smiths in Britain. Women of my grandmother's generation were married off young, no IVF programmes needed then. My father is one of eight children, and my mother one of six.

When it came to my marriage, I was only introduced to suitable boys from the *satyavis gaams* (twenty-seven villages) because that is where my ancestors came from. Herding confined the gene pool to certain groups, no different from the class system in Victorian England or the tribal system of certain African, Middle Eastern and Asian lands. The more affluent six-village blokes (blocks) were too posh for me, and the poorer *nana gaam* (small villages) blocks not good enough. Sadly, there was no talk about love, friendship or about being soulmates. Such ingredients are vital, in my eyes, to a sacred relationship such as marriage. My friends always asked me what I was looking for in a suitable boy? I consistently replied, 'When my mind, heart, and groin kick off together in harmony in his presence, I'll know we are matched.' Poor choice of formula, methinks. One is still waiting. Sigh.

On enquiring with my friends about how they made a quick decision about something so sacred, they invariably replied, 'It just clicked. It just felt right.' Intuition is a powerful thing. My brother is blissful in his arranged marriage. Sadly, it never ever felt right for me. Hanging out with potential husbands waiting for the 'click' to happen or convincing myself that I had heard a noise became the norm. *All this coming from the mind, with a disengaged heart and a disinterested groin.*

I almost agreed to marry someone because he genuinely liked me and it would stop the judgements of being 'too picky' and an 'educated snob' being darted my way. What hurt most was watching my mum's face as my friends started getting married and random people said to her,

'Well, your daughter is rather podgy, so it's difficult to find her a man,' or worse still, 'This is what happens when you educate girls.' My parents had to endure such nonsense from the birth tribe. The truth of the matter is that in the end nothing clicked for me in spite of meeting up with umpteen prospective husbands, all from the twenty-seven villages in Gujarat state, living in the leafy suburbs of London.

I recall a poignant conversation with my mother as my lack of marriage interest was causing the family stress. 'Bina, what is it that you are looking for?' she gently asked.

'Love. Friendship. My soulmate, Mum,' was my honest response.

To which she gently replied, 'Well, I don't really know what any of these things mean. To me, marriage has been about personal sacrifices, tolerance, and acceptance.' This meant diminished personal choice and limited freedom, a bit tough for someone like me who likes to dance with the fairies. She continued to say, 'When I left home, my parents said to me, "Don't do anything that will bring us shame."' She thankfully continued. 'Your father and I will never force you to marry anybody. Do what is right for you.'

I will forever love my beloved parents who showed that, in the end, their love was real. They gave me permission to individuate, a priceless gift from a parent to a child. Mum went on to add a golden nugget: 'If love was so important in the success of marriage, why do so many nuptials in the Western culture, which are supposedly based on free choice and love, end up in divorce? Arranged marriages last. There is joy and happiness in them if you choose to see it that way.'

All of this was very true, as there are arranged marriages that have lasted forever and continue to do so. I often wonder if a lot of marriages, whether arranged or loved, have an underlying theme of resigned acceptance rather than soul-connected joy where two people work towards bettering two paths. This is not cynicism on my part. Bruce Tift, psychotherapist and author of *Already Free,* marries Western psychotherapy beautifully with Buddhist psychology. He highlights how in reality relationships between partners can be the most challenging aspect of our daily lives because of the unrealistic expectations each puts on the other. To show up lovingly 100 per cent all the time is just not humanly possible. What a relief. *I am open to commitment with a man but the hermit in me would struggle with showing up through thick and thin.*

In hindsight, my need to hold an idea of constant happiness in marriage (and life in general) was a formula for failure. I was hung up on a version of romantic relationship that was off the reality scale. Too many Mills & Boon soppy narratives had hijacked my head. My favourite film at the time was *Love Story*. That Mr O'Neal, ooh la la. In my naive head, I desired the perfect relationship. A husband should be a smart, educated, professional man who could be introduced to my family and friends with great pride and an overinflated ego. Hello, Cultural Parent. In this utopian relationship, autonomy would mean no aggression, no confrontation, no criticism, no pressure to maintain a certain body weight, no pressure to be the hostess with the mostest, no fallouts with the in-laws and extended family, and certainly no divorce. Where would I put the shame? This illusion for the off-the-scale-reality relationship was fuelled by the presence of a certain young man in my life. I met him whilst at university. He was the wrong colour, the wrong caste, the wrong religion, and therefore impossible to consider as a husband (shame, shame, shame). He was a wonderful friend and soulmate, a potentially perfect husband, but just not up to the tribe's standards. Ouch.

What do I mean by soulmate? For me it means being in relationship with someone who mirrors my inner world, where a silent sacred language exists between two deeply connected human beings. This person 'really gets you'. They understand the workings of your mind, heart, spirit, and soul. They see beyond your physical limitations such as the scar on the face, the excessive fat around the waist, the podgy thighs, and the stretch marks. Instead, *they see your inner light, your real potential.* They honour your pain and vulnerability, hold it safe, and offer an unconditional acceptance of what is. When in their presence, it can feel like a dance – sometimes a waltz, at times flamenco, and at other times disco dancing.

This relationship is far from perfect but makes room for the good, the bad, and the rather ugly, of yourself and the other. In fact, paradoxically, that's what makes it perfect. I have the privilege of several such soulmates amidst members of my blood family and dearest friends. They come in all ages, shapes, and sizes. Soulmates are not bound by man-made parameters. Marriage with a soulmate seems worth waiting for. Such relationships do exist. My brother is lucky to be married to his twin flame. Just a few months ago, we were sitting in a pub, downing our spirited drinks, masks off, and sharing from the heart. It was music to my ears when my brother, a man of truth, spoke lovingly of my sister-in-law and proclaimed with such intense authenticity, 'She is undoubtedly my soulmate.' She wholeheartedly embraces everything about him that is wonderful, mediocre and ugly, with fierce love. I was rather envious when she recently bought a book of Rumi's love poems for him. How wonderful to be in marriage and in love. Sigh.

Observing marital relationships has taught me that authentic love may involve curtailing some choice and personal freedom for the genuine benefit and blossoming of the relationship. It is not just about the chocolate, roses, and quality of the champagne bubbles, or about the size of the sentimental card on Valentine's Day. Superficial chants of 'I love you, I love the dog, and I love chocolate' in one breath are just that – superficial. Relationship is about co-creating. It has a quality that is dynamic, free-flowing, and constantly changing. Authentic love, stripped bare of ritualistic chocolate hearts and roses, can fuel personal growth through honest, often painful, yet constructive dialogue. Courageous conversations are required to recognise that each of us has unique physical, emotional, psychological, and spiritual needs. Yet we struggle with expressing these needs. I should know.

In certain circumstances, talking a lot without really communicating much is one of my default settings. The chatter is part of my defence system. In keeping up the verbal diarrhoea, one does not have to face the silence with its tsunami of unsettling emotional feelings. I do not have to dig deep to overcome my shyness (I know, a struggle for anyone who knows me to imagine), risk humiliation, and engage with the difficulty that is needed for true effective communication, connection, and change. I cannot go there so why try? Instead, I project my limited attitude and cynicism on to others with statements like 'Human beings are just conditional, fickle, and needy, in it for themselves'. It then dawns on me that I am talking about myself, or my ego at least. Ouch.

There is another layer to it. Besides difficulty in being able to embrace the good, the mediocre, and the ugly which seems central to rich human relationships, my inability to enter into marriage was because of a deep internal disconnect with allegiance to the birth tribe and a desperate need to break free. It seems that my unconscious had decided to pursue an alternative path. Who needs marriage? Who wants to be oppressed for dreaming beyond the patriarchal tribe's claustrophobic dreams? *Why hang around where you do not belong, especially as there was potential for a loving marriage elsewhere in another realm?* At some stage, without really appreciating or understanding it, I had entered into sacred marriage with God, with another wisdom, with the Buddha, with the Universe, a most sustaining Life Force. This union felt far more anchoring than the human existence at the cultural myth level. The thought of treading the earth with a man through an arranged marriage magnified the feeling inside of me which screamed, *I do not belong here!*

This realisation emerged on peeling back my huge emotional onion and paying attention to my four bodies (mental, physical, emotional, and spiritual) holding all my painful stuff. The tears came torrentially cascading down my face. They cried and howled for that part of me that has felt disconnected with a sense of not belonging to many things, people, and situations in my life but belonging so painfully, and yet blissfully, to a higher truth. It obviously came at a price. Worth paying? Meet Buddha's confused baby.

Reflections

What are your views around marriage? Arranged or not.

How does gender influence the dynamics in relationship?

How can a relationship hold autonomy and intimacy simultaneously?

Chapter 8

The Buddha: Confusion, Clarity, and Painful Blissful Realisations

I love Buddha. You perhaps love Buddha. Who is Buddha?

My first encounter with the Buddha remains crystal clear. I was around twelve years old. My mother, in her wisdom, decided that her children would benefit from learning about religion, particularly Hinduism, as that was our ancestral heritage. Instead of dragging us off to Sunday school or to the temple each week to listen to tedious sermons, she bought us illustrated magazines that chronicled the mythological stories of Hindu gods such as Krishna, Rama, and Shiva. The recurring theme being that good always conquers evil. Amidst the stories and illustrations of mighty battles fought in gruesome fields was the story of Siddhartha Gautama, the future Buddha, a handsome young prince born into a Royal Hindu family. As per religious tradition, priests drew up astrological charts to ascertain the child's destiny, the date, time, and place of birth being central to this process. If unfavourable events were predicted, rituals and sacrifices to the gods could be performed to negate harmful events and avoid unnecessary suffering.

Karen Armstrong, an internationally acclaimed religious scholar, gives a comprehensive account of the enlightened Gautama in her book titled *Buddha*. Astrological charting revealed two possible outcomes for his destiny. He would either grow up to be a *cakkavatti* (universal monarch) or become a saint. His father, Suddhodana, filled with despair at the thought of his son joining some god squad (or, more correctly, monastic life) and losing his kingdom to a stranger, desperately tried to protect his son from life's existential experiences beyond the opulent, decadent, and safe palace walls. But Buddha found his father's elegant house 'crowded' and 'dusty'. Armstrong (2000, 1) describes how 'he had a yearning for an existence that was "wide open" and as 'complete and pure as a polished shell'.

Thankfully, for purely selfish reasons, I am glad his father's plans failed. Siddhartha did escape the palace walls and observed that *dukkha* (suffering/pain) was central to life. Ageing, sickness, and death were part and parcel of being human. Certainly no one was spared from death. He attributed the causes of *dukkha* to ignorance, cravings, greed, attachments, and desires. Human psychology was driven by constant wants and needs. The idea of *nirvana* (or *nibbana* in the Pali language of that era) is central to Buddhism and refers 'to "extinction" or "blowing out": the extinction of self which brings enlightenment and liberation from pain' (Armstrong, 2000, 186). This state could be attained by waking up to the knowledge of the transient nature of all things, essentially, from the illusion of permanence. Nothing lasts forever.

Siddhartha went on to become the father of Buddhism, the Enlightened One, the Buddha.

In Buddhism, self (*anatta*) as a separate tangible entity does not exist. I do struggle with this, as all my ramblings are about living from the heart through one's authentic self! The Buddha would not be too enamoured by my partiality to positive psychology, another illusion. No need to feel guilty. *We can think for ourselves* and not accept every idea around his teachings. I trust that the Buddha, who gained mastery over the so called 'monkey mind' (central to human existence where we are incessantly jumping from thought to thought), would not mind.

The psychological potency of Buddhist teaching was difficult to process in my youth. Yet there was a sense of understanding something very important. Suffering was central to the human condition. The idea that no one escapes existential angst felt bizarrely soothing. I was not singled out to suffer the horribleness of human beings. That did not stop it feeling personal and eroding my sense of self-worth for years. But now, external validation is starting to feel rather impersonal, and in that shift, I feel rather expansive, as if I can breathe, freely, calmly, and steadily amidst the suffering in a way that I have never before.

There are reams of documentation about the Buddha's life lived around 2,500 years ago. I am not an expert on his teachings but am completely seduced by ideas and descriptions such as 'true nature', 'bringing the mind home', 'calm abiding', the 'wish-fulfilling jewel' (compassion), the 'heartbeat of death', the 'innermost essence', 'an unfolding vision of wholeness', 'the *bardo* of becoming' and 'intrinsic radiance'. These concepts are in Sogyal Rinpoche's epic book *The Tibetan Book of Living and Dying*. I found them life-changing. The Buddha's teachings are open to varying interpretations as are all religious doctrines. This is evidenced by the number of schools of thought and traditions (Mahayana, Theravada, Vajrayana, Kadampa, Zen, Tibetan) stemming from his teachings. It is in experiencing his messages, so simple at one level and profound at another, that have helped me make giant leaps into a grounding, joyous, and calm space amidst the obstacle race that is life.

Central to Buddhism is that impermanence abounds – be it the seasons, the dark, the night, the moonlight, the sunlight, the physical body, sickness, health, wealth, sorrow, grief, poverty, happiness, joy, pain, suffering and so on. Everything emerges and then seems to perish. What profoundly impacted me as a child were the qualities of dignity, serenity, calm, and wisdom that were inextricably linked to the demeanour of the Buddha. The artist who created the illustrations in those religious magazines gifted by my mother had captured these qualities perfectly. They became an image I carried in my mind and heart from then on, the facial expressions *mirroring an internal state that felt worthwhile aspiring to.*

The enormity of this meeting did not impact me for years, but a seed was sown. The Buddha had been unconsciously adopted as my eternal soulmate. Having buried his wisdom deep into my psyche, a path towards liberation, beneath the chaos and suffering, had begun. I just did not know it then. Now I do, life seems to have a renewed purpose. There is a distinct spring in my step. It has been a long journey, with a lot of wandering. Thankfully, I am coming home as aptly put by John Tolkien in a line in the poem *'All That Is Gold Does Not Glitter'* from The Lord of the Rings.

Not all those who wander are lost.

How enlightening. All that time I thought I was lost, I was simply wandering new paths to new destinations.

Suffering can mean different things to different people. What do I understand suffering to be? How can it be defined? Thinking about the bigger picture and then homing in to the personal feels helpful. It is like a big onion. There are layers of suffering. Hopefully, we can peel the layers, overcome the stinging blindness, shed the tears, and reach the core of our 'intrinsic radiance'. Have you ever looked at the core of an onion? It has this beautiful luminous quality to it – just like you and me.

The concept of suffering has permeated the entire history of the human race. Texts on anthropology, sociology, biomedicine, humanities, theology, philosophy, psychology, politics, and a whole lot more speak of it. It seems to be the essence of art, drama, theatre, film, novels, and increasingly, social media communication. Pop psychology and New Age material espousing negation of this human angst abound. Mainstream news is rife with suffering. Depression, suicide, and euthanasia speak about the intolerance of this human experience. It can all sound rather bleak, but the truth is that it exists. Just switch on your gadgets, television, PC, laptop, tablet, smart phone, or that fancy watch. Any will do. Connect to the World Wide Web. Start watching. You will be bombarded with images of broken hearts, displaced human beings, poverty, starvation, dismembered limbs, and ruin after ruin of what was once called home. *We cannot deny suffering exists. We really cannot. Just like we cannot deny that peace, hope, compassion, connection, courage, wisdom, love, and happiness exist.* Phew.

At times, I feel drenched in existential angst. There seems to be a lot of chaos. The world has become a small place. Advances in technology allow for speed-of-lightning communication, travel, migration, terrorism, and war. Dark forces are propelling people of one land to flee to the land of other people, and suddenly human beings are feeling threatened, violated, and alienated in their own homes, streets, and neighbourhoods. Television news flashes speak about chemical and biological warfare. Often attributed to clashes of culture, religious, political and social ideology, it can leave us feeling angry, stormy, terribly frightened, and vulnerable.

I certainly have become acutely aware of my territorial human nature which resents sharing and caring for others amidst my own increasing insecurities. *Yet in my heart of hearts, I know that planet Earth belongs to everyone.* The territories and sense of entitlement are man-made features. No amount of positive thinking can eliminate the fact that there is some brutal stuff going on in the world, and it is causing the human, animal, and plant kingdoms a lot of turmoil. Back to the onion, this is layer one. The world feels at war. It is out there somewhere, especially for those of us privileged enough to live on certain parts of Mother Earth, safe from the constant bombardment and venomous shelling of hate and plastic. Sadly, for many, they are right in it. That is their world. Let us pause for a sincere heartfelt concern for fellow human beings caught up in that world. Pause.

On to layer two, this begins to feel personal. It could really happen. It is not too far away. Traumatic events may occur. Loved ones may die. Relationships may collapse, jobs and homes may be lost, and our health may deteriorate. The reality is that within my extended family and circle of friends, cardiac disease, cancer, depression, diabetes, and Alzheimer's disease are common topics of discussion. We all know someone affected. There seems to be no immediate end in sight. Gulp. On top of that, we are constantly being bombarded with advertisements around disease and how to prevent it, in between the ones that tell us about incontinence pads! 'Go organic!' one screams. 'Have regular scans!' screams another. 'No carbs,' says the third. 'Eat these pills,' says the fourth. 'Superfoods can save you,' says the fifth, 'Do 10,000 steps,' says the sixth, 'Sleep at least 8 hours,' says the seventh, and so it goes on and on and on till I just want to scream! So I do. Scccrrreeeeaaaammm! Please feel free to do the same if you need to do so. It feels rather cathartic as I connect with a primordial sense of injustice and the desire for change.

All this fear based stuff goes roller coasting into my psyche to permeate the deeper layers of the onion where other narratives of suffering already reside. Depending on how big your onion is, this can lead to meltdown. My onion used to be ginormous but is looking a bit better these days, especially since engaging with this verbal detoxing. Peeling the layers of our onions can help ease the hurt. The Buddha had this wonderful analogy of the two arrows. From my understanding, the first arrow is the existential arrow where we do not have much control over what is thrown at us with a world at war. However, the second arrow can either propel us into a dark, depressive cloud or project us into a colourful rainbow, so to speak.

This second arrow resides in our minds. We can use it to create more suffering or to diminish it. In some situations, extinguish it, forever. Oh, yes please! This second arrow carries our attitudes, thoughts, feelings, beliefs, and more importantly, controls our actions. *It speaks of choice – to go up the healing scale or down the wounding one.* I do not wish to make it sound easy because it certainly is not, especially as a lot of our struggles reside in the unconscious. It takes patience, perseverance, heartache, and sheer determination to programme this second arrow of choice towards our liberation rather than our extinction. It is possible. Here I am, doing just that, with some evidence for it.

My life script never went to plan. Stuff I was told as a little girl by my Cultural Parent turned out to be a lie. I was supposed to grow up in a harmonious extended family, find a nice husband to provide material and emotional comforts as well as help birth a couple (at least) of beautiful children. We would live a joyous family life, look forward to the marriage of our own children, and the inevitable expansion of our family with grandchildren. What happened instead? Every time I hoped for marriage, for security, for intimacy, for love, for motherhood, the joy of nurturing and loving a child, that hope got cruelly dashed. Unlovable was the message received. A life only half lived was the message absorbed. By mid-age, I was supposed to be comfortable in the knowledge of being cared for (by my children) into old age and not suffer isolation and loneliness. Nearing the end of my life, fear was something that would be peripheral to my existence. Dear me. What went wrong? Here I am at fifty-six years of age, marriage-less, partner-less, childless, living on my own, having to earn my own money and pay my mortgage and bills. Add to that the challenge of looking after ageing parents with their increasing emotional, physical and existential fragility alongside my own increasing emotional, physical, and existential needs. How awful is that?

Or should I say, having choice and a voice, how did it all turn out so well?

Why am I filled with so much gratitude and grace for my life? Why is it all okay amidst the existential suffering? Hope and light seem to be bursting through the dark clouds. Courage, calmness, and clarity seem mine to have and hold rather than just fear, agitation, and confusion. How can this be possible?

I believe it is largely down to embracing the Buddha's wisdom of detaching myself from ignorance and challenging long-held cultural beliefs. Contacting my 'innermost essence' has brought me to right here and now, to this page, to this amazing creative experience, and to you. Carl Rogers, father of Person-Centred therapy and author of one of my favourite books, *On Becoming a Person*, hit on it when he explained the concept of the self-actualising tendency. That part of us that intuitively strives for innate growth and realising our human potential. This tendency (inner light) becomes concealed under the layers of confusion that life throws at us, and can propel us into acute darkness. The layers make us numb and dormant. We experience our lives as being so remote from what our heart desires, that we go into disarray.

The arrow of exerting choice can ignite our self-actualising tendency fiercely and take us to a place of profound healing where amidst the long-held, conditioned ideas and beliefs about how we should be, we can connect with a deeper truth. I am free, if I choose to be. If I can abandon man-made conditioning and connect to that realm of *non-judgemental loving space* called consciousness. Rumi, the thirteenth-century Sufi mystic and poet captured this for me in a stanza from one of his poems, *A Great Wagon*:

> Out beyond wrong doing and right doing
> There is a field (my interpretation - of Human consciousness)
> I'll meet you there.

Consciousness can mean many things to many people. On sitting in meditation, one of the tools for liberation offered by the Buddha, the wisdom of my inner world envelopes me. This is when I stop 'doing' and start 'being'. To be honest, there are no bright shining lights, angels or rainbows to be seen as described by many. There is just a sense of blissful stillness and acceptance, a feeling of *'this is the truth'*. In this space, there is no war, external or internal or stinging onions. In this realm, I understand what Shakespeare spoke about where all the world's a stage and us humans being mere actors on it. In this instance, the Universe becomes the audience, watching us all at play, *encouraging us all to see beyond the limitations of the man-made scripts, nudging us along to write our own stories* and in this process, connect with humanity in an expansive way, to realise what is so beautiful about being human, amidst the suffering.

How else have I had a glimpse of consciousness? It is by honouring my gut instincts and holding in awareness two thoughts of inquiry. Firstly, what is my intention? Secondly, what is the motivation behind my behaviours? Some clarity has emerged by honouring an inner nurturing voice rather than the critical voice that annoyingly booms out negative messages. This boomer insists on blaming and shaming us by telling us that *we are not worthy* and *not good enough*. *That voice is one to definitely ignore.* It takes time to do so but never give up because there is a much more loving and supportive voice, amidst the anxiety and chaos, that whispers to us from the Universe.

This voice can speak directly to our heart or symbolically through events often described as synchronicity. I have lost count of the number of times when I have been in the right place at the right time when least expected; when a motivating song being hummed under my breath suddenly starts playing in a cafe; when people with the right answers or support literally collide into my field; when everywhere I go, an image of the Buddha will come out to stalk me as in recently when sitting at an airport transit lounge, the most ginormous image of the Enlightened One suddenly caught my eye. It was beaming at me from a digital screen advertising some random stuff and reminding me to lift the veil of ignorance by dropping the victim position in my sitcom drama of life. Then, there have been books with answers that I need in order to resolve a struggle which literally fall off book shelves and into my lap. On and on it goes. There have been few coincidences for me.

It has helped enormously that I have a tendency to never give up on life. I mean never give up. Persist with your dream. A cherished wall plaque reminds me of this every day,

> Sometimes on the way to a dream,
> we get lost and find a better one
> (source unknown).

I have experienced this precisely in my life. Do not buy into the illusion of failure, even if it means being isolated and lonely at times. Solitude can be mistaken for isolation and loneliness if we live in a world that never stops. How can we recognise an opportunity for growth if we are drowning in our story? Use this time to reflect and contemplate on what really matters to you. What are your possibilities? Why are you sabotaging yourself? What can the Universe do for you? What can you do for you?

The problem with existential angst is that it can be overwhelming. It feels personal, especially self-worth being a constant struggle. Over the years, deep in my heart and gut, I knew I was lovable. There was no shortage of love from diverse sources. But I felt desolate at times. This was inextricably linked to the fact that I was looking for love in the wrong place, externally rather than internally. Then the gems arrived. *When I stopped wailing and crying, stepped out of being the wounded victim, tore up that fake life script, ignored ridiculous religious ideologies, rebelled against the aspirations of my Cultural Parent and the biological ones, I saw what had transpired surpassed my wildest dreams.*

My life was blessed with far more than what had been lost in that man-made life script. My human instinct to survive, to blossom, and to break through ancestrally redundant cultural barriers brought glorious opportunities to me. I was fuelled on by what Eric Berne, father of Transactional Analytical psychotherapy, aptly describes as the 'arrow of aspiration' in his classic book *What Do You Say After You Say Hello?* My inner light led me to my 'secret garden' which housed my creative dreams and yearnings. Deeply held limiting beliefs were challenged. This led to a wonderful career, travel, owning my own home, spiritual enquiry, freedom of expression, and now on to the birth of my own well-being business in middle age when culturally, I have been programmed to start thinking about retirement! Stuff that I say. As for this writer that has emerged from hibernation, that's just another story! It's called the Icing on the Cake! Excuse me for a minute as I go off for a swirl and a twirl!

Caution. Insights have been a while coming, and along the way, errors have occurred. At times, ego and genuine human default mechanisms have got in the way of progress. By ego, I mean that part of me that surrenders to the illusion that I am better and more deserving than others, worse still, that I am special. We are all special. Not a single one of us came tagged as good, bad, or not special. These labels were assigned to us by man-made ignorance and the need for control and power. We need to abandon them and reconnect with our 'innermost essence' free of such narrow definitions. It is best to *part with our deluded self* that loves projecting our stuff onto others. I could run a master class: Poor Me; Rich You. Well, none of that anymore. 'Rich Me and

Rich You' is the mantra. Let us just not weigh it in 22-carat gold as we Indians like to do. Careful. Burglars abound.

Errors can be undone. Let me share. The Buddha's central message towards liberation from existential suffering was through a mental attitude of *maitri* (loving-kindness), *karuna* (compassion), *mudita* (sympathetic joy), and *upeksha* (equanimity, even-mindedness). I started trying to embrace these qualities wholeheartedly on a ten-day silent Vipassana (insight meditation) retreat over two decades ago. On arrival at the venue, my worldly possessions were handed over to the support staff for safekeeping. This meant abandoning my mobile phone (the brick!), books, magazines, knitting kit, anti-inflammatory pills and potions. It was to be a ten-day journey with myself. My mum was genuinely concerned about my survival, being the chatterbox that I am. Then there was the 4am wake-up call, another concept rather alien to me. Thankfully, I survived even though, at the time, death felt real. *Nothing gave me more proof of the fact that my mind could be my greatest friend but also my worst enemy.*

At one point amidst a meditation (or was it hallucinations), I saw myself as Superwoman. There she was, effortlessly fixing fragmented planet Earth, swinging from one wounded fragment to the next, gathering the pieces towards wholeness. Interesting how I saw myself as Superwoman, the need to be perfect and heroic ever-present. The correct label at the time would have been Rescuer Extraordinaire or Wounded Warrior.

Back in the real world following the retreat, I endeavoured to respond to every situation with love, kindness, compassion, and sympathy. What a fool. How naive. How bothersome. *The problem was that whilst focussing on the mind, my heart had been unknowingly abandoned. It shut down as I was busy intellectualising emotions rather than feeling them.*

In those early meditative days, I disconnected from the fact that loving-kindness, compassion, and sympathetic joy were heart qualities rather than intellectual outpourings. *More importantly, these qualities first needed to be directed towards myself.* Being in relationship with others came naturally to me, except with potential husbands. I could be affectionate and play the clown, which was my way of being loved and accepted. Sadly, the reality was that an overactive engagement with the mind, coupled with a poor engagement with the heart, created imbalance within my mind, heart, body, and spirit. Feelings were shoved deep into the psyche. Wounds were protected by layers of fat. In the world of psychology, small doses of denial, deflection, dissociation, repression, contraction, and sublimation-defence mechanisms of the organism (me!) to survive stopped me from thriving. I disconnected from my true (uncontaminated) nature for years. I just got fatter as I comfort ate through my inauthentic life which looked rather authentic at the time, but was obviously not.

In hindsight, some of this intra-psychic disconnection began when very young. I was always the podgy one who had 'puppy fat' when most of my peers were grown lean poodles. This shaming fat was concealed under baggy tents and smocked tops whilst those horrible girls, with perfect figures, swanned around in their Levi jeans and crisp, white T-shirts, showing off their neat little bottoms. I hated them. Not so loving, kind or compassionate, I see. As time and life progressed, the Buddha's teachings felt a bit incomplete. Where was the soul? I was constantly seeking it, that part of me which was uncontaminated by man-made ideology and tribal rules. I knew it was somewhere within me, but it felt elusive. Thank God, literally, for my Hindu gods who provided me with soul, the *atman*, which is central to Hinduism. Yet whilst I bumbled along in life in search of the soul and answers to 'Who am I?', 'What is my purpose on planet Earth?', and 'What is it all about?', deep in my being, my love for the Buddha could not be diminished. It is hard to deny when everywhere in my home (my temple), His images are held on altars honouring the divine – peace, calm, and dignity personified. Remember to stay peaceful, calm, and dignified, they sing. Amidst the suffering. *What I have learnt over time is that it is okay not to be any of these things when needs must.* More than okay. Feelings need to be expressed. Not merely observed and intellectualised.

Many people who know me would not recognise this as my story. Such is the power of the mask us humans adorn.

As you see, the Buddha and I go back a long way. The light has finally come on about the nature of my relationship with this wise being. I see him as an amazing psychologist and philosopher of his time, not some religious figure espousing misguided ideology. He was a realist, very pragmatic, harsh, some may feel. I accept. But he was definitely not some god sitting in heaven controlling human destiny. Along with Lao Tzu, Confucius, Socrates, and many other great, wise beings of the Axial age (around 500 BC), he was framing concepts and ideas for understanding humanity that are as relevant to today, as they were all that time ago.

What struck me through these reflections was the obvious lack of female role models on my altars, except for Mother Mary. A figurine of this divine mother holding baby Jesus is one of my favourites. I have long worked out that this symbolically represents my need for a sacred mother-child emotional connection with my own mother. Sometimes available, sometimes not, she did her best. Hinduism is perfused with many beautiful divine mother (Ma) energies such as Laxmi, Parvati, Sita, Amba, Gayatri, Kali, and Durga. Even though I was aware of all these goddesses, divine female energy with all its amazing empowering potential was alien to me. I put this down to introjections of stereotypical messages from the male-dominated patriarchal system of my childhood which were reinforced by mythological stories. The women were always portrayed as being subservient or in rapturous unilateral devotion to their male counterparts. Additionally, male priests dominated the scene at holy festivals, religious and marriage ceremonies, further entrenching this distorted belief system deep into my psyche. Thankfully, new insights around what is supportive out there has emerged. More importantly, what is *remarkably holding and uplifting within* has surfaced. Compassion for myself did not come for a while. Now it has, most profoundly in my body, in my beautiful divinely energetic feminine body that is the temple to gods and goddesses. It is metamorphosing from *Fat to Fab*. Come dance with me.

Lessons Learnt

Be cautious when interpreting any religious, philosophical, or psychological doctrine as misinterpretation can do more harm than good.

Start peeling that onion and let the tears flow. They speak for the wounds that need to be set free.

Exert that arrow of choice towards self-expression and drop the masks. Who are you? Who would you like to be? Stop lying to yourself and to others.

It is never too late to wake up, show up, clean up, and grow up!

Emotional pain? See it, engage with it, make peace with it and release it.

Come in to compassionate relationship with yourself and watch miracles abound.

Finally, honour the temple which houses profound wisdom and messages for awakening – your body.

Let's look at it.

Reflections

What powers you up in life? What makes you feel alive and stride with a sense of purpose?

What drains your power in life? Leaves you feeling listless and lost?

What could you do to power up rather than seize up?

Chapter 9

The Body Talks: Gas, NATs, Cravings and Spiritual Awakenings

The body has an opinion. Best respect it.

Think of how often we express feeling 'gutted', 'choked', 'stabbed in the back', or 'kicked in the stomach'. Other descriptions speak of a 'heart that jumped into the mouth', 'blood running cold', 'butterflies in the stomach', and 'hairs on the back of the neck standing up'. Phrases such as 'my palms went all clammy', 'it was like my heart had been ripped out', or 'I feel heartbroken' are also familiar. Some struggle to stay upright as their 'legs have turned to jelly'. So, the body certainly 'talks'.

Seeing the physical body as *solid* may be a limited view to hold, but understandable. It is what stares back at us in the mirror or in that essential 'selfie'. It is what we often talk about when we consider our self-worth. This can range from a critical analysis of our hips, flabby arms, crooked nose, balding head, podgy tummy or asymmetrical feet. Let's not forget the saggy boobs and stretch marks either. It is hard not to associate solidity with the physical body, especially as a lot of our pain is held in it. That tense muscle, torn ligament, stiff neck or cramped stomach can be agonising. You know what I mean.

In trying to make sense of 'body talk', the field of energy medicine has caught my attention. This honours the human body as an intricately connected energy system (electric field plus circuits) rather than separate entities such as stomachs, livers, lips, and hips. Do keep an open mind as a lot of it may sound like mumbo jumbo! Well-respected experts in this arena like Caroline Myss (www.myss.com) and Donna Eden (www.innersource.net) can 'read' human energy fields and identify malfunction within the body. Documented cases reveal how they accurately diagnosed illnesses without the use of modern medical gadgets, but through their medical intuition, a deep innate radar of sensing and seeing beyond human understanding. Hard to believe but in my mind, true.

PS: Any alternative therapy does not substitute medical expertise. What it does do is offer additional support towards well-being. It requires belief in something beyond the obvious, beyond reason and quantitative evidence. You always have choice. I chose to believe.

The idea of being an energetic being comprised of electric circuits makes perfect sense. Let's face it. Energy is what most of us desire each morning, particularly of the nourishing kind that helps us spring out of bed with joy, intention, and purpose. This energy helps us get going, be it changing baby's nappy for the umpteenth time, preparing the kids school lunches, getting in to work on time for that important meeting, expressing our creative ideas, checking on elderly parents, or buying the weekly grocery. How wonderful that energy feels rather than waking up to a drained body which has completely run out of batteries, where we are 'running on empty'. This field of medicine offers tools to recharge, but as I have learnt, *anything in life worth having requires perseverance, whether huge amounts of energy, that dream job, loving relationship, or a strong upper body.* I dream of the day where a flick of a switch lights me up like a gloriously adorned bright and shining Christmas tree. Wake up, Bina. Remember,

> There are no short cuts to any place worth going
> (Beverly Sills)

'Talk' of electrical (energy) circuits is centuries old. The Chinese discovered the *meridian system* which is vital to the health of every single cell in our body eons ago. When 'blocked', disease ensues. Acupuncture and acupressure work on restoring the flow of energy through these channels to resolve an array of health issues. Emotional Freedom Technique (EFT), founded by Gary Craig (www.emofree.com) and popularised by Nick Ortner as 'tapping' (www.thetappingsolution. com), draws on the wisdom of this ancient therapy. By tapping on specific meridian points on the body, whilst simultaneously engaging with emotions using certain words and phrases, stuck energy can get flowing again. An array of ailments such as anxiety, phobias, chronic pain, depression, and trauma can be managed or resolved. Cynics feel this is all a load of baloney. I say, imagine all possibilities. Even the great scientist Albert Einstein held an expansive view when he observed,

Imagination is more important than knowledge.

Other energetic fields include the *aura*. The latter refers to a subtle field of protective energy emanating from our bodies. It functions as an antenna which senses the quality of energies (light and uplifting or dense and depleting) held by people, situations, or the environment, in our vicinity. We all have the ability to access it. I do not see auras but feel connected to this intangible zone of energy through a habit of scanning any environment that I step into, whether a private or public space. The radar seems to emanate deep from within my body. What is the energy like? Does it feel light and bright, or heavy and oppressive? Are the contents within (often human beings but also furniture, decorative ornaments, wall hangings and so on) radiating uplifting emissions, or do they make me feel dull and lifeless? Is there danger lurking about? And what about my energy? What sort of radiation am I producing? Does it uplift and inspire others, or is it critical and deflating?

Another system losing importance through the East-to-West drift, is that of the *chakras*. The latter, derived from Sanskrit, mean 'wheels' or 'circles'. They refer to focal points of energy within the body which influence our mental, emotional, physical, and spiritual natures. Imbalances in these centres can lead to dis-ease. The latter seems to have particularly befriended the world at this point in time. Statistics around chronic stress, anxiety and depression abound. Therapies such as reiki, chanting, breath work, meditation, body massage, crystal healing, aromatherapy, colour therapy, creative visualisations, tai chi, Qi gong, and yoga may help realign our auras and *chakras* to create wellbeing.

More recently, I have added EFT, the 'tapping thing', to my self-help tool box towards more balanced living. It has helped enormously to calm my anxiety whilst I make a massive career transition, manage the fear of living in a world that feels at war, and deal with the daily challenges of caring for elderly parents with all their fragilities. Another golden nugget for healing includes a huge dash of self-love and self-compassion through creative writing. This verbal detox has proved to be an elixir for alchemy from *Fat to Fab. The written word is a potent silently spoken word. It allows us to have deeply healing courageous conversations with ourselves.* Words express our innermost thoughts and feelings, which we sometimes dare not to speak in case we shatter into a thousand pieces. They help release toxic, depleting intra-psychic energy out into a more expansive space where it can be dispersed forever. Gone with the wind, so to speak.

Why this personal belief in energy? I wonder if it is due to growing up in an environment living behind locked doors because the 'world out there' could be dangerous in a politically volatile region. As children, we become hyper-vigilant to energies around us to keep ourselves safe. It's an innate skill. *Childhood habits invariably carry on into adulthood.* My connection with energy may also be because I grew up around parents who were such opposites when it came to the way they carried themselves and their bodies. They radiated such contrasting energies – my dad with his ever-positive, beaming, and energetically alive field compared to my mum's more subdued one which carried hers, and the world's woes, on her shoulders. They literally sort of collapsed and caved in as she got older. At some level, their energetic bodies reflected their internal worlds. My mother suffered far more chronic illnesses (than my father) such as digestive disorders, ulcerations, arthritis, lumps, bumps, palpitations, and the like, as did many of her contemporaries.

In terms of the body, Indian women of my mother's generation seem to have an affinity for weak knees and challenging digestive systems. They love talking about gas, as in farts and flatulence. My mum and aunties were always sharing remedies for the relief of this slightly embarrassing problem from herbal concoctions to anti-acid remedies of Western medicine. I offer a theory. The gas symbolically represents deep-seated feelings around aspects of their lives being just 'full of hot air', as in unfulfilled and half lived. As for the arthritic knees, perhaps they symbolise the restriction of free movement – sadly, a current theme for my generation of South Asian women robbed of their autonomy by patriarchal dominance that just won't let go of the need for power. *How easy it is to feel mighty by crushing others.*

Talking about flatulence, current wellness literature focuses on the ecology of the gut and its crucial role in optimum physical, mental, and emotional health. It is seen as the 'second brain' and has created an industry unto itself with all sort of diets, bacterial pills, potions, and advocates for colonic irrigations (ouch!) for boosting gut health. '*My healthy microbiome*' is the new mantra. Never mind *Om*. It has literally saved the life of Kris Carr, wellness activist and cancer survivor of *Crazy Sexy Me* fame (www.kriscarr.com). Andrew Weil, MD, was talking about this over twenty years ago. He presents plenty of evidence for the role of diet in healing the body in his book, *Spontaneous Healing: How to Discover and Enhance Your Body's Natural Ability to Maintain and Heal Itself.* Sound nutrition is the key to sound health. Again, not a new concept but one we have forgotten due to the powers of advertising and use of sugar to grip our taste buds into addictions by the food industry. I can certainly recall the euphoria of that scrumptious ice cream laden milkshake, with its partner in crime French fries drizzled with heaps of tomato (sugary) ketchup! Saying that, in this transformation from *Fat to Fab,* cruciferous vegetables feature far more on my menu these days, out of choice rather than necessity. Bliss and cauliflower steak with peppercorn sauce have arrived.

There is ample evidence that by altering our lifestyle and diet, we can fight a whole load of diseases. The good news is that we do not have to be victims of our genetic make-up. Deepak Chopra and Rudolph E. Tanzi explain exactly why and how in their excellent book *Super Genes: The Hidden Key to Total Well-Being.* It really is worth a read. What feels most empowering is the increasing evidence that 'diseases for life' as per the medical model are proving to be reversible. That's just amazing. Intermittent fasting is providing a panacea for conditions such as Type 2 Diabetes. People are coming off medications they have downed for years. This mind-blowing stuff is central to Jason Fung's and Jimmy Moore's book *The Complete Guide to Fasting.* Giving our internal systems a break from constant food and calorific beverages promotes cell regeneration of the most spectacular kind. Interestingly, every religion espouses the benefits of fasting. Our ancestors certainly were 'fasters'. No twenty-four hour 'drive thru' restaurants for them.

Sadly, this knowledge for balanced living has been lost to my generation living a lifestyle far removed from the wisdom of our ancestors. People in the West are embracing ancient Eastern wisdom with some gusto where as Asian cultures are increasingly identifying with a Western lifestyle based on capitalism, personal freedom, and individual success. This cultural exchange seems to be fuelled by the grass looking greener on the other side. *Human beings are always looking externally for healing. That's a limited view to hold.* I should know. I did it for years until the penny dropped into my innate wisdom inbox!

We seem to be missing the point. Healing systems lie within our bodies, not necessarily just out there in the doctor's office as has been sold to us. To this end, I found the narrative of Alberto Villoldo, psychologist and medical anthropologist, in *One Spirit Medicine* most inspiring. He was brought to his knees by an illness which, according to the medical model, meant embracing death. But as he was a shaman, trained in the wisdom of ancient healing from indigenous peoples of South America, the Caribbean, and Asia, he chose this path over medical science which took him to full recovery. He is very much alive and kicking (www.thefourwinds.com) and living evidence of the incredible healing power of the human body from within.

This is a gentle calling to my birth tribe to honour the healing wisdom of our ancestors. *The Cultural Parent is not all shadow. It holds luminous teachings for balanced living.* Ancient Eastern healing systems complement modern Western living. Alternative therapies (Ayurveda, yoga, meditation, mindfulness practices, breath work based *pranic* healing, chanting mantras, *chakra* clearing, Chinese traditional medicine, reiki, tai chi and Qi gong) are being embraced increasingly for health, rather than just the medical model of resolving symptoms through electric gadgets, surgery, and pills. These ancient practices profoundly influence our emotions, which are a powerhouse for wounding and healing.

This is at the heart of energy medicine. Instead of focussing on what drug we can use to cure the symptom as in the medical model, *the inquiry is why have we lost function and what can we do to restore it? Why is energy being lost?*

Let's talk about feelings which in allopathic care seem to be belted into the back seat. *I reiterate, I am not against Western medicine at all.* Modern medicine has transformed the well-being of billions of people on this planet. Major life-threatening diseases have been conquered. I cannot deny that antibiotics can save a person's life. As a dentist, I used these agents to support my clinical interventions when needed. A recent wrist issue was made a lot better not by just positive affirmations and chanting, but a double dose of corticosteroid injections! Western allopathic medicine brings hope and quality of life to millions of people around the world. *But could it be that this approach may also be prolonging life, and with it suffering, as physical bodies can be kept going for years when the spirit and soul have long ago departed?* As Paul Gilbert, clinical psychologist extraordinaire, observes in *The Compassionate Mind* (51), 'Medicine can prolong dying, which is not the same as prolonging life.'

And what about love? The medical profession struggles with this sentiment, understandably. How does one measure love, a qualitative entity, in a scientific experiment that needs numbers and figures for validity? Love has been offered as an elixir for recovery by Anita Moorjani, author of *Dying to Be Me* and *What If This Is Heaven?*

Following a near-death experience (NDE) in 2006, she was miraculously cured of cancer that had ravaged her body. The family had been gathered to say their last goodbyes. Death did not show up. This incredible lady is now on international lecturing circuits sharing profound messages for healing learnt from her NDE. Her message? Put simply, love is a potent medicine for health, especially love for ourselves. *Choosing love over fear is key to a joyful life.* Contrary to it being a 'fluffy concept', there is a scientific explanation for this. Positive emotions such as love and laughter release uplifting neurotransmitters such as serotonin, dopamine and oxytocin into our energetic bodies. For excellent evidence about the power of positive human emotions on healing bodies ravaged with diseases such as cancer, Kelly Turner's book *Radical Remission* and resources (www.radicalremission.com) are a must. She offers incredible hope on how to negotiate that terrifying journey which begins with a cancer diagnosis. Love, meaning, and purpose play a huge role in healing a fragmented body.

Healing is not about being in a *perfect body*. It is about *feeling healthy*. The latter can mean different things to different people. To me it is about being energetic, joyful and having a sense of purpose in my steps, as well as peace and gratitude in my heart. *The word 'health' often refers to the physical body but I am increasingly paying attention to my emotional, mental and spiritual health.* When attuned to this more 360 degree approach, I can manage life without falling apart amidst inevitable existential suffering. It is not how I look that seems to bother me much these days, though I am rather pleased with what the mirror reflects back to me (grin). More importantly, how I *feel in my body* draws my attention far more than before. Intuition then guides me to my remedy for aligning my mind-heart-body-spirit using a range of healing tools shared throughout this narrative.

The field of Epigenetics, brought to mainstream audiences by Bruce Lipton, a developmental biologist, looks at how gene expression can be altered without gene modification. What gripped me on reading his book *Biology of Belief* was that in addition to environmental factors such as diet and chemical toxins, *our beliefs can actually change our experience of health* to the extent that we can recover from diseases deemed inevitable, irreversible or terminal. I guess this is what happens in the *placebo effect* in clinical trials, where people report feeling better on eating a sugar pill because they actually believe they are eating a drug which will heal their dis-ease. This encourages me no end. We do not have to be victims of genetically transmitted diseases. Phew, because I have the normal Indian ones such as cardiovascular disease and diabetes in my ancestral pool.

Caution. Some conditions are genetically transmitted which must be respected, but we do not have to be cynical about everything that is not logical and reasonable.

The scientist in me battles with my innate wisdom. I am always seeking evidence. A huge lesson learnt is that *often the evidence lies in our deep personal experiences.* We just need to stop lying to ourselves, or be open to something beyond the obvious. And in any case, when all else has failed, what harm is there in deeply trying to love ourselves anyway? As Paul Gilbert highlights in *The Compassionate Mind* (50), 'Kindness, gentleness, warmth and compassion are like basic vitamins for our minds.' As our mind resides in our body, the latter must also benefit from a surge of positive human emotional nutrients.

Based on this, alongside my multivitamin these days, I ingest huge 'pills' of journaling, prayer, mindfulness practice, angel and oracle card wisdom, smiling, nurturing food and drink, connection with soul family, tapping my meridian points, walks in nature, exercise, painting (on canvas and my nails), social media (careful!) and loving self-talk on a regular basis. They all lead to a sense of calm, clarity of purpose and wellbeing. Occasionally, retail therapy helps too. Let's not go into denial!

All the above is not 'new talk' at all. The concept of the energetic body has been around forever. Over 2,500 years ago, the Buddha (and many more before him, and after him, but forgive my bias) recognised that at their core, the entire human, animal, and plant kingdoms are made up from building blocks that also form the galaxies. Mind-blowing, isn't it? These include atoms, sub-particles like electrons, protons, neutrons, and Higgs boson. Albert Einstein said energy (E) equals mc-squared (E=mc2). M standing for mass and C for the velocity (speed) of light in a vacuum. He also said:

A human being is part of the whole. Called by Us the Universe.

Now, being no physicist, my understanding is limited but it makes sense that because the speed of light in a vacuum is huge, and even huger when squared, minute masses of matter have huge energy. That's a lot of huges! Energy can manifest in the form of light, sound, microwaves, digital stuff, X-rays, nuclear waves, and human beings for that matter. Forgive the pun. In the end, I find it hard to disconnect from the idea that we are energetic bodies living in an energetic field of all possibilities.

If all this talk around energy-based human health feels nonsensical, we can perhaps explore and understand it in a different way. This transformative journey from *Fat to Fab*, has helped me re-establish relationship with my four bodies, the mental, emotional, physical and spiritual. I realise that I had fallen prey to thinking in terms of mind, body and spirit as separate entities. And what of the heart? Over the years, I had lost connection with my tender heart-centred emotional body. If one is in any doubt about the power of our heart as a source of profound healing, I would encourage accessing the work done by the HeartMath Institute (www.heartmath.org) which provides evidence for the incredible intelligence we hold in this organ, literally.

For ease of explanation, I have described the four bodies separately, but in reality, they are all interconnected. Each profoundly impacts the other as I hope you will come to see.

In my experience, balanced lives arise from bringing all four bodies into harmonious alignment. They all need to be fuelled for us to feel alive. A key understanding is that each body needs its own type of 'food', rather than what we normally stuff down such as crisps, biscuits, donuts, and pizzas. *Often when we are 'hungry', it is not for a sandwich, a chocolate bar, or a piece of cake even though it often appears that way.* **We are usually 'hungry' (craving) for something else**: for an apology; for acknowledgement; for the love of our mother; for relief from pain; for a loving relationship; for that dream job; for something to lift the boredom; for money; for children; for better health; for rest, for security; for meaning and purpose, for belonging, for keeping fear and anxiety at bay; for a hug; for a kiss; for _____ (fill in the blank). To this end, other 'foods' exist.

When I understood at the very core of my being that hanging out with soulmates, expressing love, laughter, appropriate anger, joy, crying, holding healthy boundaries, letting go, saying 'no', self-compassion, massages, counselling support, silent walks in nature, positive affirmations, tapping, volunteering, reading, dancing, cooking, gardening, washing up, mindfulness practice, praying, swimming in the ocean, chanting, reiki, painting, reflective writing, climbing mountains, sunshine, gazing at the moon, building sand castles and *so much more were also 'foods'* that could assuage this craving 'hunger', my life changed forever. In the most magical way.

Consider the following:

The physical body needs feeding with nutritious food and fluids for maintaining its organs and systems in pristine health. It also thrives from exercise, nourishing sleep, appropriate rest and physical contact be it warm handshakes, hugs, kisses, and sex. So these *behaviours* could be seen as 'foods' that the physical body needs for health. Warning: confusion may arise from this next bit! What's fascinating me especially these days is the behaviour of 'fasting' where we periodically withdraw from eating and allow the physical body to heal from within. I never thought I would ever feed my body with 'food' such as 'fasting' but I do, and I am enjoying the benefits of it immensely.

On the other hand, evidence abounds that our physical body houses our emotional history as highlighted in Bessel van der Kolk's book, *The Body Keeps the Score*. Psychotherapeutic approach around childhood trauma focuses on this connection for healing. Memories are held in body tissues and the way people posture themselves narrate a thousand stories. Generally, to the average person, physical pain is seen as a malfunction of the physical body systems. My dental background with its emphasis on the medical model of 'cause and effect' had limited my world view. Counselling training, verbal detoxing through this reflective writing, and falling in love with energy medicine has blown that ignorance away.

We actually may *experience emotional pain* as a stiff neck, back spasm, tension headache, jaw lock or 'feeling empty'. We then binge on painkilling drugs which provide temporary relief, or stuff down the cookies for comfort eating which makes us feel even emptier. What may actually set us off on the road towards healing the physical pain and emptiness are 'foods' *that allow for expression of emotions* such as a chat with a soul mate, having that difficult courageous conversation, saying 'sorry', loving self-talk, drama, art and talk therapies, or the amazing emotional healing that comes from journaling and intuitive reflective writing shared here with you. *Spit it out of the body I say. Let it go.*

Consider: if we have just eaten a meal or a snack, and 'hunger' (craving) is gnawing away at us, it helps to ask ourselves at this time, *'What am I really hungry for?'* I don't want to make it sound easy, especially if addictions are intense (or there is an underlying metabolic disorder), but by bringing awareness to the moment, *by listening to a loving inner voice that whispers 'what's this all about?' rather than the harsh critical one that booms 'there you go failing again'*, I have been able to re-assess my options in a nurturing way.

Three tools for amazing healing rather than self-harm are awareness, forgiveness, and self-compassion.

Awareness says, 'STOP. An old destructive pattern has appeared. You have the choice to repeat it or do things differently.'

Forgiveness says, 'Let the old story go. You did your best at the time with the awareness you had. No need for shame, guilt, judgement, and self-loathing.'

Self-compassion says,'You are worthy of forgiveness. Here's a chance to do something differently for your fabulous self. Change your story, change your life.'

Profound insights have been birthed. In this moment, 'feeding' our mental body, rather than our physical one, may hold the key to liberation. *The mind is a thought generating machine and can talk us into anything at all. True or way off the truth.* This often helps address the real issue which is that 'I am bored out of my mind' or that unhelpful negative automated thoughts (NATs) are polluting ones behaviour. Perhaps we need to educate ourselves on the impact of certain foods, stress, hormonal imbalances and metabolic disorders on hunger, and stop beating ourselves up for being 'weak' and 'lacking in discipline'. Let's learn about neuroscience and physiology rather than drown in our wound-ology!

Positive strategies can be implemented with our minds rather than our mouths and tummies. How can we do that?

The mental (mind) body needs *nourishing thoughts* as 'food' rather than shame-or-guilt-based talk. The field of neuroscience has transformed our understanding of how the brain can make or break our world, literally. The poignancy of dementia or Alzheimer's disease in an otherwise healthy body cannot be missed. There is a saying in the neuroscience field; 'neurones that fire together wire together'. If we keep running old, destructive thought patterns such as NATs, the electrical circuits running these patterns get stronger and often lead to *low mood, anxiety and depression.* Fear and isolation can start running the show. Repeated storylines can become self-sabotaging and destructive.

In order to break damaging electrical circuits and create new nurturing ones, we need expansive thoughts (nourishing mental food) that can lead to illumination and transformation, amidst the suffering. This 'food' is to be found in honest communication with others, changing our stories, informing ourselves with sound knowledge, remaining curious, keeping our imagination alive and kicking, and making appropriate choices that can help us create the life we want, rather than live by life's terms. For insights into what thoughts may be driving your dis-ease, check out the *New York Times* bestselling author (wise soul) Louise Hay's *Heal Your Body*. I would also recommend reading Dr Joe Dispenza's book *Breaking the Habit of Being Yourself: How to Lose your Mind and Create a New One* which focuses on evidence from neuroscience, brain chemistry, biology, quantum physics and genetics, and outlines incredible techniques on how to rewire our brains. The title says it all.

Loving positive thoughts can go a long way. Saying that, whilst I am a fan of positive psychology, I do not wish to be positive to the point of stupidity. Reality has to be faced. No amount of positive psychology can make me the future queen of England. But from experience, by catching those NATs before they run rampant, and by reframing my outlook, beneficial physiological responses in my body (less fight and flight and more calm) are generated which lead to clarity and positive action. We can manage anxiety, panic attacks, depression, mental illness, post-traumatic stress disorder (PTSD), living with cancer, autoimmune conditions, work challenges, relationship struggles and so much more. *We can change our experience of ourselves and our life script to more fulfilling ones.* We can rewrite our story. The world need not be a scary place.

This forms the basis of Cognitive Behavioural Therapy (CBT) which has enjoyed profound success (www.evidence.nhs.uk), and continues to help people transform their lives. I certainly have benefitted from it. By gently acknowledging and challenging my self-sabotaging NATs, and paying attention to more positive thoughts, I have dared to share my inner world here and birth the writer within. It has been a nerve-racking journey, but the healing from it has been worth it. No more extra-large size Bridget Jones pants for me. What's extra-large these days is my emotional body which has an intelligence of its own.

The emotional body *is all about our feelings.* Rather than cakes, fizzy drinks and chocolate peanuts, nurturing 'foods' such as authentic loving relationships, a sense of connection and belonging, being seen, heard and understood, gratitude, expressions of love, self-compassion and general appreciation seem to keep this body alive and well. *Unfortunately, it is the one most commonly neglected and is the source of our many woes, particularly with respect to body image and constant weight struggles.* Comfort eating is all about that. Denying feelings and soothing the physical body with sugar hits which, as we all know, offer temporary relief. As I absorbed my Cultural Parent's allegiance to duty, obligation and sacrifice, I bought into the script that girls don't speak up (hence, everything must be swallowed). 'Everything' amounted to not only healthy and processed food, but also emotions such as anger, frustration, rage, sadness, fear, dread, loneliness, and lust! *When normal human emotions cannot be expressed appropriately, they need to go somewhere.* For some, they manifest as explosive rages. In others, depression – as in shutdown – arrives. In my case, they obviously stuffed themselves into my fatty tissues which graciously kept expanding to accommodate them.

It has taken me years to understand that the 'food' I need for keeping my emotional body healthy is not what one buys in supermarkets, clothes boutiques and cafes but resides within my own soul and the hearts of fellow human beings. It is called love. It is called compassion. It is called kindness. **For self and other.** By becoming aware of our emotions, we can look beyond our wounds and onion like layers of defensive attitudes, change our thoughts and behaviours and go on to create an abundance of health. As we feel loved and accepted from deep within, we start to experience optimum wellbeing.

In this journey from *Fat to Fab,* **feeling fabulous** *is what I value above all else,* because when I feel super duper, I look amazing irrespective of what the weighing scales said that morning. In feeling *Fab,* another rock-solid support arrives, which is the *ability to* **hold a fabulous attitude** *towards the trials and tribulations of life.* This has anchored me into a palpable space of well-being and joy, amidst the suffering. Connection with my spiritual body has amplified. I have always been in touch with it through my belief in Divine Intelligence which I choose to call God. The relationship is deepening. I know many do not identify with this Force at all, and that is perfectly all right. I still honour your views. For me, denying my spiritual body equates to a breathless body, which equates to death. Spiritual health is as essential as is mind, body and emotional health. It is what gives meaning and purpose to my life.

Millions of people have encountered their spiritual body through religion, but many have also done so by connecting with an inner voice which says, 'All is well, yet something does not feel right.' We can be in that dream palace, relationship and job, have beautiful healthy children, regular five-star holidays and a loving community, *but something is missing. There's an emptiness amidst the dreams, a deep hollow feeling that no one, thing or situation can fill.* I have met many such people over the years. What's that all about? I think it's about the spirit, the soul, that part of us which connects us to a greater more profound truth; Life Force, Spirit, Source, Divine Intelligence, God, the Universe or whatever you wish to call it. It can be very subtle.

I am always seeking connection with my creator like a baby seeks connection to its mother. It is a complex affair, but I will give it a go.

The spiritual body needs soul food, which can mean many things. It all gets rather confusing at times. Soul and spirit talk abound. But what does it mean? I respect that they may mean different things to people. To me they feel interconnected. The soul, based on religious teachings in Hinduism, is that part of us that never dies. It is like an inner pilot light that cannot be extinguished, whatever the circumstances. I believe it is this eternal light that helps people who have 'died inside' on being deeply wounded to 'come alive' against all odds. This light has been written about forever. Perhaps the term *self-actualising tendency*, which is central to healing through counselling and psychotherapy symbolises this inner light. It knows just what can help us thrive. Spirit is seen as eternal energy sourced from the Universe. Donna Eden author of *Energy Medicine*, describes it as 'a matrix of subtle energies that support, shape and animate the physical body, often displaying intelligence that transcends human knowing' (18). The author highlights its representation (*qi* or *chi* in China, *prana* in India, *ruach* in Hebrew, *ki* in Japan, *baraka* in Sufis, *wakan* by the Lakota, *orenda* by the Iroquois, *megbe* by the Ituri pygmies, and the *holy spirit* in the Christian tradition) in many cultures.

It represents the energetic field (back to that talk, I'm afraid!) that emerges from the Universe at birth, and then re-merges into this bigger field at death. It could be likened to how waves emerge from the ocean and then dissolve into it again. In everyday language, it is breath. Baby's first breath says, 'Hello world.' A last breath says, 'Goodbye for now.' We are just energy, drifting in and out of fields. Whilst we can touch our physical body, examine digital images of brain-mind maps, apply gadgets to detect changes in our heart physiology, the spirit and soul seem scientifically unmeasurable, but yet potently present. Millions of people have experienced the presence of these forces, soul and spirit, in their lives. We cannot all be bleeding to an illusion, surely.

Bestselling author and psychiatrist Brian Weiss presents evidence for the eternity of the soul in his book *Same Soul Many Bodies*. Coming from a medical scientific background, he used to be cynical about this possibility until a profound personal experience presented him with the evidence that a soul inhabits many bodies over lifetimes. Again, for many this may be mumbo jumbo, but as always, don't judge the book by its cover. Dive in. Experience the (true) story. Then judge. Most views accepted.

What makes for soul food? Well, anything which ignites that inner pilot light. Soul food takes me from a dull, heavy energetic field to a more clarified, lighter, and yet deeply grounded place where joy abounds. Energy medicine offers a plethora of healing modalities to feed our spirits. I 'gorge down' a five minute routine out of Donna Eden's book *Energy Medicine* when my soul and spirit feel lethargic. It gets me going each time. A relative who has Chronic Fatigue Syndrome (CFS) has become a fan. The routine invariably charges her up from that dreaded depleted state into one which allows life to go on. Whilst 'food' such as prayer, chanting, contemplation, meditation, rituals, breath work, yoga, hymns, and *bhajans* (Indian devotional songs) are obvious soul foods, I believe they extend to pieces of favourite music, gardening, landscape painting, hikes in nature, sacred relationships and frankly anything that honours the 'Thou' that resides within the 'I'. Whatever takes us into that slightly altered state of consciousness where we feel at one with the world. Mystics are the masters of spiritual cuisine. I certainly prefer it a lot more to the samosas and ice cream sundaes that I used to gorge down in seconds to tranquillise the anxiety associated with living an inauthentic life.

Kyle Gray sums it (the four bodies) up beautifully in *Wings of Forgiveness* (96):

> *Your body is that holy temple*
> *The altar is your mind*
> *And the seat of the divine is your heart*
> *The temple is incomplete without the altar*
> *An altar is bare without its source*

Here's a calling to rephrase the mind, body, spirit movement as *the mind, heart, body, and spirit dance.*

My journey from Fat to Fab can be measured in many other ways. The most obvious to the eye being the changes in my physical body. As for my mental, emotional and spiritual bodies, I barely recognise them. This holistic transformation has taken me completely by surprise. New insights have emerged.

Some people eat to live and others live to eat. Which are you? I used to be the latter for a long, long time. That is not a typo. It really has been that long. Those of us who live to eat often have a poor relationship with food. We eat too much. We know we are doing it, and it is not what we want to do, but we just cannot seem to help ourselves. We are driven by a possessive force that is hard to extinguish. In extreme cases, we get labelled with that term *eating disorder.* We are then obese, bulimics, compulsive bingers, or anything in between.

The reality is that a lot of us do not get labelled that way at all. We do not fit the medical model of a body-image disease. In fact, we are to be found functioning well in society, going about our business with great zest and gusto, our size sixteen, eighteen, and twenty-plus bodies stuffed into Lycra to create an illusion, to prop up the lie, to abate the shame and keep our secrets intact. It does not work. We still get labelled, just in another way. *Fat, fatso, fatty* are terms familiar to me and to millions of men and women out there. We justify our pathological behaviour as 'comfort eating'. Nobody understands us, especially those stick insects who can eat pasta for the entire population of Italy and not put on a pound. Crush.

I comfort ate for years, suffered the humiliation of being told to lose weight, otherwise nobody would marry me. Who wants to marry a fat Indian girl? The Cultural Parent would not approve. Thin is in. So, on to another programme to ditch some weight. Yet nobody married me – the story of my life. This led to another cycle of self-battering and diets that promised me that stick insect look. Eating cabbages for a week, or grapefruit for a month felt promising, but by day three, I would pack it all in because my body would be violently sick. It had got used to the sugary stuff to fire up its engine. A vicious cycle of fat thighs, slimmer thighs, double chins and single chins, huge waists to slightly huge waist was a way of life for years to come. Somewhere on this journey from *Fat to Fab*, came an aha moment. *Eating actually anaesthetises us.* As we layer up with more and more fat, we literally distance ourselves from what really matters, our feelings. Our emotional body. The heart centre numbs up so that we do not have to endure the pain and humiliation of being unacceptable to a world obsessed with perfect brains and beautiful bodies, never mind their dull minds.

Externally, I was all smiles, hugs, and kisses. Internally, a part of me had died, my emotional body deprived of nourishing 'food'. How do I know this? Counselling training, personal therapy, and this writing process provided a potent verbal detox. Clarity arrived. The courage to face up to my reality, rather than prop someone else's up, had blown open the lid of deception. The *truth* emerged. I really was unable to contact the affection that was given to me where it should matter – in the depths of my heart. I knew that many people loved me, but therein lay the problem. It was knowledge. The seat of that is the mind, not the heart. To be truly loved, you have to feel it. How can you feel if you are numb and desensitised? When you are busy being a Rescuer

Extraordinaire? When you do not recognise what 'burn out' means? When chronic fatigue immobilises you? When you feel you are here for others, and to be there for yourself is a selfish act rather than what it is, self-love. *What is wrong in loving and nurturing the divine pure spirit that is you?*

Answers on a postcard please.

The key lesson learnt is to never give up on finding the path to liberation. As mentioned before, I would 'eat' every emotion and stuff it somewhere deep in my body because I just could not be bothered to deal with it. This became easier than protesting. I was exhausted with the role of Rescuer Extraordinaire. I was exhausted with my life script, trying hard not to remain a spinster and conform to society. I was exhausted with living up to being a good child to my Cultural Parent. Working long hours to pay the bills and eating meal after meal on my own were equally depleting. *I simply was exhausted of everything but comfort eating.*

Unknowingly, whilst verbal detoxing through talk therapy and reflective writing, a process of 'unfolding towards wholeness' had begun. Suddenly, intuitive 'aha' ideas emerged out of my consciousness. The honour-all-four-bodies approach that I have shared with you offered alternative ideas for those misplaced hungry moments. When *I stopped numbing my physical body with junk food and started honouring it* with other 'foods' something amazing transpired. My shut down heart (chakra) burst open to the healing frequencies of this verbal detox. I started writing in a way like never before. Verses, not of the Kahlil Gibran and Rumi gold standard but still vaguely poetic, cascaded across my horizons. The whole soul food hot pot together resulted in a most profound awakening best explained in verse.

A quiet joy out of nowhere
Embraces my spirit
A welcome visitor to my soul
Bruised and battered

Whilst negotiating life
A gentle reminder
That nothing lasts
Every experience and emotion
Becomes the past
A chance for a new beginning
Right here
Right now
A quiet joy
Again

A veil of ignorance lifted as I put on a new pair of glasses through which to visualise, and experience the world. The result? My body stopped being smothered by that fatty shield. An urge to express myself with positive abandon arose. I often catch myself doing a little twirl here and there quite spontaneously. Looking in the mirror is an absolute joy and pleasure. Self-loathing has gone. Additionally, my gut instinct, housed deep in my belly, seems rather sharp, and my internal radar is appropriately sensitive to my needs and those of others.

The area around my heart feels expansive. Breath arises expansively from my belly and chest area rather than being restricted to the throat. The choked feeling has subsided. Palpitations and tingling hands do not send me into a panic attack anymore, or galloping to the doctors to be diagnosed with some ghastly disease. Rather than feeling like a vulnerable animal being hounded by some monster towards death, sensations in my body send me straight to internal inquiry. What's that about? What's my body trying to communicate to me? What situation in my life should I pay attention to? What old pattern of behaviour is repeating itself? What can I let go of? What is my true nature trying to whisper to me?

I have learnt that mind, body, heart, and spirit are one, and yet at some subtle level, they are four. Feed each one appropriately and let the dance begin.

When I sit with these reflections in my heart, rather than in my mind, waves of wisdom seem to burst through. I am part of a huge tribe worldwide which is experiencing similar feelings irrespective of race, colour, creed, caste, religion, gender, political leanings, culture, childhood experiences, and so on. Like every human being, I feel sadness. I feel pain. I feel sorrow. I feel hope. I feel yesterday. I feel tomorrow. I feel fear. I feel anger. I feel confusion. I feel vulnerable. I feel joy, I feel loving-kindness, and I feel compassion. Then that *golden moment arrives,* a most liberating feeling of being free. This journey of self-discovery has taught me that *I can feel shame, guilt, self-loathing, hate, resentment, and vengefulness, but because I have a choice, I choose not to.* There is no need. I am true nature whose central quality is non-judgemental, deeply loving and accepting of what is. The good, the not so good and anything in between. Remove the labels. Who are you?

What of this spiritual awakening? It is an incredibly tough journey which stretches mind, heart, body and spirit to the limit. *Do not underestimate it. At the same time, embrace it.*

Journal clip:

Dearest Universe,

There's a fire in my heart. It's reaching fever pitch, and I feel terrified. What's going on? I feel like I am having a mini stroke on my left side, which is feeling tingly all over. Altered sensations have been the norm on this side for years, but this is far worse than it's ever been and I feel so anxious and just want to cry … So, I do … I am exhausted. Really exhausted. Spiritual awakening is turning out to be a tough business that no one prepares you for. Where is the bliss? Where is the stillness? Where is the equanimity? The happiness? The joy? The knowing? The ananda? The rainbows? The butterflies? The angels? All there is is a steady drip of snot from the nasal passages and floods of tears of pain, grief, fear, and the feeling of drowning and falling into some dark place. Am I depressed? Or do I have a menopausal hormonal depression or a mental illness? Whatever it is, it's a deeply lonely place to be. It's all very confusing, deeply congesting and choking.

Yours all snotty and confused, Bina

A huge realisation dawned on me that day. The numbness and sensations of paralysis in my body were actually mirroring my feelings around my life position at the time. I knew in my heart that sustaining my current life was not an option anymore. Needing to break free and begin again, I was at war – with myself. Whilst not seeing myself as a warrior, descriptions of the path of a spiritual warrior do resonate with some aspects of my own journey to date. One has to be willing to die to old habits, patterns of behaviour, judgements about oneself and others, tribal conditioning, and to the critical aspects of the Cultural Parent. In this dying, space can be created for our 'innermost essence' to emerge. A nature which speaks of wanting to live from the heart with passion and joy rather than dully just plod through life. This nature, which at its most pure form is loving, kind and tolerant, can also be courageous and fire us up positively rather than destroy us. *Tapping into this wise awareness dilutes the narcissistic me and allows the spiritual warrior to blossom for the highest good of all.*

This warrior recognised that my soul does not want to live from a position of duty, obligation, and sacrifice as taught by my birth tribe, but prefers a framework based on compassion (courage to embrace suffering and kindness towards myself and others), connection (where 'we' and 'I' can live harmoniously), and co-creation (both our needs matter). *As I am painfully learning, the spiritual path is not an easy one.* You have to become no one to become someone. Go naked. Expose the lumps and bumps and stretch marks and all. The breakdown has to come before the break through. I have never felt so dissociated with myself as I do whilst on this awakening path, having to ground myself over and over again with mindfulness breath and soothing intra-psychic babble, gorging myself on soul food rather than on chocolate chip cookies.

It can get desperate. At one hopeless point, seventeen candles lit the altars in my home. This may sound ridiculous, and it is, if the symbolism in the act is missed. Lighting each candle meant more light. More light meant less darkness. Less darkness meant more clarity. More clarity meant possible choice for change which was what my mind, heart, body and spirit were crying out for. I never thought this would be me. Gripped by anxiety that made me feel as if I was having a stroke, feeling so scared, lonely, vulnerable and frightened. The truth is that leaving addictions (in my case food) means facing our fears. Fear creates anxiety and addictions are great at tranquillising this human condition, temporarily.

Here it is, *the tough bit.* I do not eat to numb myself anymore so I feel, feel, feel, and it hurts, hurts, hurts, and sometimes I think, for the millionth time again, what is all this about really? What is this existence all about? Why does it cause so much angst? Back to Shakespeare's observations, if the world is a stage, who is in the audience? Who am I entertaining, and why am I entertaining anybody? What is the purpose of it all? Really? Can someone out there please help me.

Helped, I was, in ways that can only be imagined. *The reality was that a significant amount of the support needed was held deep within.* When I listened and learnt to trust an inner wisdom, my mind-heart-body-spirit came into divine alignment. I was able to make shifts and take decisions that previously would have drowned me in fear. Where is the evidence? For one, I have shed around fifty pounds of fat without starving and fad diets. Secondly, giving up my profession, financial security and elevated societal status with it, after thirty years, has been possible. Thirdly, daring to birth a new business in middle age, which goes against my childhood life script, is further evidence of this alignment. As for writing and publishing this book. OMG! I've done it! *It felt like when I dared to jump into the unknown with absolute faith in whispers from the Universe, help arrived in the form of a million stars, stuffed with wisdom and healing messages which exploded and scattered onto these very pages that we have shared.*

As for my soul. I remain in deep contact with it as a cherished friend, companion and fellow voyager that has been with me for eternity. Kahlil Gibran (1883-1931), that most illuminated poet and philosopher pins it down succinctly in *The Prophet*:

> That which sings and contemplates in you is still dwelling within the bounds of that first moment which scattered the stars into space.

I have absolutely no doubt whatsoever that this 'first moment' will stay with me even when my physical body has perished. Please do not ask me how I know it. I just do. This illuminating and transformational journey has taught me that some things cannot be intellectualised or explained in scientific rational terms. Some things are beyond explanation. The human mind has not got the capacity to explain all of life's complexities. We can have a jolly good go. We can imagine, theorise, intellectualise, and memorise. I certainly have. All that has done is put me on one big merry-go-round. Every time I dismount the ride, another brick wall stares me in the face.

Notably, when I start from a position of 'I don't really know, but I am open to understanding and creating meaning for my purpose on this planet', the frontiers of life seem rather expansive. An opportunity to ride into the horizon with multiple illuminating sunrises arrives. I am anxious about some of you rolling your eyeballs and saying, 'Really? Don't be silly.' All I can say is, 'Do you understand to believe, or do you believe to understand?' I chose neither. I sit in the knowing.

Well, what on earth does that mean? I hear you say. I hope this helps. Another verse.

> Why does it matter
> What others think
> When deep in your heart
> In the Knowing
> Where the Truth shines bright
> And what matters most

Comes to light
Be who you are
A bright shining star
In search of meaning
With grace and gratitude
Embrace the learning
of Earth's Life School
Then, sit in silence
In the Knowing

Now, I fearlessly feel because emotions such as anger, self-doubt, and guilt need not be stuffed down into my sacred body. Neither do I need fresh cream donuts to numb myself at a rate faster than the speed of sound. Newer options have emerged for balanced living. I seem to have a better perspective amidst the inevitable existential suffering from which none of us can escape. You can have a jolly good go at it but 'constant happiness' will be the illusion. So, my new mantra is,

The Human Being gets Agitated
The Spiritual Being sits in the Knowing

Final Thought

Life is here to be loved and embraced to the full, not plodded and bombed through as is happening for millions all over the world. For those of us who are privileged enough, let us cherish the freedom we have and never ever take it for granted. We really must not. If you are feeling fragmented, perhaps it is time to honour-all-four-bodies rather than just the one staring at you in the mirror or 'selfie'. Perhaps your heart is shut down. Open it. Or your soul needs connection. Please reach out. Or those negative thoughts say you are 'unlovable and weak'. Gently push them away and invite the loving ones in over a cup of tea. Do not give in to the illusion that you are worthless. Get curious. Who are you? Underneath all those man-made layers, who do you wish to be?

Reflections

Which of your bodies do you feed the most? Mental, emotional, physical or spiritual? How could you balance their needs?

What fires up your spirit (energy) to embrace life to the full?

What does freedom look like to you?

Chapter 10

Family: Blood versus Soul

Love and soul connection abound.

They say 'blood is thicker than water', but that may not be the case where people are on anti-coagulating blood-thinning medication, or if water is cheekily disguising itself as slush or ice. Then it may not be true. It is a matter of perspective and form.

My cousin is a big fan of this sentiment and often recites, 'In the end, blood is thicker than water.' Her view being that when chaos and catastrophe arrive, it is members of the closely shared DNA club that can be relied upon to rescue the situation to provide solutions, nourishment and healing. Come what may, a parent, sibling, first cousin, second cousin, aunt, or uncle will turn up to save the day, even if it's at 3am Greenwich mean time. In my case, this is rather feasible. I have an army of blood family.

My father is one of eight children, my mother one of six. All fourteen adults embarked into marital relationships. Besides one aunt who remained childless, successful reproductive liaisons resulted in numerous children being delivered on Mother Earth. I have around thirty first cousins at the last count. Besides a few, each one is known to me. I grew up with some in Africa and forged genuinely connecting relationships with the ones who grew up in India. My father collected thousands of frequent flyer points as we burnt the carbon footprints on holidays to the motherland. My parents tried to honour connections and keep ties with family 'back home'. My first cousins delivered around fifty-five children between them. We are a fertile tribe. Our closely shared DNA club members reside in many corners of the world: India, UK, Africa, Australia and the USA. At present, four generations of family are alive. We have some of the cutest babies joining our club. The herd is alive and kicking.

Here's where it gets more challenging. Besides these first cousins, I have a whole layer of second blood family, cousins of cousins, so to speak, some of whom I feel closer to than the ones first in line. It gets more complicated. According to Indian culture, the entire contents of a village in India are considered to be a part of one's blood family. It does not matter that you were born elsewhere. The village and family still belongs to you through the ancestral cord. So much so that it is considered a sin (incest) to marry anyone from the same village as your forefathers and foremothers.

In days gone by, life meant sitting around wood fires, discussing the harvests, the sun, the moon, and the stars (sigh) and honouring tribal bonds. Blood family was indispensable especially in times of crises. Allegiance to the framework of duty, obligation, and sacrifice as outlined by the Cultural Parent was crucial to survival. Stepping out of tribal codes for correct living came at a price not worth paying, such as death. Blood was indeed thicker than water and faster than digital streams. There was no social media to expediently gather foreign troops to save the day. You were stuck with blood family. What a challenge amidst the joy.

In case you think that I am cynical, bitter, and twisted, which is possible, whilst blood family can be intensely loving and come to the rescue during an existential crisis, *it is often the source of our strife rather than the cure for it.* My childhood and adult experiences have shaped this view. Some of the most venomous and irritating people pushing us to the cliff edge reside within the immediate blood pool. Why is that? It is because the ties that bind are invariably contaminated by expectations, duty, obligations, and power struggles rather than loving-kindness, compassion, and unconditional love. Parents have expectations from children and vice versa. Siblings often have rivalry issues because they just do. Extended Indian families often demand conditional support especially where elders impose their outdated values and belief systems on the younger ones. It amounts to one large chain reaction, atomic and toxic. I should know having been raised in such a family.

Nuclear family can create deep angst, too. My personal existential suffering has often stemmed from experiences with my parents and sibling. I am not the first, or the last, to do so. It just hurts to admit it. We do not want to betray our near and dear ones, but it is a common universal international human condition. Family of Origins therapy recognises this and offers a panacea for healing. We are emotionally tied, for better or for worse, to members of the family unit in which we grow up. By recognising this and working through challenges individually and collectively, past traumas can be laid to rest. When my father lost his way and his business, intense pain and suffering descended on our family. Some members of the blood family, who could have supported us, were nowhere to be seen, betrayal and abandonment at the fore. Again. In fact, it was one of the youngest members of our extended family, and a dear family friend, who showered us with compassion and saved the day. This experience taught me that blood family can be lethally infected, and ageing does not necessarily make you wise. One does not chronologically mature into something glorious like vintage wine. It seems that we can develop deep aromatic flavours of wisdom by facing our frailties and fears head on. Whatever our age.

During our family crisis, my mother, in her vulnerability and loss, relied on me for emotional support when I would rather have had it the other way around. After all, I am her child. My brother, a man of sensitivity and honour, consumed with anger, became emotionally unavailable for a while. As for my father, *denial* is a word that comes to mind. We were all drowning in a sea of duty, obligations, sacrifices, and expectations, never intentionally wanting to harm the other, but in the end doing just that.

But a cloud always has a silver lining, should we wish to see it. Ours is a tale with a 'feel good factor' ending. Why? Because in the end, we had the necessary courageous conversations to piece together our broken hearts. We learnt to accept the good, the bad and the ugly. Of ourselves, and the other. We were also blessed with authentic relationships that tied our hearts to our beautiful soul family. We survived. In fact, we more than survived. We have come to thrive. This is where my motivational attitude to life has come from. *What can I do to thrive rather than just survive?*

Regarding the soul family, it is crucial to existence. I believe it will become increasingly vital for the survival of *Home sapiens.* What is it? This family does not exclude members of the blood tribe, far from it. Some of my closest soul confidants are genetically linked to me. From my observatory deck of life, what sets a soul family apart from a bloody one is that the former does not act out of obedience and conditional love. It works on the basis of a deeper humanitarian model which respects sameness, differences, and unique ways of being. The soul family comes together in a co-created relationship rather than an enforced one, where diverse points of view are valid and not boxed into conditional compartments labelled 'you owe me', 'wrong religion', or 'pungent colour'. This family is not controlled by the shadow aspect of the Cultural Parent which can strangulate free expression and creativity with its suffocating outdated man-made tribal rules. 'We' and 'I' can live harmoniously together. To promote this symbiosis has become a passion.

Please do not misunderstand me. The Indian Cultural Parent has many beautiful attributes. Not all unconscious conditioning is violating and fragmenting. I love the Indian code of value for family life and care in the community centred around rituals, customs, and traditions celebrating life's cosmic dances. My culture with its distinct language, fashionable vibrant attire, gourmet of mouth-watering and eye-stinging curries, heavenly classical music, literally excellence, home of Bollywood and contribution to scientific discoveries makes me very proud.

What else? The ethical principles ingrained in our spiritual scriptures, deep respect for a life force called *God,* the embracing of prayer, sacred chants, and the *Patanjali* yoga sutras pave the way to balanced living. Oh yes, and compassion and care for the elderly is prime. I absolutely love all that.

Long may these attributes be passed on from generation to generation. We need them more than ever before amidst the one big melting pot created by capitalism where the power of celebrities, 'fake news', brand names, giant food stores, and commercial chains of coffee culture cafes have been allowed to arrest the heartbeat of local communities. Globalisation, at times, feels boring and dull. When I go to India, I would rather not eat pizza, noodles, and burgers. I would rather go to Italy, China, and the USA respectively for those. Back to soul family.

The urgent need to expand soul family is because the existence of blood family, as experienced for generations, is diminishing. Biologically related families are shrinking. Consider my own. My father had seven siblings; my mother had five. I have one, and between us we have no children. My older cousins with children, have a maximum of three, the norm being two. In the younger generation, single-child families prevail, and in some cases, no children are planned. Restriction in growth of traditional Indian families is being driven by economics and changing belief systems which my ancestors would find bewildering. How can any woman not consider having children? Well, why not? *Where in the world is there a rule book which says that all women should have children, that without children life cannot be fulfilled or lived to its highest potential?* The truth is that people like me who do not have children, are more than happy to adopt, legally or not, children already present in this world and support them.

I feel responsible for the legacy left behind for the next generation. There is this gnawing desire to make planet Earth a worthwhile place to inhabit for future generations. If reincarnation is my destiny as per Hindu religion, then I am more than interested in making 'Earth School' worth coming back to! The ego, the 'what about me', ever-present, I see. In the bigger picture, Divine Intelligence may be planting the seeds for slowing down the growth of *Homo sapiens*. No human being deserves to suffer, so I say this with caution in an attempt to make some sense of what feels rather senseless. Perhaps natural disasters, attributed to climate change, and man-made wars are raging everywhere to bring us all to our senses and face the truth. We really cannot go on like this. We will implode as a race or explode. Terminology can be confusing as English is my second language. I guess I am trying to say that we will become like the dinosaurs – extinct. The suffering that will go with that may become unbearable, as it is for so many currently caught up in barbaric man-made conflict which has left millions adrift at sea, seeking that safe shore. You are not forgotten.

So why must we focus on the soul family? Well, as highlighted, blood family, traditionally a robust support system in our time of need, is diminishing. Worldwide, the cost of living and need for material comfort has accelerated. Increasingly, parents feel they can only do their best for one child. They are too economically and emotionally stretched to think beyond providing for their first born. As a young cousin recently explained to an aunt who was persuading him that he ought to seed another child, 'Aunty, that's a recipe for divorce. I cannot do it.' This is not because younger people, often called the 'snowflake generation', are weak, offended easily, and have no mojo. They are facing the reality of living in so-called First World developed countries in the twenty-first century. The need for increasing materialism to define success means something has to give. Forgoing parenthood seems to an increasing option (if that's what it can be called) for many, though other factors are driving this trend.

Economic migration has resulted in couples living in big cities minus extended family. This means having no support for child care, which was ever-present in previous generations irrespective of culture. Living in close-knit communities within the extended family system meant children just grew up with several significant carers such as grandmothers and aunts. On a recent visit to India, I noticed how the villages felt empty of youth. Older people were to be seen everywhere. Where were the young? On enquiry, many had flown away in search of the good life, or just life, either into the cities or abroad. *Sadly, in spite of city life with its promises of riches, for many, the good life is really not that at all.* Dilemmas abound. Economic constraints corner people into working longer and longer hours. Home is a house shared with ten other people who are at the mercy of unscrupulous greedy landlords. Mothers are forced to stay at home, looking after their child as their wages do not match up to the costs of child care. I am all for mothers nurturing their babies. Saying that, choice matters. For stay-home mothers, isolation and loneliness in the absence of family support can lead to depression. It may also mean having to go down the work ladder as the days of the one permanent job for life are long dead and buried. When women are fighting for equality in the workplace, this is the perfect weapon for male-dominated work cultures to resist change. Women cost a lot as they have babies. It's a shame that the womb is not a transferable organ into men to help balance things out. But it is what it is. That does not justify gender discrimination under any circumstances.

Talking of wombs, another factor reducing the size of blood family in many cultures is to do with women having children later in life. Conceding that my mum was right is uncomfortable, but here is one of those moments. She dished out some sound advice when I was busy resisting an arranged marriage (and my ovaries were heading towards their sell-by date). Her advice felt offensive amidst my search for that utopian soulmate husband. I remember brushing her off as old fashioned, but she was far from that. She was maternal wisdom personified. Mum highlighted how tough it was bringing up children, both physically and emotionally, and how the body changed as women got older and fertility dropped. Things could just get tougher all round. Parents in their forties may find that at the prime of their life, they are stretched having to consider the well-being of not only their young children but also of their ageing parents. This is a big ask and a challenging task. In fact, this stretch is evident amongst communities where people are living longer and having smaller families. The care of the elderly is becoming a global challenge. There are not enough young people around to support the old. Countries like China have softened their policies on single-child families in realisation of this fact. Younger people are needed to support the ageing population. So how ironic that in westernised societies, migration, economic constraints, and evolving belief systems are creating the very scenario of reduced family units that is being reversed in the East. We all need support. Traditionally, Indian families have heavily relied on blood family to enrich their lives and lend support come hail or storm. A sea of change is necessary. We need to gather our soul family. We need people we can turn to in our time of need come noon or 3am at night, the first responders, so to speak. We just know everything will be all right with their support. They often arise from the places one least expects.

I learnt this the other day. There I was, full of self-pity and snotty flu, feeling pretty dire and lonely in my bed. No one cared. No one was there for me, or so I thought. A visit to my regular florist down the road forty-eight hours later, and a quick chat with my lovely neighbour, revealed that both were more than happy to get that 3am call if I ever felt vulnerable and in need. It was a genuine offering from the hearts of two people who instantly became soul family members. The limitations were of my own making. I struggle asking for help as it feels like a sign of weakness. On the other hand, why am I so keen to help others? *It feels like other people's weaknesses help me stay strong or more rightly, appear strong. That is a very limiting perspective, and I have just deleted that view in the here and now.*

The concept of diminishing blood family made me reflect on my soul family. Who do I see as members of this nourishing clan? I realise that it extends far further than I had ever imagined. Members do not have to be restricted to the 3am first responders. Some can lie on the periphery of our existence yet enrich our lives beyond expectations. Nurturing human connection is available far more than we know.

Regarding my soul family, there are the obvious members: Ma, Pa and my brother. Having made our peace with the turbulence of the past, we are thankfully united. My sister-in-law and her extended family are definite members of this nourishing clan. We have spent wonderful time together in India, eating scrumptious meals, downing oodles of exotic ice cream, sleeping under one roof, and generally just feeling joyous in one another's company. Then there are beloved friends and cousins, with whom I have regular meet ups and deep connection. Some souls just drift into my life occasionally and yet, on meeting, we were never apart – priceless. I recently attended a family wedding abroad where several members of the closely related DNA club had descended on hot terrain to celebrate the marriage of a beautiful young couple. Indian weddings present an opportunity to invite Bollywood glamour into our lives. The bride's parents, the couple, and the wedding planners put on a fabulous show. The attention to detail was breathtaking. Hospitality was at the fore. The bride looked stunning, the groom dashing. Beautifully cladded women in their fusion frocks were in abundance, as were dapper men. The aroma of scrumptious food was intoxicating. The wine, especially chilled white, my favourite in the heat, thankfully flowed in abundance. We danced the nights away with joy and laughter.

I returned home from this soulful experience with a palpable feeling of having healed somewhat in my heart. A seed of genuine love had been sown as us 'multi-destination cousins' breakfasted over side-splitting silly narratives, caffeine fixes, the inevitable Bombay mix, and heart-clogging waffles. This blood family had felt alien to me when I was young due to conflict between the adults. We used to meet up and exchange niceties through the masks. Connection was offered on a cultural framework of 'oughts', 'musts', and 'shoulds' running the show, which meant there was no real connection, just the superficial hellos and goodbyes. It was a case of 'them' and 'us'. But now, a birth: as adults, we were able to set our own rules. We did not have the older generation telling us what to do, controlling our every move. This transformation meant there was genuine connection between us. The hurt of the past felt softer. The future looked brighter. No arrogant power wielding behaviour or bloody noses surfaced, just plenty of laughter and soul talk. This could be seen as one layer of the soul family.

Friends offer a second one. Children I grew up with in Kenya as part of a large expat community are some of my nearest and dearest, ever present with their unconditional love through thick and thin. In spite of living on diverse continents, whenever we meet years on, time just dissolves into space. We just take up conversations left ten years ago. I recently hooked up with a couple of friends after twenty years. Literally minutes into our meeting, we were riding into a Californian sunset, chatting as if we had just come off the phone twenty-four hours ago. The atmosphere was buzzing with soul talk. The masks were off, and our raw hearts dared to expose the joys and the angst of our existences over the past two decades. Giggles ignited our spirits. I really felt drenched in love. I could just be myself, warts and all. What a relief.

As for my precious girlie friends who I have known for forty years. We are the sort of Indian version of the *Sex and City* sitcom, minus much of the frivolous sex, to the best of my knowledge. We are Indian after all. Grin. If you have ever watched this show, you will understand what I mean. The ladies engage in endless chats about their lives through the good, the mediocre, and the downright naughty. Three friends are married, and then there's the one who isn't. Dear Samantha who is still in search of that utopian romantic soulmate, just like me. She is rather lovable, flaws and all. And so am I - I just did not know that for a long time. These friends mean the world to me and can be counted on as first responders 24/7. What a gift.

Further soulful relationships have been forged through university and in the workplace. The essay assignments and job descriptions were dumped a long time ago, but the bonds of friendship and camaraderie ever-present and strong. Some of these relationships go back to three decades ago at least. Some are just a few years old. The phrase quality over quantity comes to mind. They hold a special place in my heart, especially my dear bestie mates Katy, Sarita, Khushboo, and Alice. These mates are not physically present in my life on a daily basis, but I feel them in my heart. The experiences shared together are priceless – the fun, the laughter, the giggles, the holiday under the stars in a freezing Indian desert, the endless soul journey chats through late nights, the beach-babes (not!) holidays, the sangria moments, the detoxing ones, poignant sharing of hopes and dreams and mending of our broken hearts.

Just the other day, I was sitting with four soul buddies in a restaurant squealing over a memory from a past holiday where the SPIF (sticky palate, itchy fanny) syndrome was conceptualised. Essentially, if you have ever been on safari and ridden through endless hours on hot dusty roads, you will identify with this. How silly things can make for so many giggles and laughter! This is what soul family offers; silliness, joy, and just a wonderful feeling of being alive. Priceless, priceless, priceless.

Not all of us have such large families and friends to call upon to nourish our souls. This is reflected in the loneliness and isolation which are heart wrenching dis-eases of the twenty-first century. But we have to start somewhere. *It is never too late to connect with others if we can only change our perspective.* Let me introduce the less obvious members of my soul family, the ones who sit on the periphery of my life and have transformed it when I have been able to mindfully stay in the moment and acknowledge what their presence means to me.

Neighbours can make us or break us. Fortunately, my neighbourhood has a wonderful heartbeat. The hellos get shouted across the road, and conversations are exchanged over garden fences as we go about our very separate, and yet very together, lives. *Narratives have always been an important vehicle for sharing of human experiences which weave the tapestries of life.* On sharing personal stories, the emerging themes are familiar. Everyone seems to carry in their hearts feelings of joy and sadness, peace and war, hopes and disappointments, successes and failures, good health and illness, anxiety and freedom, isolation and connection, loneliness and belonging. There is an innate tendency for optimism and pessimism. Some see the glass half full, and some see it as half empty. Interestingly, the ones for whom the glass is always half full seem to be able to ride the roller coaster of life with courage, calmness, and clarity even when all seems rather vague and potentially lost. This neighbouring soul family gathered at my home for a Christmas lunch. Joy and wine, in keeping with the festive spirit, were shared over great chatter and laughter. It left me with a sense of belonging beyond the obvious.

Other members of this nurturing clan include shopkeepers, cafe owners, the laundry lady Firdosh, my mind-body-spirit shop buddy Athena, my energetic osteopath Izzy, my gorgeous hairdresser Diva, the delightful manicure lady Paloma, and the chatty postwoman Pat. They all turn up rain, shine, or snow to run their businesses locally so that I have a comfortable life. Little chats adding up to real connections over the years. *A sense of belonging to a community is most enriching and necessary to live a joyful life.* Don't take it for granted. And for those who assume that spinsters like me miss out on men, we don't. I have two most wonderful men in my life; my handyman Augustus and car mechanic Adonis. They are talented souls. One helps to maintain beautifully the sacred sanctuary which is my home, and the other keeps me safely on the road come snow or storm. No job is too big or too small. We have had wonderful chats over the years, and they are definitely cherished members of my soul family. Not all men are vulgar or vile.

Now we really get to the edges. Meet Flora the cleaning assistant, Peter the weatherproof newspaper seller, and Jessica the concierge lady with her beautiful smile and curly golden locks who used to meet and greet me near my previous workplace.

I really miss the daily banter with these illuminated souls. They could brighten up my most miserable day. Flora was one of my favourites. She usually came to my work place as I left after an exhausting ten hour day wishing Scotty would beam me home as he did on that famous sci-fi show *Star Trek*, the hour commute west just filling me with dread. When all seemed lost, into my field came Flora. This most uplifting soul taught me a thing or four. She was a single mum holding down two jobs and living in humble dwellings in the so-called deprived area of the inner city. There was nothing deprived about Flora. On the contrary, she had this incredible capacity to see the joy in her life amidst the struggles. Gratitude was her strength. A day break to the beach with her daughter, a chilled glass of wine after a hard day at work, watching some chick flick curled up on the sofa, seemed to power her up. No self-pity chat here, no moaning about lack of money and opportunities or concerns for the future – just gratitude for the present moment. I love Flora. We are still in touch and a catch up over coffee is well overdue.

Regarding Peter, the man with a twinkle in his eye and a newspaper at hand, come rain, shine, hailstorm, or thunder. This amazing man faithfully turned up outside the train station to greet me as I emerged from the bowels of the earth that is the London Underground. He was always ready to have a quick banter about the weather. Underneath the superficial chat, I sensed a genuine soul connection. Peter had the gift of staying in the present moment and engaging with it day in and day out. One could say he was probably on autopilot. I know he was not. People on autopilot do not have that amazing, shiny bright light twinkling in their eyes. Their eyes are usually dull and lifeless, a bit like mine have been when I have spiralled into those autopilot moments as we all do.

To be honest, living life minus twinkles in the eyes has lost its appeal. Bring on the sparkles, I say. In the early days, I missed the point of my encounter with this twinkly eyed stranger and hardly even noticed him. He was just another human being for me to negotiate past as I rushed to work in the land of root canals. But as the months and years passed by, Peter became an important part of my soul family. I noticed how I looked out for him bounding up the station steps. I genuinely missed his positive uplifting energy when he was away, and I am so grateful our paths had crossed in this way. He taught me a thing or four, just like Flora did. You do not have to be in some jet-set job with oodles of privileges to be happy. The latter is an internal event. As for Jessica, the receptionist with the golden curly locks, she always made the effort to acknowledge me no matter how busy she was. Her smile said it all. No words were necessary. You matter, she said. You matter. How good it feels to matter.

Finally, I do wonder if it is just plain luck to be blessed with such good fortune and extended soul family? I am not so sure. Investing time and effort into all these relationships, over the years, has borne sweet fruits. What started out as just friendly superficial banter became truly nurturing as time went by. I realised that soul family is to be found all around us if we ignite awareness that it exists. If we can drop the 'nobody loves me' and 'I am alone' life positions, which come from our own vulnerabilities and human needs. Social media, when used wisely, can bring a supportive soul family into our lives. Saying that, for me nothing beats face-to-face connection. As the young will remind me, that's more than possible, too, by just hooking up online. Technology: I struggle, but cannot deny it is changing my inner and external world view dramatically.

Thankfully, besides the human soul family, there is that other huge powerfully energetic one that exists beyond earthly existence. I call this family God, the Universe, Divine Intelligence, and the Life Force. When fuelled up by this energy, there is no difficulty that cannot be faced, or no path that cannot be walked with courage. When the blinkers come down and my connection with soul family is unplugged, I feel depleted, drained of power, hopeless, and the dreaded plod, plod, plod, drip, drip, drip rhythm of life looms larger than ever. No, thank you. Had enough of that.

I hope you are encouraged to go in search of soul family, especially if you are feeling isolated and lonely. Which would you rather? To live on life's terms or negotiate your terms with life? To be connected or lonely? To live as an isolated 'I' or dance with the 'We'? The choice is yours. Reach out. Reach in. You are not alone.

After all, no man or woman is an island.

Reflections

Who do you consider to be members of your soul family?

If you are feeling isolated and lonely, how could you step out of this way of being?

What could you do to connect to people that empower you?

Chapter 11

Ageing: The Agony and Learning amidst the Cherished Cups of Tea

Rocking into Older Years. Let's Do It!

I have a soft spot for elderly people. It is getting softer as I age. Funny, that. Old age equates with end of life so it may be helpful to acknowledge that we are all born to die. Amidst the diverse cultural, religious, socio-economic, environmental and political nuances in the world, that is one destiny we cannot escape. Rich or poor, living in a First World country or a developing country (whatever that means), like all narratives, the story of our journey on earth will end. We will eventually succumb to the cosmic process of death. Scientific endeavours may be able to keep the human body and mind going for longer, but eventually it will perish. Return to where both came from. I have heard the phrase 'for you are dust, and to dust you shall return' at funeral services. I think that sums it up for me.

This may all sound bleak as fear of death can transport us into despair. In my moments of 'what's it all about?', the fact that time is limited at the physical level offers relief. How many repeated behaviours and experiences can one endure? Especially the ones filled with self-sabotage and regret? On a more optimistic note, the certainty of death makes me search for genuine meaning for my existence on Mother Earth. Who am I? What am I here for? What does my heart desire? How can I live with joy amidst a world at war? What can I do for future generations?

At times, sensibility stops me from posing questions for which umpteen answers exist, or none that are plausible at all. Time is ticking, best get on with life rather than just ponder on it. Why not just embrace life in all its vibrant, mediocre, scary and rather bland dimensions? Because that is life. Who hasn't been bored with life? You know, that drip-drip-drip, plod-plod-plod, drip-drip-drip, plod-plod-plod kind of existence. It feels like death, but it is not. In this moment, that is the last thing on my mind. Life feels full of meaning and purpose. How could it not be? The truth is that I deserve a fair share of my good and I am here to seize it. Just like you can, amidst the suffering. This is a key lesson learnt on the journey from *Fat to Fab.*

Acute anxiety around death of my ageing loved ones has diminished somewhat. Knowing that far from us all being on Shakespeare's stage, dictated to by someone else's scripts, we, *Homo sapiens,* human beings of divine intelligence have the opportunity to edit and create our own scripts. This really powers me up. *We can release ourselves from the drip and plod of life and leave a narrative behind that will inspire and support future generations.* Yet we are in danger of living in a primordial fight-and-flight mode which is about survival. I should know, as not that long ago, I was starting to 'run on empty'. It is a common theme in society today.

Watching my parents and their friends negotiating older years has taught me what a thousand books could not. It really has been a momentous education. Recently, I was sitting with six people who had a collective age and life experience of around four-hundred-and-eighty years! Having one of those, what I call, cherished cups of tea, a few moments, over a brew, that leave me with a new perspective and a better understanding of the labyrinth that is life. The youngest person present, besides me, was seventy-eight years old. There was a delightful uncle in the throes of early stages of Alzheimer's disease. He could sing the most wonderful *bhajans* (Indian hymns), fluently recite passages from the Hindu scriptures, belt out entire Bollywood songs of old, word to word, but could not remember that donuts may have holes and cupcakes, well, cups! Or what month it was and that I did not live in the same home as him. Oh, and that I was not married, that old tedious tune again.

As we shared a poignant moment over a cherished cup of tea, he started talking about his illness with full awareness. It brought a massive tear to my eye when he said, 'You never ever imagine in your life that your mind will one day forsake you.' I felt a big squelch in my heart. How profound was that. I could sense he was terrified of what was to come. He knew that something was terribly wrong. Autonomy was abandoning him. How can our intelligence betray us? That is tough. Still sipping the same cup of tea, I had a conversation with another uncle who had been a mathematical genius in his lifetime but could now not remember his own phone or door number. It was difficult to have a chat with him most days as the mind was scattered and out of reach. These two heartfelt exchanges left me full of gratitude for my mind that is a powerhouse for choice and reminded me to never take it for granted, especially the unconscious part of it which houses the shadow side. One minute, you are fine; the next minute, you are in free fall.

I would highly recommend reading Wendy Mitchell's heart-wrenching yet courageous account of her journey through Alzheimer's disease *Somebody I Used to Know*. It made my heart weep and eyes smart over and over again. Mind, friend or foe?

Back to the scenario of four-hundred-and-eighty years of life experience, besides malfunctioning minds, there were other numerous ailments present in the room: arthritis, swollen ankles, bent spines, gastric leakage, weak hearts, and so on, just too many to list. It occurred to me that if I was taking all these wonderful human beings on holiday accompanied by their various drug protocols for survival, the chance of being arrested for drug trafficking remained rather high!

Engaging with older people is crucial for a life well lived. That means engaging with ourselves. After all, we are ageing even as we read this. Spending significant time with my parents' generation has been an illuminating experience about what this process called ageing entails.

It can be challenging. In the current climate, more than ever before, older people struggle to be valued for who they are. I concede to my increasing sensitivity around this issue. *Am I eventually to be seen as a burden to society rather than a human being who made a valuable contribution to the world?* Senior citizens, old age pensioners, retired people, the golden oldies and the elderly are labels often used to describe ageing people. Some feel okay. Some rather gloomy. Older people experience discrimination when seeking employment and are often discounted by a work culture that glorifies youth and brains, rather than experience and wisdom. In this fast, technologically spinning world, everything seems to be very instant and rather transient. I cannot be a hypocrite. Patience with older people, at times, can be a struggle. Especially when they are going deaf and have flatulence problems of the unimaginable kind. I have to remind myself that they may not be *cool* anymore but are fountains of knowledge that have kept the world going for a long time. In fact, older people are the very ones who have created the opportunities and amazing possibilities for us younger ones. They can learn new skills such as surfing the net, if given a chance.

The expanding frontiers of neuroscience reveal that the human brain has the capacity to rewire and establish new ways of being into older years. Essentially, our brains exhibit neuro-plasticity. Unfortunately, within Indian families, surrender to *bhagya (destiny)* and *karma* (fate) impedes people from living life to the full. In my culture, the brain seems to stop rewiring to expanding frontiers when you are old, at sixty-five years of age. There is a sort of chronological compartmentalised attitude, rather than a biological way of approaching life. Time is taken very seriously, and the mind gets boxed into a conditioned way of existing where one is born, grows up, goes to university, finds a financially rewarding job, then enters the institution of marriage, then produces children and then looks forward to these offspring taking care of you as you retire. In your mid-sixties. It is not a good formula.

Being around thriving rockers and rollers well into their eighties has taught me that there may be choice as to how we age, especially in the light of evidence that certain lifestyle choices around stress, nutrition, physical exercise, sleep and optimum emotional health enhance our general well-being. Compassion (for ourselves and others), connection (through authentic relationship beyond man-made barriers where 'I' can dance harmoniously with the 'we'), and co-creation (where we each have a say in the future of our lives) rewires the brain in amazingly nurturing ways. There are many possibilities about how we can approach the inevitable. We can be stuck in the past, wait for the future that never arrives, or we can engage in the present.

From my experience which is the only truth I know, the past is invaluable in teaching us transforming lessons about living a more authentic life. *But we must wake up from the hypnotic effect of the Cultural Parent.* A way of life established by our ancestors holds no relevance to our contemporary world today. Yet by the very nature of this parental phenomenon we become stuck in a time warp by holding onto attitudes and belief systems that simply do not matter anymore. *Conversely, we have abandoned the deep wisdom of our ancestors which helped them live fulfilled and happy lives.* They held a profound love for Mother Earth and did not disrespect her by polluting her with potent toxins and strip her insides bare by deforestation and the like. Our wise ancestors did not pump their food with artificial poisons to make an extra buck or two, nor did they choke the oceans and its beautiful residents with plastic as we are doing. They would never have reduced themselves to such desperation and alienation from their 'innermost essence' which honoured the very earth they walked on.

While dear Mother Earth struggles for her well-being, the inter-generational struggle for Indians globally stems from childhood messages around mandatory 'premature parenting'. Indian children are, consciously or unconsciously, introjected with the idea of a duty of care, to look after their parents as they approach old age, their sixth decade. On the contrary, in contemporary Western culture in which we reside, a sixty-something-year-old is middle-aged rather than old. There is still a lot of mojo put into fun and independent living. You should see my fellow sixth decade of life aerobic junkies belting out their moves in the over-fifties class I go to. Their message? Move over, you young thing!

In years gone by, this formula of mandatory 'duty of care' may have been appropriate. When my ancestors lived in remote villages in India, the average lifespan was a couple of decades lower than now. Certainly, by sixty-five years of age, life would have been lived to the full. My forefathers, as far as I know, were farmers and probably shed blood, sweat, and tears as they toiled the land, which was sheer hard, laborious physical work. Their bodies and minds may have fallen apart rather sooner than later. Death would have released them from a tough existence.

Having been to India as a child and visiting the villages where my parents grew up, I recall how my grandma and her mates would sit on a communal porch at the end of a hard day, sharing their stories and snuff (form of tobacco). They were tired and yes, they were ready to retire from life's chores. They were exhausted by the physical and emotional labour of life. Dare I say, many women were also depleted from sexual labour as girls were married off forcefully whilst in their teens, and had birthed several children by their mid-twenties. Ouch. So perhaps for that generation it was a blessing that in your mid-sixties death was close. I am a positive person. But why suffer unnecessarily?

My maternal grandma died at the age of sixty-four years. My paternal and maternal grandfathers died at the age of sixty-five years and fifty-six years respectively. Interestingly, my city dwelling grandma lived to nintey-three years, cared for by an aunt with a failed marriage, rather than by her sons as per Indian tradition. In the current climate, the responsibility of caring for ageing parents is shared in a certain way. Sons (there are exceptions of course) seem to provide the material comfort of the home, but it is often the daughters and daughters-in-law who put in the emotional and physical mileage in caring for parents, often to the detriment of their own well-being. Women seem to do all the multitasking around keeping the wheels of family life oiled and functional.

Interestingly, the birth of a baby boy is still a necessity for true happiness in traditional Indian families. A baby girl is more joyfully received when she arrives as a second sibling to an older brother. The outrageous underhanded practice of female foetal murder is a reality, concealed under the banner of 'knowing the sex of your baby' helps ease choice over the colour theme of the baby nursery. Indian parents, to this day, will abort a female foetus if they prefer to have a son. That just stinks. It is this major cultural flaw, not beautiful baby girls, that needs extermination. *How ironic that rules, made by men, justify the killing of divine female energy from which they themselves have arisen.* Time to raise the shutters boys. I have compassion for your plight, but such barbaric prejudice against my divine right, and those of my fellow sisters to exist, cannot be condoned.

So back to Indian people with this mentality of retiring from life so young. The inevitable, such as creaking knee joints, wrinkling skin, discolouration of teeth, the saggy bottoms, and the like, do arrive. This can be normal. It need not be with all the current health information on optimum health and longevity. Sadly, what seems to arise with the cultural belief that old age starts in your sixties is illness, especially anxiety and depression. It may be linked to isolation, loss of meaning, and loneliness, which is a feature of modern living. Time to retire and then do what? In days gone by in India, fathers (not mothers who kept on slaving over the unpaid jobs of a housewife) retired from working, but because of the all-under-one-roof system of joint-family living, life was centred around the household and its numerous activities. Everyone lived in one melting pot. This may have created a double-edged sword. Isolation and loneliness were not problematic as concepts of personal growth and the expression of self or the 'I' were not encouraged. On the other hand, collective living, based on inter-generational stories from my grandmas and mum, created a feeling of suffocation.

This concept of individualism is a foreign policy adopted from the West. In Indian families, it is all about family. It is your hobby! Focus is on 'we', rather than the 'I'. But we need to change and create balanced living where the 'we' exists in harmony with the 'I'. The concept of retiring from life in our sixties is not a good plan. Why? For one, families are getting smaller and being split up in pursuit of the good life to continents all over the world. Many of us will struggle if we cannot create some sort of individually grounded identity because our blood family, 'we', will not be there to prop us up as they will be busy living their dream. By having confidence in our sense of self, we can connect with people beyond our blood family and create our soul family who will help us flourish.

If we cannot embrace a multicultural family, we will struggle with isolation and all the dire consequences of that. Secondly, thanks to advances in medical science and the financial needs of pharmaceutical companies, we are living much longer than previous generations. The current average age of the older people in my family is eighty something. If one retires in one's sixties, then there's the dilemma of what to do for the next couple of decades. Of course, as we have choice, it need not be a dilemma. We could see it as a wonderful opportunity to embrace life using one's experience and wisdom for some serious rocking into older age. But first, cultural belief systems need to be re-examined and re-framed. This view comes from my own personal experiences.

When my parents reached their mid-fifties, the theme that dominated our lives and that of the society we lived in was marriage. My parents, understandably, looked to my brother and I to find spouses, engage in reproduction, and expand the family lineage. They were delighted when my brother got married. At least one of us had got going, and they looked forward to having grandchildren and joy in their life. When my sibling decided that he was not born to expand the family tree in this lifetime, my parents were shocked. I was not helping much by pursuing the can't-do-arranged-marriage theme. With both children busy individuating, putting their 'I' before the 'we', the goalpost had moved. Into outer space. Dreams and ambitions were lost. My parents' scripts got wretchedly torn up. Something they had been told would happen in their lives from when they were very young disappeared into thin air, just like what happened to my script, just torn up, never to be experienced, and to be accepted with as much dignity as possible. They had to accept my lack of marriage, with all its inferences (no wedding, no baby allowed), and reluctantly embrace my brother's decision to live childfree and authentically which, after all, is a healthy way to be.

Sadly, this up-in-smoke life script brought my mother to an emotional and physical standstill. Whilst all her friends talked about their grandchildren and were busy with extended family schedules, my parents' schedule was severely restricted. They did not know what to do with themselves. In spite of my father's attempts at individuation, which he had managed to achieve to some extent, his Cultural Parent had embedded in him a need for the family unit ('we') to stay united. My mum, in parity with women of her generation, bought into the 'we' too. The concept of 'I' was nowhere to be seen.

Sadly, my parents could not motivate themselves to create other opportunities in life for themselves. Their 'I' struggled to see joy in a world without the extended ancestral line. They needed a 'we'. So, they clung to me, and I clung straight back, as it was my duty, after all, to care for them. In any case, there was no husband or children for me to cling to. Becoming their 'we' was the least one could do to make up for the lack of marriage, for the failure to produce grandchildren which robbed their happiness, and probably caused them to feel a sense of shame though they never ever voiced that to us. They had obviously failed the Cultural Parent in some way. All their friends had grandchildren. Indians have no sense of boundaries and would ask my parents what was wrong with me and my brother. Or assume that fertility was an issue. My mum even expressed a sense of being punished for bad deeds in a past life. That's *karma* for you again. Sob.

Under the fat, I sat with my own angst. This is the power of guilt and shame. Underneath these toxic emotions, there was seething annoyance directed at the Cultural Parent, and my ancestors, for normalising social constructs that were far from normal in my life. My Buddha heart struggled. It took me forever to stop resenting this fact and come from a place of love and compassion. *The Indian Cultural Parent places too much emphasis on happiness and personal fulfilment being a family event.* Everyone out there in the tribe is born to make you happy, to fufill your dreams and desires, to look after you forever and never abandon you to a nursing home. Sadly, inter-generational challenges are causing a lot of angst.

Children of the next generation are in the throes of confusion around their own identities. Are they Indian? Asian? European? American? Australian? African? Or actually British Indians, American Indians, Australian Indian, African Indian or not Indian at all? And with that, what defines their cultural lives?

British Indian children, certainly from my background (which I consider rather privileged), want to go hopping around the world in celebration of the 'gap year' and return home to flat share with their buddies and have some fun. They do not want to stay at home to care for their grandparents or go to Mother India on every vacation to visit relatives and force connections which a lot of my generation did. These children want to experience different cultures and all that it brings. They certainly do not want to be forced into an arranged marriage. Furthermore, they want to invest in their own homes rather than buy into the all-under-one-roof joint-family system of communal living. Without being accused of betrayal. Interestingly, men and women of my generation seem to be having alternative British Indian needs, too, which are rather 'un-Indian'. Men want time out to go on all-male golfing holidays away from the family. They do not want to be constantly earning money, providing for the family and giving their hard-earned cash away to resurrect temples in India. The women want to cook less, hoover less, care less, and pamper themselves beyond what is considered culturally reasonable in the midst of rescuing husbands, children, and ageing parents.

The addiction of the older generation to their identity and way of life is understandable, but this presents a lot of confusion around identity for my generation and the one below. It is stretching families ties and bonds to the limits leading to stress, chronic fatigue, and resentment. People living under the same roof may be together physically, but their souls are miles apart. Disconnection abounds. The older generation feel they are being abandoned and their sacrifices have not amounted to much, and my generation are trying to not fall off a very wobbly bridge that connects our subculture (Indian) to the dominant (Western) culture.

In my case, parts of me are so Indian, but parts of me are so English. Who am I?

So how can we resolve this angst of caring for ageing parents who are increasingly fragile physically, mentally, and emotionally? They need a lot of support to negotiate life. Putting them into nursing residential care is a taboo, emotive to the hilt. A friend of mine shared her deep pain with me a while ago. Her father in-law, with severe dementia, had been cared for by my friend and her family for a while. The children had left home leaving her and her husband with a very vulnerable and unpredictably behaving human being under the same roof. My friend would find her father-in-law naked on the floor, disorientated and distressed. Whilst carers would come in to help out during certain parts of the day, the family simply could not afford twenty-four hour care. Being part of a culture that is so prudish about sex and any exposed sexual organs amplifies the angst. No Indian daughter-in-law is culturally equipped to care for her father-in-law's exposed body parts. It creates great embarrassment for both. In her case, the husband was not around to help out much because he could not bear to see his father this way. Great.

A decision was made to place dad in a nursing home where he would be cared for in the way that he needed to be, to give him some quality of life, to keep his dignity – all well until relatives started pouring in to visit this vulnerable person. Then the damaging conversations began: How could they? How could they put their father in such a place? How could they abandon uncle like this? What a breakdown in our culture there is. No family values left. And on and on and on.

How easy it is to make judgements when you are not willing to take on the vulnerable person under your roof? How easy to project your lack of compassion on to someone else who is actually fiercely compassionate but came to the end of her tethers with caring for a mentally, emotionally, and physically fragile man?

I believe a lot of us are more than happy to care for our parents when biological ageing truly kicks in as it does towards the end of one's life cycle, in the seventh or eighth decade by current standards in my family. It is annoying when this is expected of us early on in life when we are in the midst of trying to understand ourselves and negotiate wisely, or not so wisely, through the complexities of life. This is not about being mean or selfish. Human growth and development studies show that this is a normal response to growing up as we make the journey from childhood to adulthood to parenthood. Life, especially now, with the www.com culture can present us with so many personal and professional opportunities to realise our full potentials and give back to society, not just the family. It is important to grasp these chances with both hands. It means letting go of other hands, namely those of Papa and Mummy, much to their angst. They are happier surviving in the one big hot melting pot, brimming over the stove, firmly holding onto our hands. Holy smoke!

The reality is that the world has become one huge expansive amalgamated mass through the World Wide Web. We can moan and groan about the technological revolution, but it is an essential part of twenty-first-century living. I was late embracing it all but have succumbed. It is a great way of reaching a wider audience to spread a message, nurturing or toxic. Following on from the landing on the moon, the birth of this superhighway has been another gigantic leap for mankind. People have access to possibilities that simply did not exist before this world-changing phenomenon. There are so many ways to live life and express yourself, so many possible identities to adorn. Multicultural exposure is sending us off on tangents that would bewilder our forefathers and foremothers. *Twenty-first-century living demands a different cultural framework from our ancestors if we are to live balanced lives.* For me this means optimum physical, mental, emotional, and spiritual well- being, where in my hearts of hearts I know that the good life is not just about chasing materialism. For me, it is about being able to wake up each day, knowing in my very core that my life has meaning and purpose beyond the 'oughts' and 'shoulds' of my birth tribe, that I have a safe and peaceful abode to call home, whatever the size, a beautiful soul family to connect with, and that my compassion extends to myself and others. This all seems to equate to feeling calm, collected, and quietly joyful, not stressed and burnt out, which is in vogue these days.

I am not here to be unkind or critical of my ancestors or my parent's generation. They did the best they could. It may not always seem that way. But the truth is that they are a product of their history, as I am of mine, as you are of yours, because:

Every Single Human Being
When the entire situation is taken into account has always at
every moment of the past done the very best he or she could
and so deserves neither blame nor reproach
for anyone, including self.
This, in particular, is true of you
– Anonymous

Source: Lapworth and Sills. 2011. *An Introduction to Transactional Analysis* (5).

It seems like there is some serious stuff we need to look at. Not through a utopian lens but a realistic one. History can repeat itself, or be learnt from and rewritten. Can we achieve this by igniting constructive reflexive (two way) dialogue and appropriate action within ourselves and others? Can courage, clarity and vision for a better world be borne out of genuine heartfelt compassion and kindness for ourselves and fellow human beings? Especially for those nearing their twilight years. *A framework for living hung on fear, duty, obligation, and forced sacrifices need not cascade down the generations.* We have choice. We can have a say. Every adult is a Cultural Parent to the next generation. Let us engage in courageous conversations. For the sake of our beloved children. Over many cherished cups of tea or coffee if that's your brew. Fancy a brew?

Reflections

How do you identify yourself to the world? What labels are you most comfortable with? Which ones would you rather abandon?

How do you view older people? Have you had experience of being around them? If so, what has this taught you?

How would you like to be viewed and treated by the youth in your older years?

Chapter 12

Culture: The Tide is Changing. Surf or Drown

Peace on Earth. What can We do?

In asking the question 'What does culture really mean?', I did not imagine travelling on this voyage of life scribed here. The phrase 'in my culture, *we...*' had been central to my existence, the significance of which I had not fully understood. What has become obvious is that the *'we'* was a powerful belief system around tribal identity which drowned out the *'I'*. Drowning is not something to aspire to. But surfing is, according to Jon Kabat-Zinn (1994). To live a balanced life, it is helpful to compassionately ask ourselves. Who is 'we', and who am 'I'? How can *both* cohabit creatively and thrive rather than just survive?

The tide is changing. A resurgence of fiercely determined matriarchal energy is challenging and dismantling patriarchal formulas of the past, rather slowly but surely. I am not an extreme feminist who wants to annihilate men who have every right to roam planet Earth. They are battling with an identity crisis as feminine power starts encroaching on their centuries-old comfort zone, 'superior species'. If they are not busy being macho-men-masculine-hunter-gatherers-conquerors-wheeler-dealers-providers for their women and children, who are they? Buggy-pushing-cup-cake-baking-dishwasher-loading-nappy-changing-dads? Surely not. Well, why not? *Perhaps it is the definition of masculinity that needs a radical makeover, alongside the feminist uprising* that is quite rightly demanding equality across the board.

The need for Indian women, and women in general, for that matter, to be recognised for their crucial role in developing a loving, more tolerant society is way overdue. We need to stop being ostracised from the tribe because we dare to exert choice through our voices. We need to stop being aborted by female foetal murder, forced marriages, honour killings, sexual exploitation, and domestic abuse. How best to do it?

Social dysfunction is often attributed to ignorance and lack of education, and is projected by the better off onto those from socio-economically disadvantaged backgrounds. It is all about power. The reality is that social disintegration and disgraceful abuse is not confined to the poor. I know of several educated women in my community who have been victims of domestic abuse. It is rife across the board and driven by an aged phenomenon – patriarchal bias. This is not creating a better world. We are drenched in anxiety and woe at this fragile time. Male leaders (dictators?) rule the majority of the planet. Dire knee-jerk decision-making is creating social, political, economic, and environmental war zones. Check out the news for evidence of this erosion. Amidst the 'fake news' lies truth. Daniel Coleman in his bestselling book *Emotional Intelligence: Why It Can Matter More Than IQ* offers the idea that creating a balanced society needs perhaps more emotional intelligence (empathy and compassion) than intelligence (logic, knowledge and analytical prowess) as measured by IQ from both men and women. The wheels of change can be slow and remain stagnant. Back to one of my favourites (unknown source):

> If you always do what you have always done,
> you will always get what you always got.

No thank you. We need to do things differently by understanding the complexities of what drives human behaviour. It seems like we need a *new compassionate culture* to avoid extermination where loving kindness is not seen as some fluffy girlie emotion but something that makes genuine connection between individuals possible irrespective of gender, age, creed or colour. The truth is we are all losing. Our sanity. Mental health issues are climbing the ladder of most common dis-eases in the world.

What does culture really express? There are many definitions available out there. This journey of self-discovery led me to endless possibilities for viewing culture and its impact on individuals as well as on society. It is easy to get bogged down with other people's world views. The core human need to belong to a tribe and to herd with others is so primitive. *But courage is called for.* Creating a vision by connecting with our 'inner radiance' seems like a good place to start. I seem to have tapped into an uncontaminated part of me that is desperate to see beyond the contracted horizon of childhood conditioning. What is normalised in childhood is taken, for better or for worse, into adulthood. It isn't all helpful but the wonderful thing is that we can harness the good, and forgive the ugly.

Based on this, we need a framework where *'we' harmonises with a compassionate 'I' for self, and others.* It seems that focus on personal growth has been misinterpreted and given rise to the *'narcissistic I'.* The so-called 'Me Syndrome'. This formula is not working. Time for a new approach. What can we do?

Curiosity around how cultures emerge may help. How are economic, political, environmental, educational, and social constructs normalised? I am bewildered that the mind of a single human being such as Hitler could create a culture of abhorrent violence towards millions (the Holocaust). And all this without social media, which can now speed up this process in seconds. It seems that we, the human race, are very slow learners because millions continue to be violated as I write this. Are we really learning from history? I could sink into despair, but I am choosing to remain curious and hopeful because amidst the horror, I see thousands of acts of kindness going on. The human spirit is heroic.

Are rules for life unconsciously absorbed, consciously learnt, or imposed through conditioning? How did race, ethnicity, or skin colour be put into a hierarchal framework? How about attitudes and belief systems towards sex, gender, and sexuality? Where do they come from? What about power-based systems such as class and caste? How about heritage, customs, and traditions? Language and attire? Food and beverages?

Particular mannerisms? How do they contribute to cultural identity? What are we referring to when we say someone is very cultured? Are they people who can recite texts from the arts, history, mythology, philosophy, psychology, biology, phrenology, and all the other ologies? As in we think we are speaking the English language with them, but they are speaking some other type of English language which we cannot fathom. Can culture be bought with money, or can a poor person be cultured?

This fiercely honest journey reveals that it embodies the above and a lot more. There are so many questions and so many possible ways of viewing it. Socrates of the famous saying 'The unexamined life is not worth living' would approve.

It takes immense courage to examine our lives and walk our talk, to be able to stand on the periphery of the conditioned herd. What is our talk anyway? Is it our original talk, coming from an inner wisdom or just someone else's talk that we have taken a ride on? Does this talk create joy, peace, and a sense of purpose in our lives, or are we dead wood?

A plethora of cultural changes have infiltrated my birth tribe since it took its origins in a small state in India called Gujarat – from the widely dispersed geographical places that we inhabit, to our eclectic accents, fusion dressing, music we listen to, people we socialise with, the actual way we socialise (eating out a lot more as opposed to home cooking by the domestic goddesses!), rituals and traditions we embrace and reject, our views around family life, religion, education, arranged marriages, sex, sexuality, and a whole showcase of things. The list is endless. *The Indian culture is being diluted and simultaneously being reconstituted into a new framework. I see this as a wonderful opportunity to draw on both Eastern and Western cultures* that we are privileged to have access to, and create a new holistic, fused culture that is nurturing and fulfilling, one that allows for individual, as well as collective, balanced living, where 'we' and 'I' can live in harmony. How can we create this?

From where I am sitting, there is a need for copious courageous conversations inter-and intra-generationally at this time, not politically correct chat which is stifling human growth. *My generation needs to be brave and bold.* We need to engage with our children and immerse ourselves in to their world view, however difficult and painful this may be. It may surprise us that the youth often hold a much wiser world view than us older beings who have allowed life to obscure the truth. I love having chats with young people, as they teach me something new every time, especially about the power of social media! Far from what I hear amongst my generation (include me in this) that young people do not know how to communicate, I am waking up (finally) to the fact that they are incessantly communicating verbally and non-verbally with the aid of the WWW (World Wide Web) in ways older brains cannot imagine. Digitally based ways of communicating feel rather alien to us who are familiar with black-and-white television, cassettes for recording music, Alexander Graham Bell's creation called the telephone and the bucket-and-jug version for 'showers' to clean off the grime from playing outdoors 24/7!

How can we genuinely create change?

Well, we could be responsible Cultural Parents who sow nurturing seeds for future generations. We could liberate ourselves and our children by discarding restricting patriarchal frameworks around duty, obligation and sacrifice and injecting our body, minds, hearts and souls with matriarchal energy embracing compassion, connection and co-creation.

How? An offering:

The current South Asian framework:

Based on *duty, obligation, and sacrifice* = musts, shoulds, oughts, and have-to culture which = guilt, shame, blame, anger, fear.

I propose a new framework:

Based on *compassion, connection, and co-creation* = 'I am sorry for your suffering. I am not a competitor but a fellow traveller who wants to create a mutually beneficial outcome for our wellbeing' which = living joyfully and peacefully in Integration Street rather than on Segregation Avenue.

Utopian, some may say. I disagree. The giant oak was once a little nut. I believe my nut has great potential.

A cultural revolution is underway and talking about it without judgements, guilt, blame, and shame is essential. I increasingly try to walk my talk and engage in courageous conversations with my parents and their peers, as well as my contemporaries, fellow travellers, work colleagues, the extended soul family, and the children in my life. Here's a glimpse of emerging themes bubbling in the Indian (South Asian) cultural revolution curry hot pot.

NOTE: *I know of similar conversations taking place in other cultures too. The more we understand what's going on within our conditioned minds and open them up to new ways of seeing and being, we may be able to create healing cross-cultural partnerships for the Highest Good of All.* **We can become Multicultural Parents rather than confine our selves to being a Cultural Parent.**

English and the Mother Language.

My blood family is scattered over five continents: Africa, Asia, North America, Europe, and Australia. Many children of the next generation, in spite of being born and brought up in an Indian family have never been to India and eat a traditional Indian meal probably once a week, if that. They do not identify with the rituals and customs that have defined their ancestors for centuries. They cannot speak their mother language (in my case Gujarati). For my generation, English is our second language. Most of us speak fluently in our mother tongues, having grown up in close-knit Indian communities in Africa and India before migrating to lands of opportunity.

For the next generation, English is their first language, French and/or Spanish often being their second one, which means there is a vacuum created with loss of language. Many Indian grandparents do not speak English so cannot communicate with their grandchildren. *This leaves rich stories of another way of being left suspended in time and space, lost forever, ancestors diminishing into the far horizon as their voices become a mere whisper, stories of heroes and heroines forgotten forever.*

The impact of loss of language was brought home to me at a recent family bereavement. As per Hindu rituals, the final rites of a dead person include an open coffin ceremony at the deceased person's home before their cremation. This ritual is overseen by a Brahmin (usually male priest) to honour the onward journey of the departed. There is a lot of soul talk as per the Hindu religion. In this instance, the family invited a priest over the day before the funeral to explain what rituals would be performed, their significance, and what death signified for us Hindus.

The older generation engaged actively with the sermon as they were familiar with the priest's language (Gujarati and Sanskrit), which included passages from the holy book, the Bhagavat Gita. My generation 'sort of' understood the soul talk. I was frustrated at the obvious exclusion of other ideas and possibilities around death. The theory of quantum physics was swirling around inside my head, and Buddhist teachings kept popping up when least invited. The spirit of Jesus seemed to be nearby, too, trying to get a look in. What was so potently present in the room was a total lack of interest (personified by the bored, glazed looks, the yawns, the glancing at mobile phones) in any of this stuff by the younger generation who did not speak the mother tongue. It was all going over their heads. What a missed opportunity.

This was the perfect time for courageous conversations in English, an increasingly common language. It presented an immense opportunity to engage with the children and ask them their views on death. What was the impact of seeing their grandmother die? Where had she gone? She had been walking and talking a few days before and now was no more. What would they make of her body lying in a coffin with serene stillness? What were their thoughts on this entity called the soul? What did they actually believe happened at death? These conversations would have to happen in English, the new mother tongue for young British-born South Asians.

Some would consider this ignorant on my part. Surely, I should be encouraging our children to learn their native language. This is desirable but not always workable. The external influences are just too potent. *Parents have got enough 'oughts', 'shoulds' and 'musts' on their plates without having to add 'failed on another count' to their list of imperfect parenting.* My peers feel guilty that their children do not speak the mother tongue. It is okay. In the big picture, it really is okay. We can be sad about it but need not drown in shame. Scholars and cultural shifts will keep language going as we are seeing in the new additions to the Oxford dictionary each year. We must brace ourselves for change. Thankfully, sufficient sacred texts, full of wisdom, have been translated into English. Slight distortions due to the lost-in-translation phenomenon will have to be accepted. Interestingly, English is the favoured language of the middle classes in India. Culture is marching on.

And march on it will because that's the law of nature. The only guarantee in life, as the beloved Buddha has taught me, is that of change.

Overstretched 'duty of care'

My generation have particularly borne the brunt of this ideology to the detriment of our well-being. The stark truth is that our parents are expecting us to do what most of them have never done. My parents' generation migrated from India, leaving their parents behind in the motherland snugly enveloped by the community safety net. They never lived with, or cared for, ageing parents on a daily basis. A periodic phone call 'back home' hardly amounts to that. At my age, they had a sense of incredible freedom with which to live their lives in the promised lands they had set up home in. They never endured the agony of having to juggle work life with home life in the way that my generation has to. The women were the homemakers and the men went out to work, managed the finances and provided the homely comforts. Roles were well defined. Now, male and female roles are losing their boundaries as men and women are breadwinners. Notably, what I have observed within my culture is that women are still expected to be the homemakers and keep the domestic, as well as the physical, psychological and emotional well-being of the family, young and old, running smoothly. Men genuinely feel they are contributing to this system, and some are. But it remains a minority. Coming from their predominantly analytical and linear-thinking left brains, they seem to have colluded with the Cultural Parent regarding their superior status and material-provider-only role in the family. This imbalance is creating conflict and feelings of being overburdened, particularly amongst the women. Life has become a huge juggling act between the demand of professional work, domestic order, meeting social commitments (which can be endless, the larger the family), educating the children for that good life whilst also caring for often vulnerable-and-dependent ageing parents. Domestic calendars have multiple entries with endless visits to doctors and hospitals which can keep bodies ticking over for years. Quantity of life over quality of life is an increasing topic of discussion.

A big voice in my head keeps regurgitating the phrase *'We all may be alive, but I am not sure that we are truly living.'* What's that about?

Contemporary medical health care seems to be a victim of its own success. It reduces impetus for addressing the cause of our symptoms such as excessive stress, poor diets, lack of sleep and exercise, and suppressed emotional needs. The advent of the digital highway has dissolved home-work-life-boundaries. Fourteen hour working days have been normalised. Hello, *Homo burnout*. There is a pressing issue. Educated South Asian women hold down highly responsible and demanding jobs. But they juggle two hats. Western versus the Eastern. When at work, they are an intelligent individual with autonomy. When they return home, they are daughters, daughter-in-laws, wives, sisters, mothers and grandmothers abiding to the rules and regulations of a patriarchal driven cultural framework where the show must go on, come rain or shine.

Now women have not only their grown up children to look out for alongside the aged parents, but they also have grandchildren to accommodate somewhere within their day. As they say, a mother's task never ends. In case you think I am cynical, bitter, and twisted, which I can be, it is a fact that a lot of women take care of their grandchildren out of love. The truth is that they also do it out of duty and obligation to their children, that toxic framework again. Suddenly, just when they thought they could step off the domestic hamster wheel and have a bit of 'me time' to pursue their own interests, they find themselves back on another roller coaster with no brakes. This has been expressed to me on several occasions, so it is not a figment of my imagination. The absolute opposite scenario exists where the children and grandchildren have fled the nest to faraway places, leaving parents of my generation suffering the aches and pains of the empty-nest syndrome. They feel utterly lost. What shall we do now? Having lived the eternal 'we', the 'I' is lost at sea where sharks prowl in the form of anxiety and depression. Any ideas how to create balance?

Answers on a postcard please.

Loving Dependent Living (as opposed to Old People's Homes)

What really tugs at my heart is the sad feelings expressed by both sets of parents, whether from full nests or empty ones, is that they cannot rely on their own children to look after them in the twilight years. I do not have any children so my journey of self-sufficiency began a long time ago. A sense of betrayal is in the air. All those parental sacrifices seem to be amounting to nothing. Sigh. A lot of chat around retirement homes with carers and home help abounds. A sense of dooming abandonment prevails. The new generation are too busy reaching for their dreams, and the 'we' they have allegiance to is not the 'we' my generation identify with, which is around meeting the needs of blood family and the extended Indian community. 'We' and 'me' for the youth are merging into one.

There are valid reasons for this. Western living is birthing a generation of Indian children who are gently drifting away from the ancestral framework of duty, obligation, and sacrifice, partly because my generation are exhausted with this formula for living so are not singing it too loudly to their children, and partly because these children have been birthed on a western land with its more liberated conditioning of independence at a young age. Their unconscious minds harbour a right to independent living, where they confidently pursue dreams and goals beyond blood family, far more than my unconscious mind ever did.

But there may be a price to pay. Endless stories from parents around feelings of abandonment abound. The children have become rather autonomous. My generation of girlfriends would be seeking permission from parents regarding a holiday (strictly girls only) or to attend a party with friends where some had dangly bits below the waist (as in boys). The current generation tend to just announce to their parents their 'in relationship with non-Indian' status randomly, and their plans for cohabiting with partners. That means moving out from the family home, having premarital sex, and getting on with their lives just as their westernised friends do. Fair play. We can't have our cake and eat it, too.

Does getting older have to mean such pain? As for that word **retirement,** *I would rather not have it in my vocabulary. Why retire from life? Why not thrive forever?* With the ageing body, saggy bits, chipped teeth, and wrinkly skin? Why not thirst for knowledge till our last breath? I feel the need to think alternatively and creatively, to keep fear at bay. Age will bring its challenges. But there is hope.

The science of Epigenetics reveals how we can influence cellular functions in our body through our thoughts, beliefs, and actions. Bruce Lipton outlines how this is possible in his book *The Biology of Belief.* 'Change your story (thoughts) and change your life' seems to be the message. It is not all mumbo jumbo. If we can think more uplifting thoughts, we produce more uplifting hormones (oxytocin) and neurotransmitters (dopamine and serotonin) into our bodies and these create healthier cells at every level. As previously shared (chapter 9), this knowledge of life (energy medicine and psychology) appears to be embedded in all ancient cultures. Industrialisation, capitalism, and the Western 'modern' way of living have removed us eons from this fountain of well-being. It may help to embrace this wisdom and knowledge, now more than ever, to help us thrive rather than just survive.

As Atul Gawande so wisely observes in *Being Mortal* (29), 'The advances of modern medicine have given us two revolutions: we've undergone a biological transformation of the course of our lives and also a cultural transformation of how we think of that course.' Essentially, we have learnt how to survive longer and longer and manage the effects of that through the medical model, but this may not always be creating happiness. He is encouraging us to think about old age in a different way. Rather than being institutionalised and being pumped with medical interventions, *focussing on reducing isolation and loneliness have proved to be healthier interventions.* Hence my idea of loving-dependent living if we need it in our twilight years. But what can we do to pave the way to independent, healthy, balanced living till then?

Adopting a positive attitude towards downsizing professionally and personally has been rather supportive. After years of being immersed in a successful but highly stressful career, I have given it up to follow my dream of living from the heart. A dear dental colleague who is burning out and has been forced to make certain changes in his life said to me, *'I would rather be chasing zen than money.'* I hear you, soul brother. I hear you.

It seems like if we can keep our minds and bodies going by more balanced living in our earlier years, there is scope for ageing well and living independently for longer. Saying that, if we have to live in a shared community with some help from others, does that mean our children have abandoned us? I propose we embrace a concept of loving-dependent living based on a new cultural framework of compassion, connection, and co-creation with forward thinking and planning so that both parties (children and ageing parents) can live harmoniously. This calls for courageous conversations around decay and death which is particularly urgent as many families now consist of single children. I am encouraged by the seeds being sown where older Indian people are living in communal homes and providing companionship to one another with the help of carers. They prefer this to living with joint family where they spend most of the day in isolation and loneliness (as the rest of the family go to work) with the Indian soap opera channels for company. We need to think more creatively as a culture about managing older years. Otherwise, it really is all a bit of a slippery slope towards ill health, resentment, broken hearts and family breakdown. Most undesirable.

Mental Health

The brain is an organ within the body as is the stomach, liver and heart. Generally, if a person falls ill with cancer or colitis, kindness, compassion, and support from others is usually forthcoming. On the other hand, any malfunctions relating to the brain (and, hence, the mind) seem to create shame, guilt, and embarrassment for the person affected and their family. Mental health issues are a challenge in all cultures. There has been a big drive recently in the UK (Heads Together campaign, www. headstogether.org.uk) to raise awareness around these health issues in society. They are rife in the South Asian community. But we struggle to acknowledge that. Why? Why are we so ashamed to be honest about mental health issues?

I guess because when a person's mental health is affected, their behaviours can be rather unpalatable to our senses. It can be extremely frightening, heart breaking, and tragic. Who wants to own up to the fact that their child, sibling, partner, or parent can go into a rage like a bull in a china shop, sleep endlessly day after day without showering or brushing their teeth, start ranting on about the aliens next door, or run around the garden wielding a knife, panty-less. What will people say? What will people think? It can be so gut-wrenching.

In the Indian culture, the burning question would be 'who will marry my daughter or son knowing that her or his sister/ brother/mother/ father/grandmother/grandfather/aunt/uncle/nephew/niece has bipolar disorder?' It's all about family honour again rather than about the individual. There's the teachings of the Cultural Parent for you. *Keep family honour intact even when a son or a daughter's soul is weeping and down on its knees. How heartless can this parent be?*

What is more worrying is that mental health issues can be present ever so subtly in the form of anxiety, panic attacks, low mood, depression, chronic fatigue, acute stress, and burnout. I know of so many people in my community who suffer these problems and yet run around in society pretending all is well. It usually is as long as the drugs and pills are popped on a daily basis. Again, I am not against medical support where appropriate, *but what about our feelings?* Due to the pressures of extended family systems and patriarchal domination within my culture, these conditions are so common in Indian women, yet no one is willing to talk about them because of the underlying feelings of failure and embarrassment involved, not to mention the ever-present attitude of denial. It may also be related to religiously misplaced ideology where 'fate' or 'destiny' are blamed for a person's mental health challenges, as in you suffer this because you 'reap what you sow'. Really? Stop it.

What about talking about how this impacts us deep in our hearts? Where it hurts terribly that our family is not normal-ish like everyone else's or about how this puts unbearable strain on parents and other siblings? How *vacation* is just a word that exists in the Oxford Dictionary, as is *sleep*. Where life feels like one big roller coaster with no brakes. It is tough. We must show compassion, connect, and co-create some realistic models for managing this increasing problem in our culture. All ideas welcome.

Answers on a postcard please.

From personal experience, as menopause set in and as I gave up my food props, my body started talking incessantly in the form of anxiety. The deep dread, feelings of dissociation, and racing heart would manifest just out of nowhere. On a few occasions, I was frightened terribly by a panic attack. This all shocked me as I had never experienced such feelings of loss of control before. It took immense courage to admit to myself and then to my sibling, work colleagues and close friends that I, Ms Rescuer Extraordinaire and Ms Perfectionist, was deeply vulnerable, too. *But such courage is vital as it marks the beginning of the healing process.*

The medical model offered me pills to manage my dread which helped for forty-eight hours, and then I actually felt worse. *Amidst the fog, an inner wisdom urged me to inform myself about what was the root cause of my distress,* get informed about the resources out there to support myself, and manage my anxiety (from within) which I came to realise was a manifestation of the inauthentic life I was living. What dawned on me in one of those 'aha' moments of life was that anxiety (the body's way of signalling for help) manifests when our daily experience of ourselves is so far removed from how we wish to experience ourselves. It also manifests when we live our lives in fear. When we feel out of control but keep up the masks and act like we are in control. Human beings are great actors and actresses. Recognise any of this Fellow Traveller? I am sure you do. You are not alone.

To this end, I cannot recommend highly enough that we, as a community, loosen our grip on shame, guilt, and blame around mental health and start up some courageous conversations around it. There is nothing 'wrong with us' if we need to get any form of therapy. The modern way of living has alienated the support systems our ancestors had in the villages. In days gone by, priests, neighbours, herbalists, the shamans and wise men and women would see you through a crisis. But life is very different now. We need a new vision and a new approach.

How about being open to embracing therapies such as counselling, coaching, mindfulness-based practices, art therapy, creative writing, reiki, tai chi, Qi gong, crystal healing, angel therapy, physical exercise, hypnotherapy, walks in nature, and those most wonderful practices from our rich ancestral culture, yoga, prayer, and chanting (sound healing)? Optimum nutrition is vital, too. Out with the junk (especially sugar and processed stuff) and in with health-boosting foods. Over the years, I have been open to trying each and every one of these healing practices. They have been a life line.

Now anxiety arrives and what 'we' do is have a courageous conversation over a cup of tea. *I say to anxiety, 'What is it that you want me to face up to? What are you protecting me from? What do I need to do to feel back in control of my life?'* Try it. It may take you to liberating truth.

PS. I am sensitive to the fact that professional therapies can cost a lot. In fact, in some countries these facilities simply do not exist. If budgets are tight, it may not be possible to access these services. Some workplaces may offer support as part of their well-being programme. Alternatively, please reach out for support through your doctor, local community groups, charities, faith-based institutions, and online free resources. Anxiety UK (www.anxietyuk.org.uk) and Mind (www.mind.org.uk) have a lot of supportive information. Tapping (www.thetappingsolution.com) is a fantastic tool for self-empowerment and relief from so many mental health challenges. I would also recommend John Crawford's book *Anxiety Relief* which has some very useful tools on how to manage this distressing condition. Confide in a parent, colleague or a friend. Talk to a partner. Reach out to a sibling. Do not suffer in silence. Honour yourself. You are so worth it.

And without a doubt, journaling and creative writing can help release the internal angst in ways unimaginable as this verbal detox has done for me. Julia Cameron's book *The Artist's Way* (www.juliacameronlive.com) is a great resource.

An Offering

Pick up a pen and piece of paper (or any digital gadget) right now and write.

I honour my mind, heart, body and spirit. I honour my needs. I am deserving of love and compassion. Today, I chose to recover. I chose to heal. I have the answers within. Here I go:

I would like to say ____.

Write, write, write. Spit it out. Let it go. Speak your truth. Not someone else's truth.

If I could I would ____.

Write, write, write. Express yourself. Have that courageous conversation with yourself. Or another.

Reach out. Reach in. You are not alone.

Remember, when you dare to see and name what hurts, you may be able to do something about it. The vehicle of your angst, writing paper or digital screens, will hold you tenderly in a non-judgemental sacred space of your very own making. Spitting the pain and toxicity out of your body will feel amazing. Seek professional help if necessary.

PS: *Where are the conversations on disability, learning difficulties and so on? I am not hearing them. What's that about?*

On Death

It seems inevitable that if we are going to have courageous conversations around ageing, loving-dependent living, and mental health, we need to talk about death, that time when Yama, God of Death, will jet us back to Source on God Airways. The latter has become a little feature in conversations with my parents as we poignantly face the reality of this event. To be honest, the real reason for manifesting a humorous story around God Airways is to deal with my own anxiety around losing my parents to death. Whilst preparing myself for all sorts of emotions, the truth in my heart says nothing can prepare me for how I will feel at their loss. But an inner voice says, 'Let's at least try.' It is back to exerting choice, going into denial about the inevitable, or engaging with it in a compassionate and creative way, up the healing scale or down the wounded one. You can see where I would rather be.

My father always dreamt of living to a hundred years of age until he almost died at the age of eighty-three from cardiac failure. His heart was exhausted from the trillions of beats it had produced over this period and willed the body to die. I say body because the soul, as I understand it, never dies, that part of you that is eternal energy. The same energy that drives the Earth around the Sun and the Moon around planet Earth. Mind-blowing, isn't it? Sorry. I digress. Back to my father.

Modern medicine brought him back to life again, but I noticed how he stopped talking about wanting to live for Queen Elizabeth's hundred birthday telegram and started to have anxiety around loss of personal independence, health, dignity, and ultimately death. Each day was focussed around health and the regime of tablets, blood pressure measurements, sugar readings, and diets. Instead of talking about his next exotic meal and holiday, which were the usual themes of my father's life pre-cardiac failure, the goal now was how to keep out of the doctor's surgery, and hospital stays with the repeated 'Asian meals' for dinner. As my dad was not into reincarnation, he really wondered where he would end up at death? At least my mum had a very clear view of where she was heading – amongst the stars, never to return. Here's to wishes being fulfilled.

I have always respected my parents' views whilst trying to formulate my own about life after death. What undoubtedly has helped our family is creating courageous chat and humour around the final departure. Some people may find my honesty around my parents' death uncomfortable. Should I not be saying, as all good little Indian girls do, that no matter what I will support them into their older years even if it means disowning my own needs. *I cannot do that anymore. I value myself too much.*

Talk about death with your loved ones. Do not live with regrets. God Airways arrives and departs on time, irrespective of the weather conditions over the Atlantic or the porosity of the ozone layer. I have already ordered Dad his first-class seat, with ample supply of gin and tonics, tandoori chicken, and a viewing of *Abba: The Movie*. As for Mum, I would have got into a right huff around her position before waking up to the realities of life. Fancy her saying that she does not want to return to planet Earth after all the sacrifices I have made to give her a fulfilled life. But all is well, as duty and sacrifice are not my drivers anymore. They are attributes best dedicated to the memory of soldiers who sacrifice their lives for their country out of patriotic duty. I honour and bow to each and every single one of them irrespective of their colour, creed, ethnicity, religious, and cultural backgrounds. Thank you from deep within my eternal soul for your sacrifices out of patriotic duty. I sincerely cherish the freedom you have secured for me.

While on the subject of death, another conversation worth engaging in is around customs, traditions, and rituals associated with this event. In Hindu families like mine, a thirteen-day mourning period is dedicated to honouring the dead. The bereaved family, extended genetic tribe, and close friends commune in prayer and healing chants from holy scriptures before giving a final send-off to the soul. The latter, apparently, departs on to its next voyage on day thirteen following death. This period can be very comforting as family and friends provide much-needed support from practical matters such as feeding the physical body to providing emotional and soul food for managing the cascade of feelings and emotions associated with death of a loved one or one not loved.

Again, the tide is changing. The younger generation do not feel the need to honour eternal souls over drawn out rituals anymore. Practicalities of living in a Western society where work commitments and modified belief systems including no acknowledgement of God, or a soul, are making this form of mourning pointless. A friend's young daughter found gathering for prayers and sacred chanting rather distressing when her mother suddenly died. It all felt morbid and depressing. Notably the younger generation prefer to mourn by coming together watching digital slide shows and sharing narratives of joyful times spent with the departed, all over a few beers and gin and tonics rather than in what can feel like a very religious public domain for thirteen days. Perhaps we have Irish blood in us! They do have a jolly party at the wake to honour a departed one. Some ancestors may be reeling from this betrayal.

My feelings towards this sea of change are somewhat mixed as I do consider death to be a very sacred event. I believe in honouring new beginnings for a soul on its onward journey through prayer, reflection and contemplation. The way I have dealt with my confusion is by performing sacred rituals for the departed soul within my own home, whilst also joining in the celebratory customs of new. It can be hard to resist the odd gin and tonic. May I share a verse in honour of a soul's journey ahead? It came to me in one of those sacred moments during prayer and meditation:

In the end
It was the beginning
Of a Soul's journey into eternity
Into the realm of endless possibilities
Of rebirth, nirvana or rest
Simply what was best
For the Soul's journey

I must say my parents have surprised me with their requests around death. 'No thirteen days of mourning please,' they chant. My mum wants no fuss and rituals around an open coffin. She wants to be remembered how she was when alive and at her best. We are to have a samosa-and-onion *bhaji* cholesterol-elevating tea party for family and friends in memory of her. My father's attitude is rather similar, though his menu would include an aromatic chicken *biriyani*! So be it. Hurrah. *Having had the courageous conversations, my brother and I will not have to drown in guilt and regret in case we get things wrong.* When the traditionalists get agitated and chide us for letting down the blood family and ancestors, we can serenely honour the memory of our parents. In our own unique way. With a reframed attitude appropriate to today's cultural reality and our inner truth, which only we can know.

Arranged Marriages, Love, and Physical Expressions

The other interesting hot topic brewing for cultural metamorphosis is around arranged marriages. This idea was forged by our ancestors in faraway villages in the motherland. A rational reason for this arrangement was probably around maintaining purity in the Patel gene pool. Man, not Gaia, is territorial. Mother Earth was not defined by continents and countries until man came along and created boundaries and walls to separate your country from mine. In my birth tribe, marriages were arranged between boys and girls from similar family backgrounds, quite a common theme across all cultures, to be fair. Think Victorian England and African tribal liaisons, and the same would apply.

I guess 'like marrying like' facilitated transitions, and brides could settle easily into their new families who shared similar *reet* (traditions) and *rivajs* (customs). That is how arranged marriages were sold to me. What a flawed ideological theory. Let's talk domestic violence. The latter exists in society regardless of class. Women I know bought into this sales pitch and lived to regret it as they became victims of domestic violence. The latter is brewing quietly behind closed doors in many Gujarati households. STOP IT. There is no room for such atrocities in any culture. It is up to the Cultural Parents (South Asian adults) of today to take responsibility and change this outrageous belief system and the one around child marriages.

This abhorrent practice survives in India to this day, where little children are treated as investments and swirled into a lifetime of disillusionment and trauma. *Now here is where I exert choice to feel ashamed.* I feel ashamed to be part of a culture that thinks that this is still okay. It is not okay. It is called child abuse, and it is not acceptable. This trade needs to be abolished. Indian children in foreign lands, where laws still have some clout, are generally luckier where they do not have to endure this violation and humiliation, though certain communities still practice forced marriages even when miles away from the land of their ancestors. Stop it. Stop violating God's children. Wise ancestors are crying for these misjudgements.

Thankfully, seeds of change are being planted. The tide is changing, and surf, we must. Indian children born and brought up in western lands are exposed to a multicultural society embracing people of all races, colour, religion, education, sexuality, attitudes and belief systems. Add the internet into the equation and boom. It is a scrumptious hot pot. These children are well into romance, sexual intimacy, and this entity called love. When we receive news of an engagement, we Indians, out of conditioning and habit, need to enquire 'Is it arranged?' or 'Is it a love marriage?' Increasingly, it is the latter. Communal living before marriage, which means premarital sex (and shame to my generation and definitely the one above), are becoming the norm. I am still into primitive thinking. The word *courting* comes to mind. Too old-fashioned, I guess. Whilst embarrassed to admit it, I struggle with saying, 'I love you,' and it is only recently, with my heart chakra bursting its dams, have I started to be able to communicate love in this way to others.

As I said, *what is normalised in childhood is taken, for better or for worse, into adulthood.*

This phrase 'I love you' was confined to Western films when I grew up. In Bollywood films, which were my fortnightly fodder of romantic fantasy, no actor or actress uttered that phrase. In fact, artists refused to do the kissing scenes involving lip contact. The Cultural Parents' disapproval probably made sure of that. More importantly, clothes stayed on. Sex was out of bounds. A far cry from today's Bollywood films which are part of a multibillion industry defining the twenty-first-century Indian. Semi naked heroes and heroines writhing around in ecstasy amidst dance sequences that boast sexual liberation abound. In my youth, expressions of love on screen were confined to shy glances and fluttering eyelashes between lovers. Passion was expressed in the song-and-dance sequences filmed behind fragrant rose bushes in the glorious sunshine. Sexual expression was drenched in innuendo. It never happened.

In real life, my parents never said, 'I love you,' to my brother or me or to each other. It just was not part of our culture, as was the absence of hugging and kissing, which was viewed as a very Western form of ritual to acknowledge relationship. *I am so glad this more liberal non-verbal behaviour has infiltrated my birth tribe.* The Cultural Parents' over-the-top 'intimacy expression boundaries' rightly side-lined. On reflection, love was around, but it felt more like affection, though I know now that it was love because this entity is multifaceted like a cut diamond, verbal and non-verbal, physical and non-physical, present in the silence.

Culture around romance has changed dramatically. I do struggle with the smoochy, touchy, feely, throat-suffocating stuff in public. Let me own it. Intimacy to me is something very sacred and private, not to be hung out like washed laundry. I feel compelled to show respect to my elders regarding this matter. They are struggling with this sexual revolution, understandably so.

My parents are of a generation where an arranged marriage meant you met someone for an hour or so one day, and two weeks later you were married to them and on your way to a culturally conditioned path of family life framed by duty, obligation, and sacrifice. Sexual feelings and erotic acts were confined strictly behind closed doors. In my mother's time and to this day, Indian women often have to keep their heads covered in front of men out of respect (another bother that we can thankfully do without). My parents' generation find it excruciatingly painful and embarrassing when young people flaunt their bodies and sexual freedom blatantly in front of them. When sexuality with all its varied expression has been pathologized in childhood, exposure to it can be traumatising. Not for young, loved-up British Indian children who are far more physically demonstrative and open to hugging, kissing, and expressing their feelings. The downside of raging hormones is the sexualisation of the female body. My friend's daughter once asked me if I liked the skirt she was hoping to buy when we were out shopping together. I thought it was a belt! My response to that was 'There's class and then there's tart. Which would you rather be?' Apologies for my narrow-mindedness and judgements, but some behaviours just are bothersome.

Introjection of the Western concept of intimate relationship is refreshing at some level. Human beings are innately social animals. *Physical contact, intimate relationship, and genuine connection are an important part of evolution. Being brought up the way I was is unhealthy.* Living within a tribal framework that poured shame on you if you fancied boys, had boyfriends, held hands with someone of the opposite sex, felt the urge to kiss someone on the lips, masturbate, or imagined erotic fantasies stunts healthy emotional and sexual development. It makes you a bit distant and robotic. I am not advocating premature sexual development, just healthy intimacy and confidence in one's own sexuality.

The mother archetype in me has just surfaced. Apologies if this sounds preachy, but needs must. A message to beloved children, especially young women: Kindly respect yourself and others. Showcasing your boobs in a balcony bra and revealing your posterior equator lines do not speak of empowerment. Screaming and ranting sexual vulgarities to express the feminist in you is really not helpful either. In the end, you look and sound like those vile men who use their aggression and misplaced prowess to insult and suppress you. *Furthermore, sexualising your body does not make you more successful or acceptable to society.* It may seem that way, but do not buy into that illusion. And what sort of message are we giving to little girls? That in order to be accepted and be seen as an intelligent, capable, worthy human being, they must have the perfect body? The more flesh they show, the more liberated and powerful they are? Is that what being a feminist means? That's a narrow view. It does not mean that you are more loved, successful or worthy. In any case, be acceptable and worthy to yourself first. The human being with all its wonder in you. Not the human body you are, which will diminish somewhat and go south (sag all over) as you get older. Then what will you do?

Do enjoy your newly found sexual freedom. Acceptance of premarital sex is being embraced gradually by many parents of my generation who themselves had arranged marriages. Boyfriends and girlfriends are now invited into the family home and allowed to sleep in the same bed. This is huge. A gentle request: Please be responsible in the way you enjoy this immense gift of sexual freedom. Because it is a gift. So many children still undergo forced marriages. For them, only force is real, not love. Carry on expressing feelings of love, the type of love that can overcome the tsunamis of life. I am envious of your freedom. I still struggle with the idea of living with a man outside marriage – at fifty-six. Such is the power of the Cultural Parent. Go away! I am not listening to your suffocating rules anymore.

Remarriage

Oh. Another bee has just surfaced in my bonnet. Bzzz, best release it. Here it comes. It is around the taboo of re-marriage, particularly for women who are widowed prematurely. Death can knock on our doors at any time, especially when we least expect it. It can rob us of our fellow travellers. Couples seem to have a co-dependent rhythm about their existences, be it dysfunctional or loved-up. Sudden death can produce a tsunami of financial, emotional, physical, and family crises, especially when children are involved. Women find themselves lost in an ocean of cultural conditioning which does not encourage second marriages. It is okay for widowed or divorced men to seek virgin brides, but they will not easily accept previously married ones.

I recall my own situation. As I got older and my ovaries were approaching redundancy, my parents started getting proposals for my marriage from families of divorced men or widowers. Rather than from single men (who obviously deserved fertile young brides). I cannot be bothered to react. To this day, divorced women or widows are not encouraged to find new partners. They are seen as 'soiled goods'. In any case, Indian men struggle with the liability of looking after some other man's children. That is not because Indian men are unkind. These attitudes can be attributed to Cultural Parent conditioning. *If you are prepared emotionally only just for arranged marriages, it's jolly hard to start thinking about exploring a new relationship with anyone in your forties and fifties.* Intimacy. Help. Run! This especially when your entire life script as a boy has been about 'all women are your sisters except the one you marry'.

A widowed friend in his late fifties felt he did not even know how to go about being in intimate relationship with a woman again. He had expected his arranged marriage to last for his entire life. He had never been allowed to have girlfriends when young, so the brain could not get around the idea of dating and courting a woman with a view to remarriage so late in life. Young, bereaved women end up living with their children and become devoted to their grandchildren to thankfully create meaning in life. Imagine if there are no grandchildren around for distraction as in childless families, like mine. Underneath the pseudo happiness, there is often a storm of abject pain, loneliness and isolation. The future feels bleak. This can have catastrophic consequences on people's health and well-being. I attribute some of my mother's health issues to wounds from missing out on the joys of grand-parenting. So sorry, Mum.

We all deserve a second chance at happiness. Some of us are still looking for the first. That is just my old story. Pass.

Identity and the Good Life

Globalisation and multiculturalism, with all the possibilities, bring huge challenge into our lives. Exposure to expansive frontiers offers opportunities for creating relationship outside the tribe. The result? An increasing birth of mixed heritage children into traditionally Indian families. There are plenty more to come. *Historically, children of mixed marriages often have to dig deeper as they may feel fragmented between many ways of being. Identity can be problematic.* Several of my first cousins and their children have mixed marriages. For their children, ethnicity is going to mean something extremely different from their grandparents who were of predominant Indian breed. I say predominant because the reality is that even those who see themselves as 'pure Indians' are really an amalgamation of various blood groups. The Indian label holds residues of African, Aryan, and European blood. Remove these labels, and it is back to 'who are you?' **We are engaged in a process of cultural bereavement and rebirth.** This is creating feelings of intense grief and loss for the older generations, and confusion and pain for my generation and the one next down. Best we all show up and grow up.

We need not drown in confusion, pain, and sorrow. How can race, colour, and ancestral heritage be viewed to fit in with today's contemporary world view? Children of any heritage, non-Indian, Indian or mixed, deserve a strong sense of identity. The latter being based on human qualities of love, respect, dignity, compassion, courage, kindness, tolerance and acceptance of self as well as others. Such qualities hopefully encourage children to have strong family and societal values, a purposeful work ethic, a sense of community, interest in social enterprise, compassion for the elderly, and respect for Mother Earth. It feels more expansive to be this way than just create identity around 'the good life' based on hierarchical class, caste, and tribal systems, ridiculous monetary wealth, a proper job, the posh postcode, the designer stuff, travel off to only exotic locations, and the £100,000 destination wedding. Am I being judgemental? I certainly am. Am I going to apologise for it? Sorry. But no. *Selfish capitalism embraced by the world, and hence my birth tribe, is creating a huge disconnection between the rich and poor.* There is a sense of entitlement and narcissistic tendency that this environment brings. I should know having been right in the jaws of it.

Private school education, conditioning and the need to succeed by my birth tribe's standards led me to a revered high-grossing profession. I equated all the above mentioned 'good-life' markers with being successful, acceptable, and validated by society. I had embraced this identity for years. Embarking on a deep internal journey of 'Who Am I?' and 'What is it All About?' angst, I noticed that my middle class (now there's an interesting label) contemporaries would be name dropping the current rage in *the* designer stuff to wear, *the* places to eat, *the* wines to drink, *the* exotic holiday destination to head to and *the* chefs to adore. I would not have a clue as to what they were talking about. To which some of them would say, 'where have you been?' This made me think. Was I stupid? Out of touch? Ignorant? Thankfully increasing self-love and self-worth reassured me that I was far from any of these things.

The truth is that I feel slightly agitated and disorientated from a certain way of being that used to feel so normal and ordinary. I struggle living in a world where the moral compass seems to have been discarded, where inequality is blatantly on the rise, where a person thinks it is okay to earn obscene amounts of money to prop up their egos and bank balances, where the rich justify their position by giving to the poor.

'Those uneducated people are ruining our lives' is a theme I have heard over and over again. I notice how it really annoys me. My parents did not have formal education either. That does not make them stupid. The two beautiful souls who support me to care for my elderly parents did not have the privilege of higher education. They are far from stupid and are in fact emotionally intelligent, which according to Daniel Coleman of the famous book *Emotional Intelligence* may be more important to creating civility on our streets and sustainable communal life than just massaging the IQs. There is a genuine disconnect between the haves and the have-nots. Where intellectual, so-called educated people dismiss the voice of the working classes. 'What do they know?' they shout from their large wheeled tanks. 'They (as in the working class) who have not made informed choices about their future and ruined ours.'

This attitude was very apparent during the Brexit vote in the UK, which is the deepest arrogance because it implies that working-class people, or anyone who voted for change are stupid. That if they hanker for a different way of life, they are ignorant and racist; that if they want more they should work harder because that's what we achievers do. This is from people spending money on one meal, on a regular basis, equating to a man's weekly wage in which he has to sustain his whole family. I struggle with all this. It is causing me inner conflict. I just cannot sit with it anymore, especially as people from all walks of life, young and old, Eastern and Western struggle with making a living and being able to keep up this charade of what has come to be seen as a 'good life'. We need a vaccine for the *affluenza virus*. I would be first in the queue. I crave for a different way of living. Some addictions persist.

A rather straight talker of a friend told me to stop being holier-than-thou. Ouch. Another equally wealthy friend said that one must 'not feel guilty about my privileges' and that 'variety was the spice of life'. Another piped, 'One must make a profit.' I understand all this and accept this is my personal struggle. *I am not against people having wealth as long as there is equal opportunity for people to create some of their own,* where jobs that seem dull and mediocre to the high fliers are assigned a decent wage. As one of my previous dental patients, a retired banker, said to me, 'The problem is that in my time, I earned around five times more than my secretary, but now that figure is five hundred-fold!' Yikes.

I do struggle with such disparity and am trying to negotiate my life through it as are increasing numbers of people around the world. It encourages me no end to see that people are starting to write about this. Tami Simon, founder of www.soundstrue.com and someone I admire, is consistently promoting business with heart. Notably, there are an increasing number of books on the shelves of popular bookshops around post-capitalism, and the need for a new world order, especially for business with heart. Yes, please. Why?

Because *Homo sapiens,* if not careful, are on their way to *Homo burnout.*

This awakening has sent me off on a quest to work out how to keep afloat. How can the partly-socialist-partly-capitalist personality that is me thrive, rather than just survive? How can the Buddha's Middle Way be honoured which I am deeply committed to? How can the Spiritual Being that seems to be bursting out of my very seams be birthed? How can I not be holier-than-thou but be an authentic and genuine peace activist in my desire to create a fairer society? Without offending the Haves which I seem to be able to do with ease! The vision of sacred activism resonates deeply with me. It is at the heart of Andrew Harvey's book *Radical Passion. Sacred Love and Wisdom in Action.* Love and compassion in themselves are not enough. What we need is 'Love in Action' to create authentic positive change. But even as I share this, an inner critical voice is brewing. 'You think you are more special than others.' To which my response is, 'No.' Thankfully, after years of agonising and self-doubt, *I have learnt that some low frequency thoughts are just not worth putting any energy into.*

I simply believe we need to re-define the 'good life'. What does it look like to you?

Answers on a postcard please.

Sexuality

While we are on the subject of cultural awakenings, can we please wake up from denial around diversity in sexuality. Gender differences are still considered an illness by many.

There are homosexual, lesbians, bisexual, and transgender people within Indian society who lead double lives because of the taboo of expressing themselves in any other way than that accepted by the Cultural Parent. I know of several people leading lives of lies. Behind closed doors, they may be who they are or sadly, may not, depending on their circumstances. In public, deception is the name of the game. I have heard stories of Indian parents threatening gay sons with exclusion from inheritance and emotional blackmail, using threat of suicide as a weapon for their child's destruction.

I once supported a homosexual client who was spiralling into depression because he was being forced into an arranged marriage to maintain his family's reputation. *A South Asian tribe will sacrifice an individual to keep its honour intact and spit that person out with no remorse or compassion for their plight.* Never mind the ripple effect of such a forced liaison. What of the bride who may marry this man? What about her dreams and aspirations? Imagine the betrayal of finding out that your husband prefers to bed a man rather than you? That the children you dreamt of birthing will remain unborn? Secrets and lies. What's the point?

There are people who do not identify themselves as men or women. Anthropology has revealed that multi-gender systems exist. The term *intersex* seems to be cropping up everywhere. On scouring the internet, as one does, an intersex person may be female, male, both, or neither. They may identify as straight, gay, lesbian, bisexual, asexual. Essentially, they may view themselves as he, she, or they. From a psychological perspective, being intersex in a society that has very well-defined social constructs for gender creates existential angst. Identity issues are complex.

In India, the term *intersex* has been used to describe *hijras,* who are legally recognised as a third-gender. The law does not stop them from being discriminated against, marginalised, and exploited by the sex industry. They are feared somewhat as they can be seen to represent bad luck. I first encountered *hijras* at a family wedding in India when quite young. I was rather mesmerised by these beautifully dressed people with square jawlines wearing ornate saris, sparkly jewellery, and bright lipstick. They proceeded to perform a flamboyant dance routine outside the gated wedding venue. Sadly, the show did not go on for too long. A wad of cash was hurriedly donated to them by the bride's parents, and they were ushered off into oblivion by the security guards. The parents did not want their daughter's married life to be blighted by the *hijras* evil energy. *Superstition and fear are powerful drivers for propping up prejudice.*

I find the younger generation are much more open to embracing sexual diversity than my generation who struggle with the truth. In the UK, websites supporting Asian LGBT people speak for themselves. There are a lot of Indian children who lead agonising double lives. *We are all children of the cosmos deserving of respect whatever our sexual orientation.* Please let us not ostracise our children for their sexual diversity. The problem with this is that the secrets, lies, and shame that accompany denial can be passed down for generations. A man or woman should not be defined by their sexual organs but by their capacities for being a decent human being. Is that too simple?

Booze and Fags

I have the most wonderful memory of my brother and me experimenting with fags (cigarettes) when young. I found a packet of posh fags my father's friend had left behind following a family visit and invited my brother to our own little 'try-a-fag' party whilst hiding behind a massive water tank on the terrace of our home. Not what good little Indian girls do! Whatever. There I was feeling rather sophisticated and grown up until I lit one of the cigarettes and took a huge puff. Well, fifteen minutes later, after coughing, spluttering, crying, and choking, I gave up the drug habit. In the meantime, my brother was merrily puffing away at the joints and seemed to be an expert at smoking. I just could not believe how he was denying his hobby to my mum who kept sniffing his clothes every day and kept trying to make him confess to his nicotine addiction to her in between rolling out the *rotlis* (Indian flatbread.) *Childhoods, they can be such fun.*

As for the booze, my dad is my hero. Around my fifteenth birthday, he began to offer me a martini and lemonade instead of Cokakola (Coke) or Phanta (Fanta) as the Indians always like to say. It took away any intrigue for alcohol in my latter years. My dad was obviously not a very 'good, grown-up Indian father' in my mother's eyes at the time, but hey ho. He taught me to drink with boundaries, just like he used to.

Now to another little bee in my bonnet. Can we please step out of the blame game of attributing drinking and smoking to negative Western influences on young Eastern bodies? The state of Gujarat (India) from which my forefathers emerged has a high rate of tobacco sales and smoking of *bidis* (hand-rolled cigarettes). I saw it first hand on a recent visit to India. In the past, my grandma and her lady friends used to put 'snuff' (smokeless tobacco) up their noses as they sat around on their porches, in the villages, watching the sun go down. Interestingly, today Gujarat state also has the highest amount of alcohol consumption for an 'alcohol-free state'. Surely, it's time for my birth tribe to address these issues out in the open, fair and square. We really cannot keep blaming the West and poor Western habits for our alcohol and smoking habits or any other stuff that we wish to dishonestly disown. Period. There is this attitude called 'taking personal responsibility' that one can exert. Choice is the name of the game.

The Unmentionable That Must Be Mentioned

Violations such as FGM (female genital mutilation), rape in marriage, foetal murder, abuse (in any form), honour killings, and the other unmentionables need to be acknowledged and addressed. Within my community, domestic abuse is very real but constantly downplayed. It is not my intention to discuss these atrocities here superficially. They are complex issues and deserve far more attention and introspection. But are we guilty of being bystanders to these atrocities? Can each and every one of us do something to start creating change? Do you know someone undergoing this trauma? What can you do for them? Let us not forget those caught up in violence, those adrift at sea, seeking a safe shore. As my dear friend Push reminded me, 'Behind every sensational headline, there is a human being with feelings.' Be assured that I am in intense conversation with my Cultural Parent about this matter. *Nomoresuppressionoppressionviolenceabuseandalltheotheratrocities@ stopit.com*

The Victim Position

People of a subculture may be wounded and cannot fathom views like mine. They see people like me, an English Indian, as betrayers who have forsaken their roots. I have been called a coconut (brown on the outside and white on the inside). To those who see me that way, I say, 'I love my beloved England.' Why wouldn't I? having lived almost forty of my fifty-six years in this amazing land of opportunity. It is my sanctuary. My temple. My home. *I honour this land of a dominant Western culture that has embraced my foreign Eastern subculture, and allowed me to freely express its values.* This foreign land has presented me with immense freedom and opportunities that have led me to my true nature. How can I not be grateful? Mother India is not offended by this allegiance. Why are you?

It is a fact that subcultures suffer discrimination and marginalisation. I am not denying that or condoning racism or prejudice towards any human being in any shape or form. This has caused terrible suffering for millions of people all over the world. No one can deny that tribal, ethnic, and racial tensions are themes central to the human race. I have my prejudices and a lot of effort is needed to become aware of them so that I do not act on them and harm another human being. Easier said than done. But try I must. It is not an option. My curiosity runs high for what it has meant for people of a dominant culture, with a certain established way of cultural life, to embrace people from a subculture and welcome them into their homelands and worlds. *After all, multicultural traffic is not a one-way street.* That's all I am saying to those who see me as a betrayer, a coconut, brown on the outside and white on the inside.

God

I have deliberately left the issue of courageous conversations of this Divine Intelligence to the last. Ironically, the very subject of conversation and spiritual practice that imbibed me from birth. Religiously based rituals, customs and traditions have been central to my life. Many have enriched me. Some bored the pants off me and many have made me rebel. Religion is an emotive subject. It has been and always will be. My generation and particularly the next, are struggling with it. The metamorphosis around how I viewed God as a child to my current understanding of this vital Life Force, has been shared as honestly as possible (chapter 5). My outpourings have felt embarrassing at times, but the need to speak my truth has driven me on. This is a journey of walking my talk. The masks and charades, which cannot be stomached, dropped. I may have come across as some religiously idealistic fool who has just bought into all the fluffy shining lights and bright-stars stuff. Nothing could be further from the truth. *It has been a deeply emotive, challenging, dynamic, ever-flowing, painful, agonising and yet liberating personal journey.* It continues with no ending in sight.

The most powerful influences on my life script, besides my biological parents, have been the Cultural Parent and religion. My intention is not to convert, criticise, or shame anyone but to respect diverse views, except those who kill and maim in the name of God. Please stop it.

I hold hope for a generation that has difficulty embracing God. Perhaps they are connecting to Divine Intelligence on their terms. There is a growing movement of young people who are dedicated to the well-being of the planet suggesting an emergence of connection with a deeper more sacred truth. The opportunity to travel the globe and experience diversity through different lenses has expanded horizons. Perhaps relationship with God equates to walking in the wilderness, skiing down tranquil mountains, deep-sea diving, trekking through the Amazon, or climbing Mount Everest. The mind body spirit audience is growing thanks to technological advances. Cultural barriers are coming down, and the increasing liaisons of young South Asian people in mixed-race relationships speaks of something profound. This generation is being able to see beneath the colour of skin. *They seem to be connecting from the heart rather than just engaging with fellow human beings from their conditioned minds.* Perhaps a journey back to the wisdom of the indigenous ancestors who revered Mother Earth has begun, and people are connecting to the truth via another energetic route. Dare I say it? The World Wide Web. All paths welcome that lead to peace and harmony.

Thought of the Moment

How interesting that I was not destined to be a mother in this lifetime and yet the archetypal mother in me is roaring like a lioness desperately wanting to guard her cubs (children anywhere and everywhere).

Please let us not harm our children because what is normalised in childhood is taken, for better or for worse, into adulthood.

Reflections

What courageous conversations would you like to have around the cultural and religious challenges you face?

What is your identity?

What community do you belong to?

Chapter 13

Self-Love and Healing: Beyond Duty, Obligation, and Sacrifice

Finally set free. To be me.

At a recent well-known motivational speaker's workshop, the central theme was about loving one-self as the ultimate goal of existence, the idea being that when we start with love for ourselves, we send it out to others and this has a ripple effect leading to joyful family life, more peaceful communities, and ultimately, a better world. A lady in the audience was a bit exasperated because she did not understand how she could measure self-love. Should she go shopping to treat herself? Or tell herself that she loved herself? Or just say, 'I am self-love,' all day in line with positive affirmations. *I believe we can measure self-love by considering the concept of healing.*

I am referring to that wonderful state where a sense of 'I'm okay' arrives and the journey towards wholeness begins; we are aware of being more at ease with ourselves, and with others, and where the volume of that inner critical voice, which has forever run the show, is *automatically* lowered because the brain has rewired to the truth which says, 'You are good enough. In fact, you are more than good enough.' Self-love means that we notice our stumbles and catch ourselves before we fall. And even if we do fall, we seem to be able to dust ourselves off and journey on. Healing does not mean being forever free of worries and enjoying perfect health. We are faced with constant challenges of the human existence especially in a world with increasing environmental toxins, economic challenges and the haves having a lot more haves, and the have-nots not much at all. *But healing says, 'I choose to thrive rather than just survive.'*

And how do I know that healing has occurred for me?

Well, my physical body is trimmer (not perfect) and feels healthier (more energetic) than it has for as far as I can remember, the need to feed it with excess food gone, vanished into thin air. Who would have thought that I would crave for a green juice over a strawberry milkshake; that eating a superfood salad is far more satisfying than scoffing a triple decker club sandwich; where eating a chocolate chip cookie does not send me on to a roller coaster of guilt and self-loathing? Saying that, I don't even like those sugar laden cookies anymore. This may not be a big deal to those who have never struggled with angst about body image and comfort eating. Trust me: this is huge healing for someone who has struggled with being overweight for what feels like eternity. It really is. This gradual, yet dramatic, shift has come about by connecting with the knowledge that *what I see as 'my body' is only a quarter of the truth.* Encased within this quarter truth (physical body) reside my other three bodies; the mental, the emotional, and the spiritual which need fuelling in different ways. More than that, action on this knowledge has helped me walk across the bridge of transformation into authentic lasting change. A major lesson learnt is that knowledge and hope, in themselves, do not manifest a good life of balanced joyful living. *We must walk across the bridge to the other side even if it feels horrendously wobbly at times. More than that, we must be prepared to cross many bridges over and over again.* Life is dynamic and so must we be.

As Maya Angelou, the American poet and civil rights activist, said, 'You may encounter many defeats, but you must not be defeated.'

How do I know healing is mine to have and to hold? That I am not defeated? That I have connected to a larger Universal truth than taught to me by my Cultural Parent who has a tendency to box me into tribal behaviour not always of the most nurturing kind? The evidence that self-love has been ignited comes in surprisingly simple things like a bizarre need to offer my face for gentle stroking to the soothing wind, and caress leaves from welcoming trees. It comes in the knowing that connection to Mother Earth, an endless source of love, is real. We are connected to a most benevolent field of energy in magical ways. If we can be open to receiving it. Spending time with nature has become a necessity. In a profit-driven, business-orientated culture where everything has a price, this still comes for free. Sadly, not for millions whose homelands have been ravaged by war. So it feels even more urgent to *not take freedom for granted* and *embrace gifts from nature* on a daily basis. Parks that have been on my doorstep for years, which felt like aliens, are now soulmates. Feeling tired? Best walk off the fatigue in the park. Feeling emotionally vulnerable? Off to the park again to watch free-spirited children and dogs at play to remind myself that the potential to be that way still lies within. Full of energy? Back in a park for that brisk walk to wonder at the seasonal changes and rhythms of nature.

Why does rolling green grass and acres of fields feel so healing? It's because Mother Nature is smart. Green represents the colour of the heart chakra, that energetic centre seated in our ribcage which, when expansive, allows us to simultaneously feel and heal. By engaging with our feelings as we stroll through nature, we can access the unconscious which stores unhelpful narratives and release them. Understanding the power of *letting go* has led to immense well-being. Memories of the past need not necessarily be painful. On the contrary, being at the seaside, with the ocean mirroring a blue cloudless sky, I feel a sense of arriving home to Source. As a child, and even to this day, I love floating in water and staring at the brilliant blue flawless sky. It feels so nurturing, unconditional and expansive. Funny that the colour associated with the energy of the throat chakra, the seat of our self-expression, is that very oceanic turquoise blue. Mother Nature is deeply healing. Gardening really is therapeutic! Swimming in the ocean cleanses our souls.

What are the other signs of a successful journey from mere knowledge to transformation?

My spirit is craving to live from a place of childlike freedom. The need to sing, dance and strut my stuff out there with others seeking a similar path to mine is growing larger each day. *I am actively seeking connection with my soul family, my rebirth tribe, as opposed to solely, my birth tribe.* This shift suggests that limiting belief systems introjected by the Cultural Parent have been processed and released. I do not have to be a 'good little Indian girl' anymore to be accepted and validated. I can release her and just be me. No need to keep up with the Jones either. Best just keep up with myself. *This journey of silent but potent verbal detoxing has paved the way to negotiating my terms for living with life, by exerting choice.* We get drawn to what heals us or what destroys us. What is drawing you? What situations, relationships, and habits are you healthily or toxically attached to? Do you have a sense of thriving or slowly dying? Which would you rather be? I am choosing to heal.

Signs of authentic change need not be accompanied by a spectacular display of fireworks. It can be simple things like sitting down with a cup of tea and savouring each sip without a list of 'things to do' sabotaging that moment of peace and calm. Eating mindfully is a new habit – chew, chew, chew. When attention to enjoying each mouthful is lost over meals, it feels like a missed opportunity to enjoy bliss. Simple tasks, like hanging up the washing on a beautiful sunny day or watering the plants, leave me with a deep inner sense of joy and peace. No longer do these tasks feel like chores to be ticked off the 'must-do' list. They seem to connect with my true nature which is far more uncomplicated than what I have made it into.

Changes in relationship dynamics are a sure sign of internal shift. For instance, it is liberating to know that my sibling has my best interest at heart even though it has not always felt that way. What has felt like criticism in the past feels supportive now. Secondly, looking after my elderly ageing parents does not feel like a burden. Being around them with all their physical and emotional needs may feel overwhelming at times, but kindness rather than resentment supports the way forward. It has not been a rosy thornless ride. Compassion fatigue is for real. ***Healing and self-love mean there is no need to dress it all up to make it sound better***

than it is. I believe our paths (my parents and mine) have crossed in this lifetime for a higher purpose, and hence feel blessed to have these teachers accompanying me in the School of Life. They remain staunch companions in spite of their fragility. Sadly, some relationships are ending to make way for new beginnings. Like-minded people nourish my dreams, so I tend to hang out with them. Those who criticise harshly and keep putting obstacles in my way are being gently bypassed. It is not personal. But I have a dream to birth and need all the help I can get from my soul family. Finally, after years of seeing vulnerability as a sign of weakness, I am embracing it as an incredible strength. Asking for help and support is as new to me, as a baby is to their first crawl. Vital for growth. I accept.

All the above and more seems to have arisen by abandoning a familiar framework of duty, obligation and sacrifice and replacing it with compassion, connection and co-creation, a theme I have repeatedly threaded through this narrative of my journey from an inauthentic life to one of truth. Compassion (*karuna*) is central to Buddhist teachings which have influenced my world view for sure. However, intellectualising an attitude is very different from feeling it, and putting it into practice. To this end, having *courageous conversations with myself has been very powerful for quieting that critical voice that says compassion is all about everybody else but me.* Mindfulness practice, self-acceptance meditations, journaling, talk therapy, oracle and angelic wisdom and this verbal detox are some of the ways I have ignited fierce compassion for myself. Forgiveness and compassion go hand in hand. Diverse teachings from great visionaries (please see reference list) have helped enormously. For anyone starting out in trying to understand what self-compassion is all about, I highly recommend connecting with the wisdom of Kristine Neff (www.self-compassion.org) who says 'With self-compassion, we give ourselves the same kindness and care we'd give to a good friend.'

Why is a friend more deserving of this beautiful human quality than ourselves? What are we saying about ourselves when we do that? If it is that 'we are not deserving or worthy', who said that? Is that true? It is not true at all. It comes about because we have bought into the idea that to have self-love is to be selfish. Who taught us that? Do we have to believe the bearer of that distorted message or can we exert choice and choose another path?

Such insights suggest that self-love has emerged. With this, self-worth has blossomed too. These grounding qualities have given me the courage to give up a career as a dentist to pursue the dream of running a thriving business promoting cultural metamorphosis, social change and balanced living. With this move, I gave up a successful and secure job, and an important personal identity which was linked to my professional life for over 30 years. Being single and having not expanded my own biological family, the 'dental family' had always been a key source of support for my wellness and very sense of being. It provided me with endless affection, praise, and feelings of self-worth. Whilst the decision to quit was conscious, nothing prepared me for the roller coaster ride that threw me into free fall.

Everything that had been familiar to me for decades was given up overnight. With that went my privileged status in society, my financial security, my daily nurturing chats with dental soul family and daily contact with patients (people) who I valued as a source of great joy in my life. To help people through difficult dental procedures, see their smiles of sheer relief after positive experiences, and receive thanks for kindness and professionalism is something I cherished and dearly miss. Leaving behind a job I excelled at and having to start all over again at the bottom of the ladder in the world of counselling and coaching was tough. It was not easy to digest or sit with. This decision, whilst still the right one, created angst with an endless stream of exhausting thoughts (those dreaded NATs again!). Will I be good at my job again? Will my business thrive? Who am I to think that I can help people live more balanced and fulfilling lives? How will I manage financially? How will I juggle business and family life?

Nothing prepares you for the tsunami that is authentic change, but thankfully, even in my darkest moments, I keep striding, guided by the light at the end of the tunnel. The angst is worth it. A fabulous attitude is keeping me going. An elevated status in society, materialistic endeavours, the perfect body, and power are not central to being successful. They do not create the 'good life'. *Being loved and accepted by everybody is not crucial to existence.* Self-love, a sense of inner joy, optimum health and balanced living are more paramount. Gratitude for what I already have, inside, rather than outside, holds the key to freedom. I say this sensitively as life can be deeply traumatic and it may be hard to see anything that one can have gratitude for. But, please never give up. Keep knocking on your soul's door for courage. Keep knocking on any potential doors of support. Keep knocking on the Universe's door for support. You will be heard.

The ability to close old doors and open new ones to experiences beyond my imagination (as in writing this book) came about by fiercely challenging my Cultural Parent. The latter dished out a rather limited life script weaved around suffocating allegiance to the birth tribe. Shame and guilt were sneakily woven in to keep me culturally aligned and suppressed by the patriarch. Well, stuff that, I say. Ideally, I would have loved to marry my *anam cara* (soul friend) and have a family. I am sure that the feel of peachy baby flesh against my bosom would have felt blissful beyond what words can describe, and hand-drawn cards smothered with hearts and scribbles of 'Love you, Best Mum' messages a priceless gift. *I could go on and on, but this is about self-love and healing, not self-destruct and wounding.*

The issue is whether I was unknowingly rebelling against the Cultural Parent, under all the layers of fat. Seeds of self-love and self-worth were obviously present, as they are in each and every one of us. They just need watering. Now that mine have been hydrated, the emerging roots and blooms are simply spectacular. Negativity is being shed with quiet determination and purpose to make way for all possibilities.

Thank the Universe that my true nature (innate wisdom under the conditioned script) understood what really matters. I recently came across a growing trend which made me shudder. Apparently, women from South Asian backgrounds are so fearful of domestic violence that they are frightened to get married. Sob. Ideally, being in a loving marriage is most desirable. BUT. *As my journey has taught me, being single and childless does not mean you are flawed or incomplete.* For any women struggling out there, take heart. Courage is required. New perspectives are essential.

You can still enjoy family life and share 'love-you' messages with children. Let's face it. There are hundreds who are starved of love all over the world, never mind food. Reach out to them. Additionally, being married and showing up as the dutiful daughter-in-law who produces the heir to the patriarchal throne is not the only aspiration to hold onto in life. Wanting an education is not a luxury. It is your birth right. In fact, education has brought meaning and purpose to my life and allowed me to contribute immensely to society. Over the years, being a part of many organisations, charitable and funded, has taught me about the glorious possibilities of joyous living and sense of belonging through community. *We are robbed of life enhancing experiences when our only script is to be law abiding citizens of some out-of-date cultural framework.* Who wants to be a Rescuer Extraordinaire? No, thank you. No need to get my rewards by saving others. They have the capacity to save themselves. Whether they exert that choice is not my angst to bear.

What else has been reframed? Moving out of the family home (in my case at age forty-three) is not selfish. Premarital sex of the responsible kind is fine. Fun, frolic and sangria are not something to be frowned upon, as are having male and LGBTQI friends. Showing up at every social function to honour the ancestors is not necessary. Being a domestic goddess simply does not matter. *Most importantly, putting up with any form of abuse is not your fate or your destiny.* Trust me. It is not written in the stars. This is not your story. The Cultural Parent's boxed ideas of how South Asian girls and women should live dishonour you, never mind the family. If you are in this situation, especially if you have children, please reach out for help. Go online. Find organisations that may support you. Is there someone within the family you can trust? Reach out. Reach in. Set yourself, and your loved ones, on the path to freedom.

This calling is not about hating men. Far from it as evidenced by my ramblings in Chapter 4 around compassion for them. But healing and self-love means holding a broader perspective than the one sold to us by our ancestors. *This is about fiercely honouring my worth in the twenty-first-century.* A life partner (or companion, as well meaning Indian aunts like to call any potential male interest) is not mandatory to pay my bills, keep a roof over my head and see me into joyful old age. I am all for having a partner who will treat me with respect, dignity and love. Where we co-create rather than dictate. Anyone who wishes to see me grow and express my inner truth without feeling intimidated would be welcome. But *I will not go into a romantic relationship out of fear of isolation and loneliness or to satisfy the Cultural Parent.* In spite of fiercely protecting my autonomy, I am surprisingly open to being in intimate relationship with a man more than ever before. I sense that is because inner validation and self-love have become more reliable friends than external praise, applause and awards. *I feel anchored from within and my sense of identity and worth do not depend on being someone's girlfriend, partner or wife.*

Additionally, there is no need to burn my bra with extreme feminist ideology. Be Superwoman. There may be a fine line between self-love and self-entitlement, the one who 'has it all'. I do not have to empower myself and succeed in the world by putting men down. When I observe women being so angry and anti-men, I understand it. Men who violate women are not to be condoned in any shape or form. #NOMORE FOR SURE. But I want to gently point out that it may be more helpful if us women use our beautiful feminine qualities of empathy, communication, compassion, love, and sensitivity to address the problems of gender inequality rather than the attitudes of aggression, vulgarity, sexual prowess, and entitlement that have been used by men to suppress women forever. Yes, let us be logical, analytical and rational like men can be to have intelligent debates about how we can address what is unacceptable, but *let us not lower ourselves to their shadow side.* What is unacceptable in them resides in us. That's the nature of human beings. We all harbour male and female energies. We must not forget that lest our aggressive male energy pops out of us and violates another.

I just want to be a woman, living in harmony with others and supporting children in whatever way I can. After all, children are the future. They are the ones who will either sustain Mother Nature or be extinguished by her. I would rather they support her. Children are a gift and need carrying through the inter-generational challenges ahead, not by imposing patriarchal domination, but through compassion, genuine soul connection and co-creation. The latter means we bother to ask our children about their future. How do they see it? What matters to them most? What challenges do they face? How can we connect to create a future where we all have our say? We do not own them. They are their own entity.

No one in my eyes sums it up better than Kahlil Gibran, writer and poet, in my favourite poem that has helped me befriend my own inner child (the agitated good little Indian girl) beyond what words can describe. A glimpse:

From *The Prophet*

Children

They are the sons and daughters of life's longing for it self

They come through you but not from you

And though they are with you, they do not belong to you

You may give them your love, but not your thoughts

For they have their own thoughts

You may house their bodies but not their souls

For their souls dwell in the house of tomorrow, which you cannot visit, even in your dreams

How wonderful to have your own little secret garden where old weeds can be pulled out and new seeds planted to produce wonderful blossoms that speak of hope, give courage for action and lead to amazing possibilities.

In healing, I have sought balance, aspiring to the Buddha's Middle Way. Waves of existential suffering will arise, but they will subside. It is the law of nature. How I chose to see it (suffering), and engage with it, will determine whether I drown, or surf the wave. This process is rather tough, but not optional, if we want to thrive rather than just survive. I guess by now dear Fellow Traveller, you know where I am heading! More often than not, the negative experiences we endure have their origins in our ancestors, childhood history and conditioned habits which are deeply memorised in the brain's neural network. This often makes us judgemental, act unreasonably and treat people harshly. *The truth is that we often never know the real truth.* We don't know what has gone on for people in their childhoods and life in general. What traumas have befallen them? What losses and betrayal have they suffered? They really may be doing the best they can.

I know healing has occurred because I notice an inner willingness to think more multi-dimensionally before being judgemental about others. I don't go into my old script of 'they have abandoned me', 'they should know better', 'they are so unreliable' or 'nobody cares' because someone forgets to call me or delays their Email response due to a long list of 'things to do' or some calamity in their life. Things don't feel so personal anymore. The paranoia that ran the 'they must be talking about me' video when a large bottom was mentioned has gone. These, for me, are the subtle signs of moving on from old wounds. If I love myself, I am open to showing a loving, expansive attitude towards others. Let us agree to disagree, better than feeling deeply wounded all the time. I guess this is what I mean by connection. *Not meeting others always on our terms but meeting others on both our terms. Which may mean walking away from familiarity and relationships that serve us no more.* Scary but necessary. Connection extends to being in tune with ourselves and walking our talk.

To create healing, the brain needs rewiring. How can we do that? How can we encourage our brain to rewire towards self-love and all the freedom that brings?

Igniting awareness has helped immensely. This concept may be expressed in many ways. Words or ideas such as realisation, perception, knowledge, bringing into the field and consciousness have been threaded into the definitions. It is almost impossible to pin down accurately because all these ideas can be subjective, particularly consciousness which is a most complex phenomenon. For me awareness is that skill or intuitive human capacity that facilitates transitions from the unconscious realms into a conscious state. Robinson (1974) alluded to four stages of learning in his article on *Conscious Competency: The Mark of the Competent Instructor* in the *Personnel Journal* (Vol 53, 538-9). Awareness can be learnt. It is what takes us from unconscious incompetence, to conscious incompetence, to conscious competence and finally that most liberating place, unconscious competence. This is where we really walk our talk. Where our espoused theories match up with our actions which are genuine, authentic and transparent. Where we start coming into mental, emotional, physical and spiritual alignment. Utopia some might say. My beloved friend Nancy holds the attitude that mankind has always been stressed and diseased so there is nothing new about what we are having to face. Historians and economists may disagree. Particularly in the current climate where a businessman is President of the United States. I certainly welcome any formula that helps create an oasis of calm, harmony and well-being amidst the wars.

It seems in order to achieve that, we need a commitment to work with the hidden realms of our psyche. Carl Jung, psychiatrist and psychoanalyst, in his prologue in *Memories, Dreams and Reflections* states 'everything in the unconscious seeks outward manifestation, and the personality, too, desires to evolve out of its unconscious condition and to experience itself as whole' (17).

We all want to come out.

This suggests that the unconscious is a vast hard drive and a potent powerhouse which holds so much of our disguised personality with its attitudes, belief systems and assumptions about ourselves, others and the human race. It is the stuff of counselling and psychotherapy. But unconscious means just that. Out of our consciousness. Out of our radar and hence, often out of easy reach to create fulfilling change in our lives.

These days, time for accessing the unconscious and unravelling all the mush in there is rather limited. Life has become hectic or actually, life is still just life. Working to the three-hundred-and-sixty-five-day year and twenty-four-hour clock. It is us *Homo sapiens* who have chosen to experience ourselves as *Homo burnouts* within this framework that is millions of years old. The unconscious offers a possible panacea. I say *possible* because it harbours some of our most creative aspects and chaos too from the past. The latter, according to Jungian philosophy, possibly from centuries ago where ancestral trauma has cascaded down the generations. But get in there (often called the shadow side) and wow. It can be life changing as evidenced by my journey and so many who have walked before me and alongside me. And who will walk after me.

I believe this hidden part of us often holds answers to those key questions. What causes us to become broken? Why have we disassociated from our true nature? That uncontaminated part of ourselves that knows the truth long before it has been taught to us. Free of man-made ideas and thoughts of how to be when we already are. Free to be me. Why oh Why?

Interestingly, psychotherapy is seen as a new form of spirituality. I guess in the end, when we go into therapy, we take our ginormous mind-heart-body-spirit onion in with us and attempt to peel off the layers of our existential angst. With the support of a therapist we are seeking to answer that eternal question 'Who am I?' Under this confusion, melancholy, chaos, shame, guilt, hurt, pain, fragmentation, and annihilation, 'Who am I?' Under these moments of joy, fleeting happiness, clarity and success, 'Who am I?'

Techniques such as hypnotherapy that are popular for quitting addictions like smoking and food cravings work on the unconscious. More recently, therapies such as the Eye Movement Desensitisation and Reprocessing (EMDR) and Emotional Freedom Technique (EFT) have been used to process emotional and psychologically unhelpful material (trauma) which is often recorded in the unconscious. Alternative therapies aim to access these 'out of radar' experiences not by just focussing on the symptoms of our disease, but by going beyond into the 'unknown' which is the unconscious, held in body and mind.

A plethora of ways exist for healing. I can only really share what has worked for me - practices such as journaling, reiki, chanting, breath work, mindfulness practice, meditation, body massage, crystal healing, creative visualisations, energy clearing, tai chi, Qi gong, angel and oracle wisdom, walks in nature, mindful nutrition, volunteering, connection with soul family, exercise and yoga have certainly paved the way to liberation. Regarding specific alternative therapies, it is only by trying different modalities have I come so far. Curiosity is the key, as is a fab attitude! *What can support us to transform our inner world, and hence our outer experience for the better?*

Counselling and psychotherapy provide a genuine platform for healing. Having trained as a counsellor and undergoing personal psychotherapy has been life changing. When our story is heard, our narrative acknowledged and received without judgement, a profound internal shift occurs. We can come into contact with our fragmented parts, which keep us broken, and our healthy Self can start emerging and create wholeness over time. It is quite a magical process. But talk therapy is not for everybody. Especially around challenges like post-traumatic stress disorder (PTSD) or childhood trauma. Often, in this situation, body-related therapy may hold the answers for healing as there is ample evidence that traumatic memories are stored somatically. Bessel van der Kolk's book, *The Body Keeps the Score* is excellent on this subject.

Sometimes we just cannot articulate the words to any human being about how we feel. This is where the gift of writing comes into its own. *This is where reflective practice and the written word are diamonds amidst the jewels of healing.* They have taken me on a journey of self-discovery and catapulted me into an amazing space that has taken me completely by surprise. I have always loved writing and knew about the healing potential of putting pen to paper, but nothing prepared me for this outpouring of my Truth. Nothing prepared me for this revealing, insightful, sometimes scary but in the end, transcending journey. The writing process is a potent balm, creating authentic shift in the energetic body which, when misaligned, can manifest disease. *This tool can heal if you dare to engage with the words, and hence thoughts and feelings, that are your life story.* If you dare to be brave enough and see it the way it is.

Note: seek professional support if working with complex wounds and trauma. Please do not re-traumatise yourself. Many therapists use writing as a doorway into healing.

Reflective writing has been a most healing balm for me. It has led me to express myself in a way like never before.

> I am an ocean of experiences in search of the norm
> Amidst the howling wind and storm
> Torrential rain resonates with my pain
> A tender soul fragile and frail
> Full of sorrow and a hopeless tale
> Then Suddenly
> Clouds part
> A darting ray of sun
> Pierces my heart
> Balm on a soul
> Now less tender

A word of caution. None of this comes overnight. Beware of offerings of quick fix formulas. They may make you feel buoyed up for a while, but then that dreaded restlessness will return. Many approaches offered out there are like balms that cover a wound but do not get to the source of it. One of my greatest inner conflicts continues to be that monster, fear. Not healthy fear that stops me crossing the road when a van is hurtling down it at full speed, or that which motivates me to look after myself better, but the sort of fear that grips me so tight that before I know it, I have been annihilated by dinosaurs and swords. It is hard to sit with toxic emotions that run the endless videotapes in the head around doom and gloom, and further doom and gloom. Anxiety and panic at the fore. The harder I try to get out of the trench, the deeper it gets as the cycle of self-destruction gets repeated. *But remember, we can stumble and fall. It is okay. More than okay to do that. The key thing is to get up and journey on.*

I encourage you to gently step out of the trench of anxiety and fear. It is possible. Healing will only arise if we can get to the root of our disturbance. To this end, I found Lissa Rankin's book *The Fear Cure* a very helpful tool. She describes an 'inner pilot light', a voice of courage inside, that can guide us out of annihilation. Her view on *true fear versus false fear* is insightful. True fear exists for many. It offers a mechanism for protection for survival. It stops you going over the edge of a cliff. If you are in a violent relationship or live in a war zone, it is truer than true. False fear is one that hangs on to past experiences that are well past their sell-by date but act out as if they exist now and will do so forever. In her words (51), 'false fears show up as worry, anxiety, and rumination about all things that could go wrong in an imaginary future.' The encouraging thing is that fear, if engaged with courage, can lead us to healing. It's a matter of interpretation.

Another solution for diluting monstrous fear (and hence creating calm) is **by not buying into the idea of constant happiness.** For zillions of us, this state is a goal worth aspiring to, but it takes some doing. No easy road to it I'm afraid. That gorgeous soul the Dalai Lama seems to be there, as are other great enlightened beings out there who are quietly walking the path. I have a way to go, but there is hope.

I come closer to a peaceful, almost quietly joyful state when wholeheartedly accepting that suffering will arise. It is one of the conditions for being human.

Challenges around work, health, relationships, unexpected traumatic events, death of loved ones and so on are expressions of life itself. Climbing out of the trench covered in mud, and leaving anxiety and fear behind takes time, effort and determination. Setbacks will come. Tears of rage, frustration, and sadness will abound. Be kind to yourself. Withdraw. Immerse yourself in whatever powers you up. This may range from spending time with cherished ones to changing jobs, making certain lifestyle changes, looking for external support, learning to say no, seeking similar minded people, and most importantly, honouring your needs. This can be extremely difficult when the job pays those essential bills, children are involved or if taking care of ageing parents or other family members. But what choice is there? To carry on when your mind, heart, body and spirit are screaming in pain may only take you to despair and break down. 'Prevention is better than cure' seems a phrase worth mentioning at this time. So somehow, this process of withdrawal is crucial. Support systems need to be accessed. We need to dig deep.

When your energy is replenished, start off again.

An Offering

If you are really struggling at this very moment and whilst you find the direction to face which is right for you, hold on to this message in your heart:

Constant happiness never made anyone truly happy.

Being constantly happy would have never ignited my curiosity to ask the big questions about life. My search for the truth, for another way of being, for balanced joyful living as opposed to constant internal conflict, fragmentation, and stress have all come from some of the lowest moments in my life. *By fiercely examining my life script and challenging belief systems passed down to me by my biological and Cultural Parent(s), this moment of resurrection has arrived. Releasing what does not serve us anymore without, guilt, judgement or shame, is a key to liberation.* What may be more helpful is to hang onto the wisdom of healing practices from all cultures. Not just our own. There are plenty of resources out there. We just have to believe, look and engage. The truth is that we are all seeking inner harmony irrespective of our cultural upbringing. We are all seeking freedom, security, love, peace, happiness, and genuine meaning for life. We all desire social order which allows for diversity and quirkiness. A lot of cultural barriers are man-made rules. Time to lift those barriers. Again!

An ultimate personal tool for healing has been my intimate relationship with the Universe. My daily struggles and hopelessness have often been accompanied by insightful messages for healing from this Life Force. I have woken up to my Truth by paying attention to these whisperings, call it intuition, gut instinct, a Loving Voice (as opposed to that Critical Voice), the Shining Light, Divine Intelligence, Spirit, Guardian Angels, God, Reason, Logic, or whatever works for you.

I share these insights authentically, in the hope that you will know from the bottom of your heart that you are not alone. Far from it. Remember: the world's a stage with over seven-billion of us on it. It is rather crowded. *If you are drifting along feeling rather lost, look into the crowd and beyond in search of your soul family. Your chosen tribe. Rather than just the birth one.* Anchor into family that will nourish and power you up rather than leave you brainwashed, depleted, suppressed and depressed. Go in search and find it. Ask the Universe to support you to your destination. I highly recommend Esther and Jerry Hicks' book based on the teachings of Abraham, *Ask and it be Given. Learning how to Manifest the Law of Attraction.* The latter can be a controversial subject. All views welcome. I resonate with the importance they place on being in touch with our emotional body which for me has been a life changing event. They refer to the Emotional Guidance System as a key tool for accessing our connection to ourselves and to Source, that amazing energetic field out there full of possibilities. How energetically aligned are you to your truth? Not all the man-made stuff but to the Universal truth. Go in search of it, however painful the journey. *Remember, the evidence is in the experience.*

A final ultimate realisation. Life had become a drip and a plod because a part of me had definitely unplugged from the healing pool of Life Force energy out there. Available in seconds, ever-present, ever-nurturing. I seem to have reconnected. I feel powered up and running, Wifi signal's stronger than before. Plug in, Fellow Traveller. What have you to lose? Except isolation, loneliness, fear, anxiety, hopelessness, physical ailments, feelings of shame, guilt, regret, pain, feeling trapped, of being inadequate, and so on.

The truth is that you are far more than these limiting qualities. You are far more than a dripper or a plodder. For starters, you are courage, passion, heroic, curiosity, faith, intelligence, kindness, quirkiness, joy, peace, compassion, love, and hope. And that's just the starters. The dessert is rather divine.

I have decided to join fellow human beings (warriors for the human spirit) who are rubbing their eyes vigorously in disbelief and excitement because in the audience, observing this play on Earth, are the contents of the Universe. Billions of galaxies with moons, stars, planets, blazing sunsets, meteorites and amazing rainbow colours of light seem to be flashing here, there and everywhere. It is like an extravagant display of the poshest fireworks show. *These energetic bodies recognise that life on earth is about being part of a drama called Universal Consciousness.* In this world view, Shakespeare's earthly stage with over seven-billion *Homo sapiens*, is like a drop in the ocean. It is difficult to see where it quite begins or ends. All is in constant flow. Amidst the chaos lie possibilities. Obstacles can be overcome. Human narratives rise and fall. They speak clearly and loudly of the profoundly heroic nature of the human species. We can thrive, rather than just survive. Count me in.

What would you like to do?

Answers on a postcard please.

Reflections

Why do you believe others have the answers to your needs?

How can you create self-love and healing in your life?

What do compassion, connection and co-creation mean to you?

Endings

A Prayer

Dear Ancestors

Namaste
Thank you for our birth onto numerous shores
We honour the sacrifices you made for us and cherish your wise
teachings
So much of what you have bathed us in has held us with love
Forgive us our weaknesses and hurtful behaviours

We pray for blessings as we unchain ourselves from duty, obligation
and sacrifice
Such rules serve us no more for globalised twenty-first-century living
Grant us, the Cultural Parents of the future, a framework of compassion,
connection and co-creation
So that we may wake up to a universal truth

No child is born labelled good or bad
We are all born to receive
Freedom, dignity, respect, love and friendship
Across the waters
Across all continents
Transcending colour, caste and creed

For we know, beneath diversity lies humanity
With all its fragility, strengths and genius
Shower your blessings in to this sea of knowledge
And applaud our courage to resist cruelty and injustice

We pray that you see us as jewels of the ancestral crown
Rather than betrayers of your fruits of labour

Grant us the best
Of love and peace
Where East-meets-West-and-the-Rest

Amen

References and Resources

Articles

1. Drego P. (1983). The Cultural Parent. *Transactional Analysis Journal*, 13, p. 224-227.
2. Robinson W. L. (1974). Conscious Competency: The Mark of the Competent Instructor. *Personnel Journal*, 53, p. 538-9.

Books

1. Alberto Villoldo (2015). *One Spirit Medicine. Ancient Ways to Ultimate Wellness*. London: Hay House.
2. Andrew Harvey (2012). *Radical Passion. Sacred Love and Wisdom in Action*. California: North Atlantic Books.
3. Andrew Weil (1995). *Spontaneous Healing. How to discover and enhance your body's natural ability to maintain and heal itself*. Third edition. London: Sphere.
4. Anita Moorjani (2012). *Dying to be Me. My Journey from Cancer, to Near Death to True Healing*. UK: Hay House.
5. Atul Gawande (2015). *Being Mortal. Illness, Medicine and What Matters in the End*. Second edition. UK: Profile Books.
6. Bessel Van der Kolk (2014). *The Body Keeps the Score. Mind, Brain and Body in the Transformation of Trauma*. UK: Penguin Books.
7. Brian Weiss (2004). *Same Soul, Many Bodies*. Great Britain: Piatkus.
8. Bruce Lipton (2005). *The Biology of Belief. Unleashing the Power of Consciousness, Matter and Miracles*. UK: Cygnus Books.
9. Carl G. Jung (1963). *Memories, Dreams, Reflections*. London: Fontana Press.

10. Carl Rogers (1961). *On Becoming a Person*. London: Constable.

11. Chimamanda Ngozi Adichie (2014). *We Should All be Feminists*. London: Fourth Estate.

12. Coleman Barks (2007). *Rumi. Bridge to the Soul*. New York: Harper One.

13. Daniel Goleman (1996). *Emotional Intelligence. Why it can matter more than IQ*. London: Bloomsbury.

14. Deepak Chopra & Rudolph E. Tanzi (2015). *Super Genes. The hidden key to total well-being*. London: Penguin Random House.

15. Donna Eden and David Feinstein (2008). *Energy Medicine. Balancing Your Body's Energy for Optimal Health, Joy and Vitality*. Great Britain: Piatkus.

16. Eckhart Tolle (1999). *The Power of Now. A Guide to Spiritual Alignment*. Second edition. London: Hodder & Stoughton.

17. Eric Berne (1961). *Transactional Analysis in Psychotherapy. The Classic Handbook to its Principles*. London. Souvenir Press: Grove Press.

18. Esther and Jerry Hicks (2004). *Ask and It be Given. Learning to Manifest the Law of Attraction*. UK: Hay House.

19. His Holiness, the Dalai Lama (1997). *Awakening the Mind, Lightening the Heart*. Second edition. London: Thorsons.

20. Jason Fung and Jimmy Moore (2016). *The Complete Guide to Fasting*. Las Vegas: Victory Belt Publishing.

21. Joe Dispenza (2012). *Breaking the Habit of Being Yourself. How to Lose your Mind and Create a New One*. UK: Hay House.

22. John Bowlby (1988). *A Secure Base*. Oxon: Routeledge.

23. John Crawford (2016). *Anxiety Relief. Seasoned Professional Help*. UK: Amazon.

24. Jon Kabat-Zinn (1994). *Wherever You Go, There You Are. Mindfulness Meditation for Everyday Life*. Second edition. Great Britain: Piatkus.

25. Kahlil Gibran (1926,1935). *The Prophet and The Art of Peace*. London: Watkin's Publishing.

26. Karen Armstrong (2000). *Buddha*. Second edition. London: Phoenix.

27. Kelly A. Turner (2014). *Radical Remission. Surviving Cancer Against All Odds.* New York: Harper One.

28. Kyle Gray (2015). *Wings of Forgiveness. Working with the Angels to Release, Heal and Transform.* UK: Hay House.

29. Lissa Rankin (2015). *The Fear Cure. Cultivating courage as medicine for the body, mind and soul.* USA: Hay House.

30. Louise Hay (2007). *Heal Your Body. The Mental Causes for Physical Illness and the Metaphysical Way to Overcome Them.* Fourth edition. California: Hay House.

31. Maya Angelou (2014). *Rainbow in the Cloud. The Wit and Wisdom of Maya Angelou.* Great Britain: Virago Press.

32. Nikki De Carteret (2003). *Soul Power. The Transformation that Happens when You Know.* UK: O Books.

33. Oliver James (2007). *Affluenza.* London: Vermilion.

34. Paramhansa Yogananda (1998). *Autobiography of a Yogi* Thirteenth edition. California: International Publications Council of the Self-Realization Fellowship.

35. Paul Gilbert (2009). *The Compassionate Mind.* Third edition. London: Robinson.

36. Phil Lapworth & Charlotte Sills (2011). *An Introduction to Transactional Analysis.* Second edition. London: Sage.

37. Sogyal Rinpoche (2002). *The Tibetan Book of Living and Dying.* Second edition. London: Rider.

38. Thich Nhat Hanh (2007). *The Art of Power.* New York: HarperOne.

39. Viktor E. Frankl (1959). *Man's Search for Meaning.* London: Rider.

40. Wendy Mitchell (2018). *Somebody I used to Know.* London: Bloomsbury Publishing.

Websites

1. www.anxietyuk.org.uk
2. www.foodrevolution.org
3. www.hayhouse.co.uk

4. www.headstogether.org.uk
5. www.heartmath.org
6. www.innersource.net
7. www.juliacameronlive.com
8. www.kriscarr.com
9. www.mind.org.uk
10. www.myss.com
11. www.radicalremission.com
12. www.self-compassion.org
13. www.soundstrue.com
14. www.thetappingsolution.com

Acknowledgements

A huge thank you to Gill Donaldson and Cathy Lasher, counselling supervisor and trainer in Reflective Therapeutic Practice, respectively. Gill persisted with her encouragement for me to write a book, amidst my protests, and Cathy opened up the floodgates to intuitive reflective writing, with her style of energetic teaching, which magically connected with the writer within. I am so indebted to you both.

To my beloved parents, Nalinbhai and Kantaben Patel. I am glad I chose you to birth me onto this amazing school of life called planet Earth. It's been quite a journey and I cherish your love.

To my dearest brother Mehul. Your encouragement for bringing this story to life has been priceless. The enthusiasm, support, and time you have invested in this life-changing project have been deeply valued, and I simply could not have done it without you. Only love is real.

To beautiful Swati. You are an angel in our lives. I cherish our soul friendship dearly.

Dear Baroda Dad, Sheelaben, Urmishbhai, Nandita and Meet. It's a pleasure to be family. Holding mum and Rohan in our hearts.

Dear Extended Blood Family. Sending love and light always. May dreams come true.

To Sidney. A twin flame. Heartfelt gratitude for the unconditional love and acceptance always. Love you to the moon and the stars in the sky above.

My dear little sister Rupa. You ignited the path to much more than you will ever know. Thank you forever.

Dear Hasmukhas. You bring joy and laughter and keep me going when the going gets rough. My life would not be the same without you all. Keep up the laughter. Boys, get to work. You know what I mean!

Dear Westland Girls. The love, laughter and chats have been priceless. Here's to oodles more!

My beloved Soul Sisters here in the UK and scattered all over the world. I have been inspired by your dignity, courage and resilience. Thank you for your support come rain or shine. You Rock!

Dear Viren. Your generous spirit and artistic talents have supported me on this journey immensely. Thank you so much. I really appreciate you.

A huge thank you to Amy and Lee for taking the time to read my final manuscript and give me such encouraging support and feedback. You are cherished.

To my beloved SOUL FAMILY all over the world. There are just thousands of people who have come into my life as blood family, during my childhood, through the formal education system, in my career as a dentist, during counselling, and coaching training and practice, on holidays, retreats, workshops, on random streets, in the London Underground, at airport lounges, in aeroplanes, trains, buses, in cafes, markets, shops, businesses and in my neighbourhoods. I know that my journey to finally living authentically from the heart has been made possible because of endless chit-chats, courageous conversations and soul chats along the way. These have forced me to ask the bigger questions: 'What's It All About?' 'Who Am I?' and 'Who would I like to Be?' Thank you for all your contributions be it philosophical discussions, insightful conversations, sharing of knowledge and resources, a hug, a smile or a wink. They have all communicated something special and set me on my way 'free to be me'.

Heartfelt gratitude to the beautiful spirit Louise Hay for opening up all possibilities to living a life of authenticity and joy. Your vision and wisdom created a publishing home for authors who are able to find their voice and share their messages of the human heroic spirit globally. To all authors and fellow spiritual seekers, who have shared so generously of their knowledge, wisdom, vulnerabilities, sufferings and paths for healing so that I can walk the path to living from the heart, thank you. Ms Eternally Grateful.

To every single person involved with the publishing of my book at Balboa Press, especially Mary Oxley and Ginny, heartfelt gratitude for helping me bring my story to a wider audience.

Thank you to Hay House UK for granting me permission to use the feedback from my book proposal submission as part of the Writer's Competition in 2016.

Gratitude to Tami Simon, founder of www.soundstrue.com. I have spent hours being inspired by you and diverse enlightened speakers streamed through your podcast and audio programmes. The 'business with heart' ethos that you are promoting resonates with my conscience and supports me immensely as I endeavour to do the same.

About The Author

Bina Patel

www.binapatel.org.uk

Bina is of Indian origin and was born and brought up in Africa to the age of sixteen. Britain has been her home for almost four decades. She enjoyed thirty years in a professional and rewarding career as a dentist, trainer and researcher. In recent years, a deep desire for change forced her to stop living in her head and follow her heart's calling.

She is committed to balanced living particularly in the current climate where she observes that Homo sapiens are on their way to becoming Homo burnouts. Promoting cultural metamorphosis and social change have become a passion.

The desire to live an authentic life paved the way to counselling and coaching training and taking momentous steps forward in areas of her life which had always felt resistant to change. These included overcoming a lifelong battle with weight, a reduction in chronic stress and a change of career into the arena of well-being. Giving up a secure and financially lucrative job which provided status, validity and recognition in society was a tough choice. But possible. She is privileged to come from a loving family who supported her in this change.

Unfortunately, for millions of young girls and women in patriarchal-dominated cultures where skewed power dynamics resist any change, they can only dream of living an authentic life. Education and all the possibilities that come with that only but a distant dream. *This book is a calling to engage in courageous relationship with the Cultural Parent that potently frames our world view, and to arrive into the twenty-first century where East-meets-West-and-the-Rest in expansive ways to create a better world. For all human beings. Irrespective of gender.*

As for having the courage to write a book? Training in Reflective Therapeutic Practice opened the floodgates to her inner world which housed endless narratives around culture and the forces of conditioning. Writing and publishing a book felt daunting until she attended a Writer's Workshop run by Hay House UK. This proved to be life changing as it gave her the framework, confidence and courage to enter a Hay House Writer's Competition in 2016. The positive feedback she received from her Book Proposal submission drove her on and has culminated in this book.

HAY HOUSE UK EDITORIAL TEAM (MAY 2017)
Feedback from Book Proposal submitted as part of the 2016 Writer's Competition
(With permission)

'We found your submission to be a very powerful, inspiring and moving account of your personal experiences of growing up within set cultural rules and expectations. We found your voice to be authentic, honest and courageous, which is something that readers greatly appreciate. We found the structure of the book to be well thought-out, with your personal story balanced with exercises for the reader at the end of every chapter. Your story would resonate with many others who have been or are going through similar experiences. If you are considering sharing your message with a wider audience, it would be worth considering starting to blog about your experiences and your journey, as this will enable you to start reaching an engaged and interested audience for whom your message will be helpful and inspiring.'

THE BLOG TURNED INTO A BOOK!

22390425R00156

Printed in Great Britain
by Amazon